Saving Ella

Mercy's Angels Book 1

Kirsty Dallas

ISBN: 1489535195
ISBN-13: 978-1489535191

1

FOR KYLIE

This book is a work of fiction. Names,
characters, places and incidents are either
a product of the author's imagination or are used fictitiously.
Any resemblance to
actual people living or dead, events or locales is entirely
coincidental.

☐

☐

PROLOGUE

"Dadddyyyyyyy!" The scream that came from my mouth shocked even me; it sounded terrified, more animal than human. Tears streamed down my face, my wide eyes glued to my unresponsive dad. I reached for him with hands that shook uncontrollably no matter how much I willed them to be still. I nudged and pushed at my dad begging him to open those dark chocolate eyes and smile. This had to be a joke...a cruel, horrible joke. Daddy didn't play those sorts of jokes and that's how I knew this was real.

"Please Daddy, please, please, please wake up," I begged. His skin was clammy and cold and no matter how much I shoved his limp body, he didn't open his eyes. My heart was beating too hard and too fast as I looked around the small kitchen for help I knew wasn't there. Mother had been gone for three days and wouldn't be home til this evening. Suddenly my mind which, had been a scrambled mess of terror, became startlingly clear...phone! I scrambled to my feet slipping on the milk which flowed like a white river from the carton on the floor. I headed straight for the phone's base where the handset should have been cradled, which of course it wasn't. I clumsily pressed the button to find the handset, forcing myself to be still and listen for the beep, beep, beep of the lost phone. It definitely wasn't in the kitchen or the living room. I didn't want to leave my dad alone on the floor, I wanted to comfort him, hold his hand and let him know everything would be alright. Ambulance first, comfort second I rationalized. Casting a hopeless glance back to my dad I ran down the hall listening for the distant call of the elusive phone.

A whimper escaped my lips as I stuck my head in my room. Not there. Our small house had never felt so big and endless, the hallway a continuous gallery of photos and memories that were currently no more than an irritating blur, a taunt of happy memories that I somehow knew were coming to an end. Finally reaching the door to my parent's room I flung it open where the sound became louder. There, on my mother's perfectly tidy, perfectly delicate little dresser sat the little white device, flashing and beeping with impatience. I grabbed the phone and fumbled trying to see the buttons through a haze of watery tears. My heart still pounded so hard it hurt as I ran back into the kitchen, to the side of my dad's still body on the cold, hard floor. I almost missed the calm resolute voice that answered, the words twisted into a garbled mess. Emergency was the only word that registered.

I sobbed uncontrollably now. "M-my dad, he won't wake up." The woman on the other end of the phone was painfully controlled.

"What is your address sweetheart?"

I tried to clear the panic in my mind and think. Address, address?

"Twenty Pine Hill Road, Dunston," I spoke so fast I was surprised the woman on the other end of the phone could understand me. I held my dad's limp hand tightly now barely noticing the unrelenting tears that wet my face.

"Can you tell me if your dad is injured?" the composed voice on the phone asked. I looked at him carefully. He seemed so peaceful, like he was only sleeping.

"I don't think so."

"Okay sweetheart. The ambulance is on its way, they will be there soon. I'm going to stay on the phone with you until they get there. What's your name?"

"Ella," I sobbed, wishing, praying for the angelic sound of sirens that would soon be approaching our home.

"Okay Ella, I'm Sally. Are you home alone with your daddy?"

"Yes," I whispered. "Mom is away, she won't be home til tonight." Mom was always away or out with her friends. In fact, it had been almost a week since I had last had a conversation with her. She wasn't much for idle chit chat with a thirteen year old who had no interest in day spas or shopping.

"Okay, I want you to do something for me, Ella. I want you to see if your dad is breathing. Watch his chest and see if it goes up and down. Can you do that for me?" My eyes immediately shot to dad's chest. I had to drop his hand so I could wipe away the tears that blinded me.
"I don't know, I can't tell."

"That's okay. Put your hand on his chest, can you feel it

moving?" My hand quickly found my dad's large sturdy chest. I sat quiet and still praying for movement. With an unrestrained wail I almost dropped the phone.

"I can't feel anything." I began to panic again.

"Alright Ella. Was you dad eating anything when he collapsed?" I looked around the room for the answers.

Was he? He had been fixing lunch but I didn't think he'd started eating without me. "I don't think so," I murmured as I thought back to the moment he simply collapsed in a sickening heap to the floor.

"Okay sweetheart, I want you to lay your head on your dad's chest and see if you can hear his heartbeat." My dad's usual warmth seemed to be seeping away from his body, replaced with a frigid, cold that didn't belong in my warm caring father. My head rested against his cold chest and I tried hard not to cry, otherwise I might miss the magical sound of his beating heart.

"Can you hear anything, Ella?" the calm resolute voice asked. I listened for a moment more. There…perhaps something…I wasn't sure but there seemed to be noises. Whether they were coming from Dad's heart or not, I had no idea.

"I don't know," I sobbed. Though what I did hear now was a balm to my frantic soul…a siren!

"I think I can hear the ambulance," I exclaimed, renewed hope surging through my veins.

"They're less than a minute away Ella. Is the door unlocked?" I knew it wouldn't be; Dad was paranoid about security. I jumped up and ran to the front door. The sirens were close, their wail a beacon of hope. I flicked the latch on the door and pushed it open. Stepping onto the porch I watched the ambulance swing around the corner and onto my street. I waved my hands frantically, fearful they might miss my house. The lights on top of the ambulance flashed a furious vision of warning, the siren screamed with terrifying urgency.

"They're here." I wept with relief as help pulled into my driveway.

"Good girl, you did so well Ella. You can hang up the phone now. The paramedics will take care of your dad."

"Okay," I said with tears still falling down my pale cheeks as a man and woman in uniform raced up the porch steps. I pressed the little button that disconnected me from that calm, steady voice, watching the solemn looking paramedics as they slammed through the front door with such force that the Christmas wreath we had hung only this morning fell to the floor. I stood quietly in the kitchen watching like a useless bystander as the paramedics pumped on my dad's chest. The crack I heard every now and again was sickening to my stomach; my hand covered my mouth tightly trying to muffle my unrestrained moans. Somehow my tears stopped, which shouldn't have surprised me. I had cried a river; surely my body was now bone dry. The panic that had consumed me fell away replaced with mindless disbelief as I watched my lifeless dad. Looking about the room I took in the Christmas decorations I had been so eager to set up this morning. I had woken Daddy soon after the sun had risen on what was an unusually warm Thanksgiving. While other thirteen year olds were grumbling about how lame it was to have to spend the holidays with their families, I silently looked forward to it. Even though it was usually just me and Dad, I loved it. He worked hard all year to make sure the holidays were ours to do as we wished. Movies, picnics, hiking, skating, drawing, or just simply hanging out at home; we were always laughing and having fun together. The paramedics moved my dad to a gurney as I continued to watch on, numb, my arms wrapped around my stomach. He was gone. Somehow my heart already felt the weight of his loss. Without warning the most important thing in my world had been taken from me and I felt horribly alone.

CHAPTER 1

Ella

Hate — to feel intense dislike, or extreme aversion or hostility
Such a powerful word, such a strong emotion. To live without
hate must be bliss. I had lived with hate for four years now, four
long years of intense dislike and extreme aversion. So much
hate filled my life, it felt like nothing else existed; my heart and
soul was filled with it. For the most part, I was dead inside and
could barely remember the time when I was alive, when I had
dreams, hopes…a future. By the time I was thirteen I had it all
planned. Get good grades, study hard and get a scholarship to
study art. Eventually, perhaps, meet a handsome man who
would whisk me away to the most exotic places this world had
to offer and I would sketch. One day I would own a small
gallery and all my pictures would hang on those walls. I was
going to be an artist and nothing was going to stand in the way
of my dreams. That was until hate came along in the form of
Marcus Fairmont. Rich, powerful and my mother's new
husband, I hated him and God, he hated me. His fists certainly
echoed that hate when they connected with my body and his
eyes confirmed the sentiment. I was fascinated with eyes and
had an innate ability to read the truth in them—lust, love
happiness, sadness, hate—I saw it all in the eyes. Where
Daddy's eyes had been gentle, full of love and fun. Marcus's
eyes were full of ruthless hate and indifference.

For a time I was defiant, fighting every step of the way, refusing
to bow to his reign. I went out of my way to find trouble; bad
grades, bad boys, shop lifting, drugs, anything that would
embarrass Marcus, anything to escape Marcus. I did things I
am not proud of. Losing my virginity in a drunken stupor in the
back seat of Henry Spanner's Chevy was not an impressive
moment. Snorting lines of coke in the girl's bathrooms at
school was equally unimpressive; cutting myself repeatedly
because I had grown to hate myself almost as much as Marcus,
dumbest moment ever. My mother was blinded by her love for
Marcus, or more appropriately, her love for Marcus's money.
Marcus kept her well dressed in Prada and Gucci, sent her on
exotic vacations with her friends, paid for her new boobs, full

lips and Brazilian wax. Mother barely noticed my desperate acts of self-harm and self-loathing. If she noticed Marcus's violence towards me, she either didn't care or was too afraid to say anything. Her eyes were indifferent and unconcerned, blinded and Marcus was a damn good sweet talker.

My life had become some sort of sick, twisted game. Marcus playing the part of an anxious concerned parent and I playing the part of an indifferent and sullen teenager. He and I were the only players in this game and, for a while, he had defeated me. I was ready to give up and he would have won. That was a moment of true clarity for me. If my life was to be a game, then I'd be damned if I would let Marcus Fairmont win! He played my mother like a finely tuned instrument in the hands of a musical genius. His brow would furrow with appropriate worry when my name was bought up. He threw thousands of dollars at Dr. Fuckwad Theo who was supposed to 'fix' me. Dr. Fuckwad was exactly as his name suggested and knew Marcus had no intention of seeing me overcome my so called 'problems', he knew Marcus would continue to try and break me and he didn't care. He was handsomely paid to play a small part in this game. God how I wished I could hate my mother for bringing this into our lives. God knows I tried to, but hate was perhaps too strong a word for my mother. Disappointment was definitely something that came to mind. After I turned sixteen, I decided to run. This was the only time I fought for my freedom and tried to escape the abuse my body had become far too accustomed to. In the middle of the night I packed a bag and left, sneaking out like a thief into the night. Henry, my drug dealer slash boyfriend slash only friend, gave me a ride and helped me put five-hundred and twenty-six miles of beautiful asphalt between my step-father and I.

Henry knew what went down with Marcus and I, he knew the bruises went further than skin deep and in his own sick twisted way he did what he could to spare me that pain. He gave me the blissful escape of drugs, alcohol and sex…he helped me escape. Three days after my escape, fucking Tom Brennan, Marcus's right hand man and coincidentally local law enforcement, found us at a motel. Henry just stood there and watched him drag me away. Henry wasn't prepared to go to jail for me and though I understood why, it pissed me off. Tom delivered me back to Marcus, hand delivered right to his door like a fucking gift wrapped present. Instead of beating me, Marcus's cruelty found a new low. Marcus offered me a glass of scotch and yeah, I found that strange but being completely naïve, I drank it. To this day I don't know what he put in the liquor but it rendered my body completely useless. Through a hazy memory I can still recall what happened and how I felt, my limbs non-responsive as he knelt by my side, his eyes filled with vulgar, unspeakable hate. He whispered in my ear, his breath hot and laced with alcohol.

"I could fuck you right now so easily, Ella. That's what you want isn't it? To be fucked by a man rather than a boy? That's why you're whoring your way through this town, isn't it? I'm not going to give you what you want, Ella. You're too fucking ugly, too thin and bony, too shallow and empty. A real man doesn't want this; a real man would never want a whore like you, but I am going to show you just how in control of this body I truly am." Then I noticed the knife. Surprisingly it wasn't very big, but fuck was it sharp. "You like to cut yourself, mark your skin? I'm going to leave my own mark on you Ella and every time you look at it you will think of me and how I own you. I control you Ella."

One deep slice across each wrist, which hurt like a bitch at first, but quickly became a numb throbbing sensation as my blood pumped from my body. I thought I was going to die and I clearly remember smiling. I was going to see Daddy again, then the darkness pulled me under. I woke in a room where bright unmerciful lights glared down on me from the ceiling while doctors and nurses hovered over my bed. The looks on their faces as my bleary eyes took them in was heart wrenching pity. Everyone looked at me with pity now. Poor little Ella whose daddy died and now she's all rich and has everything and hates it. Poor little whoring, drug addicted Ella tried to kill herself. Teachers, friends, parents, doctors, they all looked at me the same. I felt like screaming, like bellowing til my throat was raw and stripped of the inequity of being accused of such a thing. Whore, yes. Drug addict? Perhaps. Self-harmer? Uh-huh. But killing myself? Slitting my wrists and letting my life simply drain from my body? Fuck no. Marcus's clear psychosis meant it was time for a new tactic and I obediently heeled. It felt like giving in and that pissed me off, but I wasn't really giving in. I was surviving. I did what I had to do to stay safe. Bide my time until I reached that golden mark—eighteen. Then I was free to leave; they couldn't force me to stay, they couldn't pay me enough to stay. Lately though, I found myself wondering if I would reach that mile stone only a short week away. Even though Marcus's violence had lately lost its sting, the way he looked at me now filled me with a new fear. I had finally begun to develop a woman's body. Over the last year my small, spindly form had developed the curves I once yearned for. Now Marcus's eyes watched me with sickening lust and I thought I had just maybe, finally reached breaking point.

My hand instinctively danced across the blank page before me, leaving elegant charcoal lines in its wake. Sketching came naturally. It was a talent my daddy discovered I had when I was nine when he found me sketching a portrait of our dog, Twisty, with Crayola crayons.

Apparently it was amazing and I truly loved doing it. Art was where my mind was free to escape; it actually felt as though I was no longer in my own body. I could be somewhere else, anywhere else. Free. Within a few long lines and some simple shading, a face took shape. Beautiful and graceful, the picture of Mrs. Flannery was for my art teacher Mr. Flannery. He had given me the photo last week, asking me if I would mind sketching a charcoal of his wife, a gift for their thirtieth wedding anniversary. He was actually going to pay me for it, my first commission. A light tap on my door broke my concentration. I knew it was Mother, Marcus never knocked.

"Yes," I said in a low, irritated voice, my thoughts wishing her away. Our relationship was splintered and delicate. In fact, it was probably more appropriate to say we didn't have a relationship; she was more of an acquaintance. The door pushed open and my mother entered. She was elegantly dressed in a tight fitting dress, heels that were much too high; her hair styled into an artful twist at the back of her head. She was pretty, my mom—high cheek bones, sharp green eyes and blonde hair that she paid a fortune for. That was the problem though; my mom was an expensively manufactured lie, attractive on the outside but bland and ugly on the inside.

"Ella, I'm leaving now. Marcus is in the den. Could you grab his dinner from the oven? It will be ready in fifteen minutes." I felt her watching me expectantly; my eyes, though, never left the page before me.

"Where are you going?" I finally asked. However disillusioned I was with my mother, I still hated it when she was gone. I absolutely hated being alone with Marcus.

"I'm having dinner with Kate, then a movie after. I will be home late." I still refused to meet her gaze.

"After I've fixed Marcus's dinner, could I go down to the mall?" Mother immediately went for her purse. She had no problem throwing money at me for shopping. Hell, she encouraged it. It was her favorite past time after all. I didn't spend her money the way she would have preferred me too though. Jeans, sweaters and sneakers were the extent of my wardrobe; I didn't own a single dress or skirt. Art supplies were a must too. Sketch books, canvases, charcoal, sometimes I indulged with paint, though charcoal was my favorite medium. But as long as I was shopping, mother was satisfied.

"I don't think that will be a problem, but check with Marcus before you leave. Here." She handed me a credit card.

"You remember the PIN?" I nodded. It was a card that accessed money from her personal account. Marcus kept a close watch on their spendings, but somehow mother still managed to keep a little tucked away to accommodate her outrageous shopping demands. She knew Marcus didn't like me spending his money. As I reached out to take the card, my sleeve slipped up revealing the ugly scar on my wrist. I knew the moment she spotted it, her lips drawing tight with disappointment. Surely the woman who had nurtured me in her womb, given birth to me, fed me, clothed me, surely my own mother would know better. I tugged down the cuff of my sleeve, gripping it tightly over the raised scar.

"Thank you," I murmured, trying desperately to hide the bitterness I felt. No, Mother wouldn't know better because she preferred to live with her head in the sand, her tucked and nipped Victoria's Secret draped ass in the air. No, I wouldn't kill myself. I wouldn't give Marcus that satisfaction.

"Don't stay out long, you know how Marcus gets," warned Mother. I ignored her. If anyone around here truly knew how Marcus got, it was me. She didn't have a fucking clue. As she turned for the door, she glanced back over her shoulder. "It's beautiful Ella, Mr. Flannery will love it." I peeked up through my veil of dark hair. For a split second I thought I saw something in my mother's eyes that I had never noticed before...pride. If it were there, it was gone already, hidden behind a heavily caked mask of makeup and indifference. Once the door was shut again, I breathed out a sigh of relief, sliding the plastic card into my back pocket. Carefully, I placed the sketch down and made for the adjoined bathroom to wash the charcoal from the tips of my fingers. Under the harsh white light of the small room I studied my reflection in the mirror. Marcus always told me I was a sad excuse for a girl, a worthless whore that only abject, drug addicted boys would dare fuck and, right at this moment, I had to admit I felt pitiful. My face was okay, I guess. My dark brown eyes hinted at the distant Asian ancestry, a throw back on my daddy's side. My hair was dead straight and parted perfectly down the center in a rich chestnut brown that apparently women paid top dollar for. My cheek bones were high, my nose slight and in proportion, my heart shaped lips full. If it weren't for the sullen expression that had become my permanent trade mark look, I might have caught the attention of nice boys. Even though I hadn't used drugs in two years I still looked like a beaten junkie. My skin was pale, too pale. The marks under my eyes so dark they looked like bruises. A bruise on my cheek had faded to an ugly yellow. A white scar about an inch long from where I hit the kitchen table after one of Marcus's hefty blows marred the skin beside my right eye. I didn't even bother to try and hide it under makeup anymore. I just pulled my hair forward like the protective cloak it had become, hiding my scar, the bruises and the misery. At least the other scars could be hidden under clothes. I might never wear a strapless dress or bathing suit, but that was a small price to pay for my life. One more week and I would be free. I was so close; the anticipation sent my heart into a tail spin.

With my hands now clean, I grabbed my favorite camo jacket and house keys from the dresser. With a deep resounding sigh, I left my room. The house was quiet, it was always quiet. Not like our old home, before Marcus. That house was small and noisy. The floor boards creaked, the doors groaned, the faucets spluttered and I loved it. Marcus's home was enormous, perfectly orderly and perfectly silent. In the kitchen I quickly pulled the chicken mignon out of the oven and dished a plate for Marcus. Pouring a glass of his favorite red I made sure the table was neat and presentable before heading for his den. At the closed door I stood a moment, the low dulcet tones of an Italian operetta seeped through the heavy oak. My mind was screaming at me to leave. Just turn and walk away, screw waiting to be eighteen, I was close enough. But he had found me so easily last time. I shuddered at the memory of what had awaited me on my return. One more week, I'd made it this far. Shoulders back and head held high, I knocked.

"Come in." No hesitation, his voice calm and confident as always. I pushed open the door. The room was subdued, the lights low. Hideous pictures of women in compromising positions decorated the walls. I hated them. Photographic art my ass. Marcus was a sadistic prick. The room stunk of cigars and it almost made me want to gag. The man himself sat at his desk, his fingers steepled under his chin.

His perfect dark hair was cut as stylish as a model from GQ magazine, his suit jacket thrown over the back of a chair. As always his nondescript hazel eyes were cold and calculating as they leisurely examined my body. When Marcus first started dating my mother, for a split second I had considered him handsome, for an older man. Not anymore. I don't think I had ever met or seen a more revolting human being.

"Dinner is ready, chicken mignon." I quickly cut to the chase. Marcus frowned, clearly disturbed by something. Shit, what had I done now? He nodded in the direction of something over my shoulder. I glanced around. Fuck. Tom Brennan sat in the leather chaise at the back of the room. He was still in his police uniform drinking a long neck, so I assumed he was not on duty. He was a tall, lean man with a nose too big for his narrow face. He reminded me of a bird and not the pretty colorful kind. More like an ugly vulture. He made my skin crawl. Police should make you feel safe. Tom scared me almost as much as Marcus did.

"Sorry, I didn't realize you had company," I tucked my head down submissively and apologized. Marcus's grin was as cold and calculating as his cunning eyes.

"Tom was just leaving." Tom stood and nodded to Marcus, moving towards the door.

"I'll call you first thing," he murmured to Marcus who replied with a nod. Tom grinned at me, a sneaky vindictive grin. "Good night Ella," he crooned in a voice laced with arrogance.

"Tom," I whispered, knowing very well if I ignored him Marcus would make me pay. Tom disappeared out the door.

"I won't keep you then." I said, more than ready to leave the confines of Marcus's dark, gloomy office. Marcus seemed to consider this for a moment before shaking his head.

"Not yet, I think I would like refreshments in here first." His eyes settled on my chest and I tried my best to ignore the fact. What the hell did he mean by that?

"Do you want your dinner served in here?" I took a step backwards ready to go fetch his meal and get the fuck away from him.

"No." demanded Marcus in the voice I knew too well. It was calm and controlled and I knew it meant business. It was his you're-in-for-it-now voice. I glanced nervously at the door, so close I could easily make it before he got to me, but then what? Marcus stood casually and rounded his desk, his movements slow and calculated, like a cat stalking its prey.

"Would you like me to bring your wine in here?" I tried again, hoping he would decide that was a great idea so I could put some distance between us. How I didn't falter over the words was a miracle. My heart was ready to burst from my skin. I didn't like the direction things were headed. Marcus shook his head slowly.

"I'm not hungry for chicken mignon Ella, nor am I thirsty." Oh God, the lustful gaze in his stare told me exactly what he was hungry for. Marcus walked right by me and I heard the door close, the quiet click of the lock. I could barely breath, my palms slippery with sweat, but somehow I remained perfectly still as I began to think of a way out of here. I hadn't survived the last four years from being stupid. There was nowhere to run, no point in screaming as no one would hear and I have no doubt Marcus wouldn't let me get close to the phone. Then I felt his hot breath on my neck.

"If you want to hit me just get it over with," I growled with the barest trace of defiance in my voice. He chuckled and the sound made my skin crawl.

"Oh Ella, tonight is about so much more than a beating and I'm going to take my time. Your mother won't be home for hours."

My body grew tense as his words began to take shape and understanding dawned, my focus sharply narrowed in on survival. My eyes darted around the room and settled on the large mahogany desk. Top drawer, left side, he never locked it. The gun sat loaded and ready. I knew it was there, I had found it months ago while sneaking through his office looking for the picture of Daddy that he had callously taken away from me. It had been there only a week ago when I decided to check again. Please let it still be there. I would kill the fucker before letting him touch me this way. Marcus's hands crept around my waist and I trembled under his slimy touch. Slowly his hands rose to my breasts and just as they were about to touch me I pushed hard and broke free. Spinning around I faced the nauseating immoral stare of Marcus.

"I know you're no virgin, Ella. You've been the town whore long enough to have some experience, but tonight, I'm finally going to give you what you need. A real man. No boys in this room Ella, only a man." He thought for a moment. "Maybe I should call Tom back. Have you ever had two men at once, Ella?" He smiled and anger quickly surged through my body. Mother fucker! All the torment and shit he had put me through over the years and to top it off he was going to rape me and he was going to ask Tom to join in? Hell to the fuck no. Determination filled my veins with strength and courage.

"Don't you dare touch me, Marcus! Not you or your fuck buddy Tom!" It's been a long time since I had spoken to Marcus this way. For too long I had been controlled, dominated but not anymore. Marcus's eyes widened with shock and I nearly laughed. What did he truly expect? That I bend over his desk and present myself on a platter? His fist connected with my face before I even realized it was coming. I fell to the floor and felt the blood leaking from my nose, down my mouth and chin.

"Perhaps we will put that filthy mouth to some good use finally," he sneered. I had to get back on my feet, prone, as I was on the ground, I would be unable to defend myself. With shaky legs I stood and turned to face him. Top drawer left side, top drawer left side; it was my new mantra.

"If you try to put your dick near my mouth I will bite the fucker off," I growled. Smack. This time I actually flew back across the desk, hitting it so hard it took my breath away. How I stayed conscious I have no idea. Splayed across the desk on my stomach I felt large hands fumbling at my clothing, pulling with determination at my jeans.

"Nooooooooooooo!" I screamed kicking and scrambling to get away from him. My fingers groped for the drawer, just a little further. I felt the cold air on my naked skin as Marcus finally pulled my panties away. His smooth, large hands gripped me with force. When I heard his zipper I thought I might throw up. With all that I could muster I kicked hard connecting with what I thought was his thigh. The curse words he muttered confirmed that it had hurt. Finding the slight leverage I needed, I was able to reach my hand over the edge of the desk and pull the drawer open just enough. Marcus gripped my hips again, pulling me back towards him. The cold metal under my fingertips was the sweetest touch I had ever felt. Gripping the weapon I kicked once more.

"Fucking bitch," he grunted and I smiled. That one apparently really hurt. Marcus released his grip on me for a moment and I was able to roll over. The shock on his face was priceless as I held the gun up in front of us, my eyes no doubt filled with fury.

"Get the fuck away from me," I gasped. My face throbbed, but I could easily ignore the pain, my life depended on it, adrenaline surged through my veins.

17

This is what fight or flight felt like—exhilarating! Probably more so because Marcus was about to experience how much of a bitch karma was...and if anyone was going to deliver that karma, it was going to be me!

"It isn't loaded you stupid bitch," Marcus growled. It was a week ago and if he was telling the truth I had no doubt he would be all over me by now. I clicked off the safety and caressed the trigger. Marcus sneered at me backing away, not even attempting to pull up his pants to hide his large dick that was quickly losing its interest in me.

"You don't get to touch me anymore, Marcus." I kept the gun steady, pointed directly at his chest. The day I found a loaded weapon in the house I had Googled everything I needed to know about guns. Turn the safety off, place your finger on the trigger and aim for the chest; big area, hard to miss, plenty of vital organs. Marcus snickered.

"You're going to run again, Ella? Remember what happened last time you tried to leave me?" I fumbled with my jeans, pulling them back up over my hips.

"I'm leaving and you won't find me this time Marcus. If you try to follow me, I will fucking shoot you. I'd rather go to jail then deal with this shit." Marcus stood back, leaving the path to the door clear and I carefully moved to it, gun still steady, eyes watchful and clear. There were no tears for Marcus, not when he beat me, not when he cut me and not now when he tried to rape me. I knew it pissed him off that he couldn't bring me to cry.

"When I find you, I am going to fuck you, then cut your damn throat and watch you die," sneered Marcus.

"You won't find me," I breathed heavily, pushing away the pain in my throbbing head.

"There is nowhere you can hide Ella. I have too many connections, I can find a fucking needle in a hay stack if I so wish. I'll even give you a half hour head start. Just enough time to eat my dinner and drink a glass of wine."
He smiled that charming smile that fooled everyone except me. I flipped the lock on the door, never taking my eyes off Marcus gun still pointed at his chest, as I moved out of the den. Slamming the door shut I turned and ran down the hall, into

the foyer and out the front door. I ran so hard I thought I might throw up and when I finally did, I wiped the bile from my mouth and ran some more.

****

Reaching the mall I tossed the gun in a garbage can and ran into the nearest bathroom. I had this all planned. At home, in the back of my closet, was a packed bag and the little money I had managed to stash with it. Thank God for Mother's credit card; I would easily pick up what I needed in the mall. The only thing I would miss were my sketches of Daddy, hidden in the bottom of my bag where Marcus could not find them. As soon as I was safe I would pick up a sketch book and some charcoal and I would draw myself a new picture. I would never forget my daddy. My nose had stopped bleeding but my eyes had already begun to swell and blacken. I washed up as best I could, zipping up my jacket to hide the blood on my shirt. I turned into the first department store I walked by and bought a back pack, some spare clothing and a bottle of water. There were plenty of stares, but I ignored them all, letting my hair hang forward as usual in an attempt to hide my battles.

After purchasing the items, using my mother's credit card, I ran to the nearest bank and withdrew one thousand dollars. As I tossed the card in a nearby trashcan, my eye caught the art supply store and my heart ached. Later, there was no time for my dreams now, they'll be no good to me if I'm not alive to relish in its pleasure. Without looking back, I left the mall. I had originally planned to take a bus and head to California. I had always wanted to see the ocean, but right now I just wanted out of this fucking town.

I had to move quickly and put as much distance between myself and Marcus as I could. At the bus station, the lady behind the desk eyed me suspiciously. She had kind eyes, sharp eyes; the kind that didn't miss a thing. She finally asked if I needed a doctor. When I said no she asked if I needed the police. Oh crap, my heart almost stopped beating.

The perceptive woman with strawberry blonde hair in a wiry curl, light brown eyes and a voluptuous body squeezed into a far too tight dress watched me curiously for a moment while I shuffled nervously on my feet.

"I just need to get out of here, please. Anywhere! Just as long as it's far from here." The woman breathed out a deep sigh.

"You running from the man who did that?" She nodded at my face. I glanced away and tried to bury the tears that threatened to escape. As soon as my gaze returned to those kind sympathetic eyes I couldn't stop them. A tear escaped, followed by another, then another. In four years I hadn't shed a tear over the pain Marcus had inflicted on me. Now, while this woman looked at me with eyes full of understanding and concern, now my fucking tears came. My throat was so choked up with emotion I couldn't even speak, so I just nodded.
"I guess you don't want him to know where you're going?" I nodded again. "I've got a sixteen year old daughter. If something like this happened to her, I would hope someone would help her out too." I just stared at the woman, unable to speak, unable to do anything but look just as I felt—beaten, physically and emotionally. "Nicky! I'm taking my break. Be back in twenty!" she called out, grabbing her bag and stepping around the counter.

"W-w-what are you doing?" I finally stammered.

"My name is Rita, you don't need to tell me yours if you don't want to. First rule in running, don't leave a trail. Buses are always the first choice, but it's a bad choice 'cause people see you on buses. Bus drivers, passengers, people at refuel stations, check stops. My husband, BJ, he's a truck driver. He's as deaf as a mule, but he's a good man and he won't hurt you." She looked at me pointedly as she led me out of the bus terminal. "He is due to leave in fifteen minutes and he's headed to Lilyvale, a small town about nine hours from here. His cousin Larry lives there, he has a rig too; does long hauls from the east to west coast. We'll tee up a drop off at his place and he can take you further away if that's what you want. He won't hurt you either. Neither of my boys can stomach a woman being hurt like this." I didn't know why I trusted this stranger. Perhaps because I was naïve or perhaps it was because I simply needed to. After all, what could be worse than what I was leaving behind? In front of me now was nothing but survival.

"Ella, my name is Ella." Rita smiled and I followed her

away from my home, away from hate—finally.

CHAPTER 2
FOUR YEARS LATER

Jax

"The thermostat doesn't appear to be working. With that storm coming in we're gonna need the heat," came Beth's raspy voice from the doorway. She needed to stop smoking. Maybe that husky tone had once been sexy, when she was younger, but now, she just sounded like the pack a day hardened addict she was.

"It's not a problem Beth, I'll take a look in a sec. It probably needs a new fuse. I've got heaps of them laying around." My eyes were fixed on the folder before me. Bills, so many bills. Mercy had been hiding them from me. It had taken me the last hour to find the folder hidden under a tray of never ending filing. I knew she didn't want me paying her bills, but fuck, I wasn't about to use the money, so it might as well go to something good like the shelter.

"Mercy will be pissed if she finds out you've been going through her files again." Beth chuckled. I looked up and grinned. Yep, she'd be pissed, if she found out. Beth looked tired. She was a fifty something year old woman who had lived a hard life, too hard and it showed on her lined face and in her tired eyes. I would take the first shift tonight even though I was dog tired myself. Beth needed a break.

"She will be pissed if she finds out. Are you planning on telling her?" I quizzed Beth as she turned to leave.

"Hell no! I've seen Mercy pissed and it ain't pretty." Beth strolled back down the hall leaving me alone in the icy office. Yep, the thermostat was most definitely not working. I ran my hands through my hair and grinned with lazy satisfaction. It was too long. I should probably get it cut, but after nine years of working for Uncle Sam and wearing his butt ugly military enforced buzz cut, I was enjoying this slight rebellion.

I stood and stretched my aching six foot six frame. Yeah, I was tall. Mercy says she has no idea where it comes from. She's all of five foot five and according to her, my good for nothing father barely reached five-six. Grabbing a spare fuse off the bookshelf I made my way down the narrow corridor and down the steep stairs to the basement. It was freezing down here and dark and damp. The dark had never bothered me and I had endured climates of both bitter cold and scorching heat before. I was the only one who would come down here. Mercy was too busy, David had no idea how to replace a fuse and Beth was convinced a ghost had taken up residence. Against the back wall was my unmade bed, the uncomfortable portable kind. And in the center of the room hung a punching bag, this was my timeout. When looking at the bruised and battered bodies of women and children got to be too much, I came down here and beat the anger out of me. I was blissfully anger free right now, so I bypassed the bag and quickly sorted out the new fuse, adjusted the thermostat and climbed the deadly staircase out of the basement, making sure to close and lock the door at the top. There were two children with their mothers who had found refuge in the shelter at the moment and I didn't want either of them stumbling down the unsafe stairwell. My nose led me straight to the kitchen where dinner was being prepared. I rubbed my hands together, enjoying the warmth radiating from the ovens. Nancy, a middle aged woman with wisps of grey hair amongst a short brown bob, took a nervous step back away from me. Nancy was new; she had only been staying with us a week and she was as skittish as a mouse. Her cautious green eyes were submissively downcast, her hands timidly linked in front of her, rubbing anxiously at her fingers. I pretended not to notice the fearful response and smiled. It was the usual reaction from the women in the shelter who did not know me well. I was a big powerful man and most of these women had run from big powerful men who had beaten the ever living crap out of them. I knew I made many of them nervous, but for the regulars, they came to realize I would not lay a finger on them. I was a diehard protector, especially when it came to women and children. In the shelter, I was handyman, gardener, dishwasher, office boy, the resident go-for and, on occasions, security. Mercy's Shelter for Abused Women was owned and run by my mom, Mercy, and whenever I returned from a mission, I would help out. My last mission was in Afghanistan eight months ago and, after many weeks of deep contemplation, I decided that this return would be permanent. At twenty-seven years of age I had seen enough death and destruction to last a life time and, to be honest, could easily have done without the misery and despair that came with the shelter. But this was Mercy's life, her dream and as she often said, "from the pits of despair they shall rise stronger." Nothing gave me more satisfaction than seeing a defeated woman regain her strength and pride. And many of the women who came to Mercy's Shelter did. When they arrived they were at their lowest—beaten, starved and desperate. Fortunately, thanks to the hard work of Mercy, many of these women left with renewed spirits, hope and a strength they had long forgotten. Of course there were some that didn't recover, no matter how much time and effort you put in; some returned to the very prick that sent them running in the first place. And then there were the few, when at their very lowest and most vulnerable, they would end their misery. I shivered at the memory of the tiny teenager I had found slumped in a pool of blood in the bathroom six months ago. Sure, I had seen death before, I had meted it out. But somehow this was different. I had tried to reach out to Sarah but she was having difficulty trusting me. Perhaps I didn't try hard enough because I had surely failed her. She was innocent, so young. She should have been at home with her mom and dad arguing about the clothes she wore and the music she listened too. Not slumming it on the streets and selling her body to buy food.

I had to stop thinking of her, for the thoughts led me back to nightmares and cold sweats. Nightmares that had once forced me to seek help for post-traumatic stress with the shelter's only therapist, Dave.

"Damn, smells good in here Mary. Anything I can do to help?" A large, well rounded woman with flushed cheeks and a toothless grin glanced over her shoulder at me.

"You get out of my kitchen boy. Last time you tried to help the oven caught on fire." I laughed loudly. I liked Mary. She told it how it was—I couldn't cook for shit.

"Now that wasn't my fault. I was so distracted with your shepherd's pie I completely forgot about dessert so, I think it's safe to say, that was your fault."

Mary laughed. "Here, taste this." She handed me a warm muffin right from the oven. My eyes rolled back in my head as the chocolate flavor burst and flooded my mouth. I let out a highly inappropriate, yet appreciative groan.

"Have you tried one of these yet?" I suddenly asked Nancy who still stood anxiously by the door. She barely met my eyes and shook her head. "Mary, give the lady a muffin while they're still warm." I didn't spare her another glance, I didn't want to make her feel any more anxious as I left the kitchen. I felt the woman's eyes on me as I walked away though. She was curious, wondering if I could be trusted, who I was, why I was here. If she was intending on staying a while, she would realize she had nothing to fear.

"Is it a full house tonight?" I heard Mary call out.

"Yep. No spare beds tonight."

I made my way down the corridor and into the large open plan room which served as a rec room, dining room and bedroom. The beds were set up on the farthest side of the warehouse, thirteen to be exact, with the occasional divider to help afford the women some measure of privacy.

The bathrooms were close by and handy. The other side of the warehouse was furnished with big old comfy lounge chairs and a couple of big wooden tables. Nothing matched, but it was all sturdy and clean. Mercy's Shelter was by no means large, but it was tidy, warm, comfortable and more importantly, safe.

"Hey Jax, I'm hungry," called out a tiny voice from the floor to my left. A little brown haired boy with big blue eyes followed my movement through the room, bouncing on his little feet with excitement. At six years old, Eli was the youngest in the shelter and had been staying regularly with his mother, Annie, for over a month now. Annie had picked up work at the local diner and had almost saved up enough money to rent a small apartment. As much as I was proud of Annie for turning their lives around and making a fresh start for her and Eli, I would be sad to see them go. Eli was a breath of fresh air in the shelter. He was excitable, carefree and always sporting an honest and innocent grin. He was one of the lucky ones whose mom got him out before he could be physically or emotionally scarred by his father's heavy handed reign. The other child currently in residence was a twelve year old girl, Sam. She was not so fortunate. Her mother had carried her under-nourished beaten body in three weeks ago. Neither Sam nor her waif of a mother, Georgia had said much since arriving. They had obviously suffered and the fact that they were here now spoke volumes. But they couldn't stay forever. Mercy and Dave would have to have a sit down with Georgia soon and plan their next course of action. Dave was the in-house shrink. In the beginning I was suspicious of his reasons for joining the shelter. I assumed my mother's pretty smile and playful blue eyes had drawn him in. But David in action was something else to behold. He loved his job and he truly cared about his patients. In the shelter he operated in stealth mode, not flaunting his fancy degree or doctor title. He was simply Dave and he was there to talk and offer advice. He was a welcomed and much needed addition to the team and the fact that he loved my mother was even more welcoming. She deserved a man like Dave after the many years of dealing with my biological father's shit.

"Ten more minutes little man. You better go wash up for your momma." Eli turned and scrambled away for one of the bathrooms. I could already feel the large open area starting to fill with warmth from the fixed thermostat. Crossing the hall to the small room that was the entry to Mercy's Shelter I headed for the big heavy front door. It was time to lock the place down for the night. Mercy had left almost an hour ago, leaving Beth and I on for tonight's watch. I didn't do night shifts all that often now, but two of our volunteers were down sick and our other male staff member, Blue, wanted a couple of nights off, so here I was. Curfew was normally late, eleven p.m., but the beds were already full and the storm was settling in. No one else would come knocking tonight.

As I reached the door I glanced through the fogged up window, giving it a quick wipe to check the street front. As my hand reached the heavy dead bolt something caught my eye. The snow and wind was vicious, blinding everything with a flurry of white. But somewhere out there I caught a dark shape moving along the sidewalk. Watching carefully I noticed it again, drawing closer to the building. Hunched over, the petite body pushing against the wind slipped on the ice and went down hard. I didn't hesitate to pull open the door and trudge out into the bitter storm. With no jacket it was crazy cold. A few long strides forward I reached the fragile girl struggling to get to her feet.

"Hey, are you okay?" I yelled over the howling winds. The tiny figure snapped to attention, beautifully slanted, dark brown eyes widened as they took me in. She was gorgeous, even under the heavy layers of jackets, the tattered old beanie and thick scarf. Her skin was porcelain white, with cheeks flushed from the cold, beautiful lips that I just knew would hold a drop dead gorgeous smile. Her eyes ran a heated trail up my body and I knew she was impressed and terrified. I smiled and instinctively I raised my hands as a gesture of calm and safety.

"It's okay, I won't hurt you. I work in there." I pointed behind me. "It's a women's shelter. Do you want to come in?" I hoped to God she said yes and said it soon before one or both of us went into hypothermia. Her eyes shifted from me to the warehouse, nervously. Oh yeah, she had that same look they all did, suspicion and fear. "We have a full house tonight, all women except for me. I know, I'm crazy to put myself in confined quarters with so many women, but I enjoy being fussed over. Anyway, if you ladies all wanted to band together and take me down, I'm sure you'd have no trouble." I allowed a small grin just to let her know I was making a joke. These scared fragile women didn't often get my sense of humor. To my surprise, a small grin escaped those pretty lips that were starting to turn blue.

"Come on in and take a look at least. It's too damn cold to be standing out here. I don't even have a jacket on, you're all bundled up and I'm freezing my cojones off."
With only a moment's hesitation, she moved forward, mindfully taking a wide birth around me. I didn't walk behind her—I knew that made the women nervous—but instead stayed slightly to the side and in front. I opened the door and stepped through, holding it open so she could follow. The warmth was welcome as I slammed the door shut on the frigid storm outside.

"My name is Jax Carter. This is Mercy's Shelter. I help run the place. There is no reason for you to be afraid here." I had said those words thousands of times, planting the seeds of trust right from the start. The pint-sized girl stood sopping wet, shivering and watching me warily. Her little fists were curled up at her side, her face a little defiant. She had anger in her. She was a fighter. You needed that strength to live on the streets, but not even her bold little stance could hide the fear. At least she wasn't screaming or fainting. It had happened before. "Come on in. You can take a warm shower and get some dry clothes on. Supper is about to be served but I'll make sure to save you a plate." I moved through the small foyer not checking to see if she would follow. She either would or she wouldn't, it was something that couldn't be forced.

CHAPTER 3

Ella

Only I would have the rotten luck to step off a bus and into a full blown blizzard. But I'd take the freezing, icy snowstorm over Marcus any day. How I ended up in Claymont, at the base of the Black Ridge Mountains, I have no idea. I was supposed to be on my way to the ocean. For four long, tiring years I had been making my way in that direction, the clear blue skies and golden sands of the ocean calling me forward. However, this morning when I pulled out my small wad of cash and looked up at the glittering lights of the departures board at the bus station, something drew me to Claymont. Rita had mentioned the town to me a couple of months ago; she had a friend there who owned a flower shop. The fact that the town now stared down at me, taunting me, daring me was surprising. Call me superstitious, but I always listened to my gut. So, here I was in the freezing snow with no idea where the closest hotel was. I was hungry, cold and beginning to feel a whole lot sorry for myself which just made me angry. I didn't need anyone's pity, least of all my own. Mind you, even if I did somehow stumble across a hotel, I didn't really have enough money for a room, but it wasn't the first time I had arrived somewhere without money and a roof over my head. Somehow I always ended up okay. I had only had to sleep on the streets a handful of times over the years and I hated it, but never enough to face the wrath of returning to Marcus. I always tried to make sure I could swindle my way into some sort of shelter, even if it was a hospital. Yes, I was guilty of faking an illness just to spend a night in the warmth and safety of a hospital. I hated the cold, I hated being homeless, I hated the fucker who put me in this position so much the thought of him burned like acid in my chest.

As I had stumbled along the street feeling miserable and sorry for myself, heading toward what I hoped was the city, I had slipped on the slick ice of the sidewalk and fell in a graceless heap on my ass. As I cursed my pathetic luck a tall figure appeared before me. Instinct kicked in and I quickly climbed to my feet, fists clenched, walls of resolve hastily erected as I faced the threat. The towering hulk of a man before me was enormous; he had to be six foot five, maybe more. His shoulders and chest were wide and nicely displayed in a tight, long sleeved shirt. Nicely displayed? Why the hell was I observing my threat's hotness rather than gearing up to kick him hard in the balls? For some reason my eyes had developed their own mind and continued to peruse the fine form before me. His long legs were hidden behind well-worn denim. His hair was blonde, that golden sandy blonde that looked like it needed a wash and it hung in his eyes in an almost rebellious style that screamed I-don't-give-a-fuck. And those eyes, so grey they were almost silver. A tiny smile pulled at one side of his lips in a playful manner. The look screamed bad boy, run, escape, but the gentle concern in his eyes drew me forward. He held his hands up, a gesture of surrender, peace and he told me the open door behind him led to a shelter. I read the large sign over the door and couldn't believe my luck; I had literally slipped across the doorway of a shelter. He joked about being the only male in a shelter full of women; he arrogantly grinned at how he enjoyed being fussed over by the ladies and I found myself smiling too. I followed him inside with my defenses alert, my fists still clenched ready to fight if necessary. I knew I wouldn't need to though, this stranger's eyes were honest and kind.

"My name is Jax Carter. This is Mercy's Shelter and I help run the place. There is no reason for you to be afraid here." Jax, his name rolled through my mind like honey.

He turned, expecting me to follow and while my mind said no, my feet said fuck off and caught up to the giant man as he strolled with casual ease through the doorway and into a big warm room. Damn he was tall. Marcus had been a big man but Jax was bigger. And for some reason, even though his overwhelming presence was frightening, I also felt curiously safe. Safe like I had not felt in a very long time.

"Do you have a name?" he asked over his shoulder. I had gone by many names over the years—Kylie, Jemmah, Melanie, but something made me want to tell this stranger the truth. I had no idea why. Perhaps my brain had frozen somewhere between the bus depot and the shelter. He glanced over his shoulder again, most likely to see if I would answer. His lop sided grin sent my heart into some crazy aerobatic somersault.

"Ella," I mumbled. His smile widened and small dimples made those roguish good looks more boyish, more innocent, younger somehow.

"That's a pretty name." He turned back to lead me through the shelter. Pretty! Ahhh geez. Well if he didn't blow my senses to hell with his cheeky grin and gentle eyes, the compliment sure as hell did it. I forced myself to look away and take in my surroundings.

As far as shelters went, this was by far one of the nicest I'd been in, but also one of the smallest. I wondered if they had room for me. A few curious gazes watched me, though not for long. As soon as my eyes met theirs they looked away, normal for places like this. Everyone was running from something or someone. Nobody wanted to give away their miserable stories with the honest truth behind their eyes. A middle aged woman with curly brown hair pulled into a messy pony tail nodded at Jax. I couldn't pick her age, maybe fifty, sixty at most? Her eyes were full of understanding; like she knew the truth and maybe she did. She looked tired and beat and I didn't doubt that she had her own demons and nightmares. She seemed as tired as I felt but her smile was warm and friendly. She showed no sign of pity. I appreciated that, I hated pity, didn't need it or want it. Only moments ago I had been filled with so much pity for myself I could have drowned an entire city in it. She was placing a plate of food onto the lap of a young girl who looked to be around twelve. The little girl glanced my way and I saw it. The shattered innocence and despair. God, I hated that I could spot it so easily. If I hadn't of lived this life I might have been able to be comfortably oblivious to such hopelessness. Would I though? Could I ignore these people, these places? People who hadn't spent time on the streets, who didn't struggle, they didn't truly understand and most of them had no trouble turning their heads and looking the other way. I would like to think I wouldn't be so callous, but maybe, if my life had been different, if my dad hadn't died, I would be one of those people who was blissfully ignorant of such a tragic existence.

"Hope you left some for me, Sam," Jax said playfully. The

little girl attempted a smile but it did not reach her eyes. Suddenly her plate of food became the most interesting thing in the room.

"Who do we have here?" the woman asked, her voice rough and husky.

"Beth, Ella, Ella, Beth." Her smile grew bigger.

"Nice to meet you Ella. You look like you could use a warm shower." I was shivering uncontrollably, my teeth almost clicking together, my fingers and toes felt numb.

"Jax, you remember it's a full house tonight?" She turned her attention to Jax, though her kind smile remained firmly in place.

"How can I forget when you keep reminding me?" Jax continued to move through the room, waving me on. "Come on, Angel, let me show you where you can wash up. I'll go prepare you a plate of food while you get warm." First pretty, now angel? The sentiments made my heart do silly things. Hold up, full house? That meant no beds.

"I don't need a bed. If I could just wait out the storm I'll go find somewhere else to stay as soon as it's passed." Jax shook his head as he led me around the rows of tidy beds and to a doorway at the back of the room.

"It won't be a problem Ella. Take a shower, warm up. I'll get you something to eat. I'll drag my bed up out of the basement for you and I'll bunk down on the couch in Mercy's office for the night." He handed me a big fluffy towel, it was soft and smelt wonderfully clean. Yep, this was officially the best shelter I had ever stepped foot in.

"I don't want you to go to any trouble. I can sleep on a couch. I'm smaller than you so I'm sure I'll be more comfortable on a couch," I argued while discreetly inhaling the scent of the fresh towel. Jax grinned.

"It wouldn't be very chivalrous of me to allow a lady to sleep on the couch while I snuggled in a nice warm bed and I am quite the gentleman around here so don't bother arguing."

"I'll be out of your hair first thing tomorrow," I said.

"We don't usually have a full house. There are a few regulars out there who only come when they need a break from home. There will be at least two empty beds by tomorrow night.

You can stay as long as you need." Suddenly I felt uncomfortable. Never before had it bothered me to bunk down for a few nights, sometimes even a few weeks in a shelter. It beat sleeping in doorways and stairwells, but standing here before this beautiful man who obviously had a home, most likely a wife with the standard two-point-five kids, dog, the whole cozy deal. I suddenly felt like the failure Marcus had assured me I was.

I clenched my jaw hard, pressing away the tears, the weak and pathetic tears that always came at the most inappropriate times. Like when Rita, BJ and Larry had come to my rescue all those years ago. Even now when I put in my regular 'I'm okay' phone call to Rita, her kindness and concern still brought tears to my eyes. Give me anger and violence and not a drop would fall, but kindness got me blubbering within seconds. I couldn't say anything, so I simply nodded.

"Door locks from the inside, so don't worry about anyone walking in on you. There are three showers in the shelter, but this one is the largest. Have you got dry clothes in there?" He nodded to my backpack.

"Yes," I growled, the looming sorrow disappearing with irritation. I knew I sounded like an ungrateful brat, after all Jax was only trying to help me, but it pissed me off that he thought I was so inept I couldn't even scrounge together dry clothes.

"Soap." He tried to hand me a clean wrapped cake of soap and I shook my head.

"I h-have my own s-soap." Damn, between the shivering, the effort it took not to cry and being pissed off, I could barely talk.

"Well, go get cleaned up. When you're done I'll be in the kitchen. Just go through the doorway on the other side of the room, turn right and follow the corridor. Kitchen is at the very end. You can't miss it, it smells amazing." I simply nodded as Jax strolled away and I backed into the large cubicle behind me, locking the door. It was simple, nothing fancy, but again, clean. It smelled a little like detergent and bleach. Dumping my bag on the small counter I quickly shed my wet clothes and got under the steaming hot spray. My fingers and toes stung from the sudden rise in temperature. It was a delicious pain, a biting warmth and reminder that I was alive.

Suck shit Marcus, Mister 'I-Can-Find—A-Needle-In-A-Haystack-If-I-So-Wish'. I smiled at the thought of Marcus's departing words. Didn't find me though did you asshole? Once the stinging pain had seeped from my extremities, I dug out my bottle of coconut body wash. I always carried my own toiletries. Living in shelters and rooming with strangers had taught me that no matter how low on cash I was, I had to have those luxuries. I quickly and efficiently washed. I never lingered under the hot spray of water that wasn't my own, there were always others who needed that hot water too. I also had no desire to see or feel the scars that covered my arms. They reminded me of my own weakness and just how low I had let my life sink. And the deep ugly scars on my wrists, I hated them most. They reminded me of Marcus, just as he said they would. They were ugly and made me feel ugly. What would a man like Jax think seeing those scars? I bet his beautiful wife had no scars. Stop feeling sorry for yourself, Ella. You're alive and you escaped. You're better off than most. I didn't have another jacket. Only long sleeved shirts and a couple of sweaters. But it seemed warm in the shelter and my jacket would be dry enough to wear come morning.

I left my hair out, as always, to cover the scar by my eye. I collected up my damp clothes and grabbed my backpack heading off to find the kitchen. Hopefully there was somewhere I could hang my wet clothes.

"Hi," came a little voice from beside me as I stepped out of the shower. He was a little brown haired blue eyed bundle of joy and innocence and as cute as a button. There was no stopping the smile that he brought to my face.

"Hi yourself."

"What were you doing out in the storm?"

"Oh, I only just got into town. I didn't realize there was going to be a storm." He nodded thoughtfully.

"Did your mom and dad bring you?" Such an innocent question and it made my smile drop slightly.

"No, I caught a bus. Have you ridden on a bus before?" I easily deflected the conversation away from family. His eyes widened.

"Sure, I went on a bus to school once." My smile was back in place. "I'm Eli." His little hand outstretched, mimicking the manners of an adult, and I politely shook it.

"It's nice to meet you Eli, my name's Ella." His blue eyes lit up.

"Ella and Eli. We kind of match."

"We kinda do. We've got pretty awesome names." Eli suddenly disappeared in a rush of excitement, squealing to his mother how our names 'kind of' matched. Floating on a euphoric cloud of childish innocence, clean and warm from the shower, I wandered through a long corridor, following the incredible smell that wafted through the air. Holding my clothes in front of me like a shield, I stepped into the large kitchen. Like the rest of the shelter, it was clean, all but a few dirty dishes. A significantly round woman laughed with a loud shrill, her rosy cheeks flushed. She spotted me by the door and I shrunk back suddenly wishing I could disappear into the corridor behind me. I hated being the center of attention.

"Come on in before this big oaf eats all your dinner." Jax had his back to me, but when he heard the stoutly woman's invite he casually turned around and smiled.

"Feeling a bit warmer now, Angel?" Flip went my heart, stupid Ella. He more than likely had pet names for all the women in the shelter and no doubt saved the truly heart melting sentiments for his wife.

"Does angel have a name?" the woman beside him asked, wiping her hands on a large apron. She gave Jax a curious smirk.

"Sorry Mary, this is Ella, she just blew in with the storm." Jax lifted two plates and put them down at a tall bench in the center of the room.

"It's nice to meet you Ella. And I mean it, get your skinny backside in here and get some supper before Jax eats it all. I mean look at him, he's the size of a damn oak, he needs all the food he can get to fill those long legs." My eyes automatically went to those impressive legs before my mind caught up and realized what I was doing. Jax grinned; I was totally busted. I knew I blushed and hated it. I put up my shields, my determined pout behind the long veil of hair that shrouded my face falling forward around me. "Here, let me take those for you. We have a laundry room and I've got a few things to wash. You have anything else that needs to be washed?" I shook my head and hesitantly handed my clothes over to Mary. I didn't like handing over my possessions to others. I had so few things of my own that I preferred to take care of them myself, that way I could be sure not to lose anything. I know they were only things, material things, but things were harder to replace these days. Money was always scarce which meant being extra careful of what little I did have. Mary winked as if recognizing my hesitance. "I will take good care of these, Ella. I'll make sure you have them back before you go to bed tonight."

Jax was already sitting down to his own plate of food. He didn't force me to join him; no expectations, just the silent offer of a meal. My backpack slid from my shoulders and I let it fall to my feet as I climbed onto the tall chair at the counter.

"I hope you're not a vegetarian. Not that Mary minds cooking vegetables, but she's got this thing about fattening everyone up and she seems to think that it's done with three food groups—pig, beef and lamb."

I took a deep breath and drew in the spicy aroma of what I think was beef casserole, with what looked like real beef and veggies.

"Yep, real beef," Jax murmured. "Not many shelters offer the real thing, so I'm told. Most the women who stay are surprised with the food. Mary's husband is a butcher. He provides us with enough meat to feed a small army. And trust me, it tastes a hell of a lot better than the food I was forced to eat in the army." I cast him a sideways glance.

"You're a soldier?" I asked the words so low I wondered if he would even hear me.

"Was," Jax wiped his mouth politely with a napkin. "I served for nine years, right out of high school. I finished up my last tour a little over eight months ago."

"You didn't like it?" I was genuinely curious. Even though he was built like a soldier, he didn't exactly look military. His hair was too long, his eyes too gentle and warm. He nodded towards my food.

"Tell you what, I'll talk if you eat." I glanced at my food; it smelled delicious. He didn't need to make me a deal to force me to eat it. But the chance to sit and listen to this beautiful man was too much to refuse. I should have been scared of Jax. I was always reluctant and cautious around men and large men like this one usually just freaked me out. However, sitting here alone in this kitchen with Jax felt unusually comfortable and there seemed to be no hostility in him, no hatred or violence. Not like Marcus where the hatred in that man's stare was almost as punishing as his fists. The violence he had brought to my world not only left me physically scarred but emotionally scarred. All it took was a raised voice for my heart to break into a panicked stutter; the violence of a fight—fists hitting, pushing, screaming—all sent me into a full blown panic attack. I had other triggers too. If someone came at me from behind, I would lose my shit; the smell of cigars made my stomach turn; big men dressed in expensive suits sent me into fight or flight mode; basically any memory that was associated with Marcus caused me to slip into a panic that would cause my lungs to squeeze close until I either passed out or regained control. "Hey," Jax's gentle voice bought me straight back to Mercy's kitchen where I realized I was rubbing my wrists as the memories threatened to drag me away from this moment. "Lost you there for a minute," he noted. Letting my hair fall forward again, protecting me from his knowing gaze, I scooped up some beef and put it in my mouth. Delicious!

"I didn't hate the army. I was good at it. Moved my way up the ladder quickly, but in the end I was more interested in saving lives, rather than taking them. Don't get me wrong, I believe in what our soldiers are doing for our country and others, but it just wasn't for me." I nodded as I greedily shoved food in my mouth. "I like to build things. I've built a lot of the furniture here in the shelter. I've set myself up a small construction company. Little jobs, sometimes sheds, I've helped build a couple of homes for friends, for Mercy, even my own." I glanced at his hands, big, strong, calloused hands. They were nothing like Marcus's soft hands that only knew violence and hate. Jax's hands were made to create and protect. I looked at my own hands. A little soft from my last job, eight weeks washing dishes; easy work, crap money. It had been a long time since charcoal had colored my fingers. Almost twelve months to be exact. Over the last four years there were only four portraits that I sketched and they currently lay safely folded at the bottom of my backpack. Sketching brought me painful memories of what could have been. However much I loved to do it, I just couldn't bring myself to keep it up.

"There you go again." Jax was watching me carefully. "Am I boring you?" he teased. I blushed like a school girl and rolled my eyes at my ridiculous bashfulness. We finished up our meals. Jax talked, I listened.

I enjoyed his voice; it was strong yet gentle and always enthusiastic, like even the most insignificant moment was important. He told me all about the shelter and a little more about his business. He never asked questions, never pried, not once. I wasn't sure if I was relieved or disappointed. When I realized we had sat talking for over an hour I was stunned that the time had passed so quickly and easily. I followed Jax back out into the common room, noticing the lights had been dimmed and most of the women had gone to bed. Eli sat at a table with an array of crayons and paper. A woman sat quietly at his side reading—his mother I assumed. I quickly made my way over to my new friend and slid into the free chair at his other side, placing my backpack safely at my feet.

"Mind if I join you?" Eli smiled and pushed a piece of paper my way. I could see he had drawn a very impressive looking bus. "The bus I came in on was red," I offered. Without hesitation Eli grabbed a red crayon and started coloring. I thumbed the crayon for a long time until eventually picking it up, my fingers caressing it almost nervously, like it might bite me or something. Then, with great hesitation, I pressed it to the page. After a few testing lines my hand took over. The worry in my mind seemed to disappear, the tension in my body lost. The world around me ceased to exist. I didn't even notice that I had reached for another piece of paper, nor had I noticed when Eli was dragged off to bed by his mother. I especially did not notice Jax sitting across the table from me, staring at me like I was some sort of mutant freak.

"Un-fuckin-believable," he gasped when I glanced his way.

My body tensed. It sounded like something Marcus would say when he was pissed off, right before he would hit me. I reached for my backpack, flight imminent. I didn't care that we were in the middle of a snow storm. Then I forced myself to be still and watch his eyes. No anger, just something akin to wonder. "Angel, that there," he pointed at the scattered drawings before me, "is fucking incredible." The tension began to recede and I gave myself a quiet reprimand for the haste with which my body turned to fight or flight mode. As I stared at those incredible grey eyes I realized I could easily fall for a man like Jax Carter and that scared me to death. I didn't do relationships, I didn't even do friendships. There was no room in my life for commitments; in fact, I had never once in my life developed what one might call a close relationship, other than with my dad of course. I had some friends, before Marcus. They disappeared about the time my bad behavior reared its ugly head and then my acceptable friends were replaced with completely unacceptable ones, like my drug dealer and his stoner friends. There were boys who easily took what I offered—sex, no strings attached, simple yet unsatisfying sex. Moments where I could embrace the fact that someone wanted me, if only for a short time and didn't involve violence or pain. Rita was the closest thing to a friend now and she was only a five minute phone call of reassurance every few months. She deserved so much more than that, after everything she had done for me, but it was all I could offer. Jax Carter couldn't and wouldn't be more than a man who gave me shelter and the sooner I got out of here and away from him, the better.

CHAPTER 4

Jax

I couldn't take my eyes off her. There was something about this girl that just drew me in. Physically, she didn't look anything like Sarah, but the fight and determination I knew she had inside was one and the same. Only Sarah had reached the point of no return, she had reached the bottom and I had failed to see it. Perhaps my attraction to Ella was an unconscious attempt to make up for my mistake with Sarah, but as a man I certainly did not miss the way my body responded to her, the want and need were undeniable. If she were another girl in another place I wouldn't hesitate in making a move on her, but here in the shelter was a completely different story. My position was clear—keep the women safe, keep them warm and fed, talk and listen—and that's what I would do for Ella, talk and listen, earn her trust.

I stared at the array of magnificent drawings before me. She had drawn Eli and Annie and a woman who I did not recognize, and lastly, me. Perfect, each and every one of them, such incredible detail. While she had been busy drawing I was able to admire her closely without scaring her off. She was so consumed with sketching she didn't seem to notice anything around her. She barely acknowledged Eli heading off to bed. Her fingers were small and slender, everything about her was petite and fragile, but her eyes were fierce. At one point her sleeve had slipped up and I got a quick glimpse of a deep scar on her wrist. It made my stomach twist with horror at the sight. Suddenly, all I saw was Sarah slumped on the stark white tiles, blood oozing from deep ugly slits in her wrists. I shook off the image that would send me into a shivering mess and focused on the little angel before me. Ella's scars didn't look fresh, but they bothered me.

She had, at some time in her precious life, sunk so deep she wanted to end it. To think a beauty like Ella had almost been lost bothered me far too much. In the short few hours I had known this angel, I had become a little obsessed. I couldn't get involved with one of Mercy's girls. Not only was it forbidden, but the women who came through the doors had too much baggage for romantic entanglements and, to be honest, I carried too much baggage for them. Most of the girls were passing through, rarely staying in town long enough for a date, let alone a relationship. And I didn't do one night stands, not anymore. I couldn't really call Selena a girlfriend; what we had going was mutually beneficial, more like I'll scratch your back if you scratch mine. Then once the itch was scratched we both went our own way. Not exactly a relationship but I wasn't screwing anyone else. The thing about war and death, it really fucks with your mind. For a short time, I thought losing myself in the body of a warm willing woman would fix all my problems. All it did was give me a few minutes, maybe a couple of hours, if I was really lucky, of blissful oblivion. No thoughts of blood, guns, explosions or fucking hot deserts. But when it was over I was right back at the start and the ridiculous game would begin again. When Sarah died I realized how disrespectful my life had become. Perhaps if I hadn't been so preoccupied with getting laid I might have noticed Sarah slipping, I might have been able to save her. I had stopped with all the women right then, Selena being the only one I allowed to return. Rubbing my tired eyes I gave Ella one last glance. No, I would not betray her trust, or that of any woman in Mercy's Shelter. I had learned to zip it up and keep my shit together. I gathered the pictures and took them with me while I went to fix myself a coffee. I don't know why I took them, some primitive part of me seemed to think they were mine. As I walked by Ella I caught her scent, a subtle blend of coconut and soap. Damn she smelled good, too good. I glanced at my watch. Three hours before I could wake Beth up for her shift. It was going to be a long night.

Even though my eyes were closed I knew the sun was bathed across my face and I squeezed my eyes closed tighter in a futile attempt to block it out. With a blink I quickly realized the blinds were drawn open and the sun was shining through in all its unholy glory. Mercy was hovering over her desk rummaging through paperwork.

"Shut the fucking blinds," I grumbled, rubbing my eyes. My stomach growled, acknowledging my brain was now awake and demanding food. First stop this morning would be The Pit Stop for their world famous all-day-breakfast.

"No, it's after ten, time to get up." Mercy's gaze never left her desk. "You know, if this place burns down the insurance won't cover us if we're over our quota and, if my memory serves me correct, last night was a full house. So how did we end up with a plus one?" I rolled over to look at my mother. She still had her head buried in that damn paperwork.

"Eli and Sam put us over capacity weeks ago. And since when do you care about that shit anyway?" Finally she looked up and smiled. My mom was beautiful. She had blonde hair and grey eyes just like me, but she was tiny, like a doll, a defiant and determined doll. Nobody crossed Mercy. The fact that her heart was bigger than Texas made her as damn near perfection as anyone could get. I threw my legs over the side of the couch. I was way too big for it and the bed that I had dragged up from the basement for Ella wasn't much better, but I rarely worked the night shifts anymore so when it came to uncomfortable sleeping arrangements, I dealt. My bed at home was a king; enormous and comfortable. I sighed just thinking about it and found myself wondering if Ella ever had a nice big comfy bed like that.

"You've been holding out on me, Jax." Curiosity got the better of me and I glanced over at my mother. She was holding the pictures that Ella had drawn last night. "If I had known, I would have put you to work years ago. These would be hanging in galleries all over the world and we would be rich." I couldn't help but laugh. More likely they would be stuck to the front of her fridge, along with all the other pictures the kids who crossed our threshold gave her.

"Our plus one did them. Pretty impressive, huh?" The need to check on Ella was all consuming as I pulled on my boots.

"Impressive is one word. She's talented. She shouldn't be in here drawing with children's crayons, that's for sure." I ran my hands through my messy hair and tried to subtly check my morning breath.

"Yeah, you stink. I can smell you from over here."

"I should, I lost my toothbrush again." I grabbed a warm can of Coke off the desk and took a swig.

"How the hell did you lose your toothbrush, again? And that's disgusting, Jax. Go home and cook yourself a decent breakfast." I belched loudly. Yep, I was quite the catch.

"Now that's impressive," Mercy grunted. I made for the door.

"I know you were in my files again. Keep out or I will toss you out of here." I couldn't help but laugh again. My mother, all bark but no bite. "And no point in rushing out, she's gone already." Was I really that transparent? Was she really gone already?

"When?" I didn't even bother refuting the fact I was in a hurry to check on Ella. Mercy looked up and smiled, that all knowing smile that infuriated me. I couldn't keep a damn thing from the woman.

"She was at the door ready to leave when I got here. Something about working finding an apartment. She hoped someone at the College might be looking for a roommate." I know the disappointment was written all over my face and right then I didn't care who saw it. "She's pretty," Mercy noted. My mother was far too perceptive for her own good. "She needs a bed and food Jax, not a date." Did she really think I would go there? It pissed me off a little.

"I'm not a greenhorn, Mercy. I know how to do my job and I've never gone there before, I wouldn't." Mercy smiled.

"I know, honey. She was very pretty though and you would have to be blind not to see the eager look in your eyes just now." I shook my head, still incensed that she would suggest I would try something inappropriate with Ella. I left her office. I needed a greasy breakfast, a toothbrush and a shave.

The previous night's storm had left a thick cover of snow. Thankfully Dave had already shoveled the sidewalk and the entrance into the parking garage out back. I headed straight for The Pit Stop for a breakfast that would contain enough oil to grease a motor or, in my case, my stomach. Benny was behind the counter arguing with someone about the price of milk. Benny always found someone willing to gripe about inflation to. I took a seat at the counter as a steaming mug of coffee was pushed my way. Man I loved The Pit Stop. I didn't even have to open my mouth unless it was to eat or drink.

"Damn, Jax, I've been looking everywhere for you," came a familiar sultry voice behind me. For some reason, today that voice rubbed me up the wrong way.

"Mornin' Selena." I took a long sip of my coffee, hoping to infuse some life into my bone tired body. She slipped onto the seat beside me and I chanced a quick look. As usual, she was stunning. Blonde hair in a perfect pony tail, makeup flawless, wearing a knock out dress that enhanced her assets flawlessly, but today, it didn't make my blood boil with lust.

"I caught Beth downtown and she told me you were at home. When I couldn't find you there, I went by the warehouse and Mercy said you'd just left. I saw your car out front. Pure luck I found you." She was smiling her deep red lips at me, looking through her thick lashes and seductive eyes and I didn't want her. I hated how she referred to the shelter as a warehouse. Sure it was in fact a warehouse, a nicely converted warehouse that I had worked on for months. But she had no respect for what it represented or the women who took refuge there.

"I'm on my way home. I just stopped for some fuel." A plate of greasy bacon, sausages, eggs and hash browns slid my way. "Supremely perfect as usual, Benny," I grinned. He nodded my way as he continued his pointless argument with some old guy at the end of the counter. I stabbed some bacon, sausage and egg and then lined it up for my mouth. When a soft hand stopped my progress I was more than a little irritated.

"Jax, that is so bad for you. It will clog your arteries and give you a heart attack." That got Benny's attention. How many times had Benny had the grease and heart attack argument?

"Or, I could just get hit by a bus when I leave. At least if that happens I will die a happy man with a full stomach." The hand was nudged aside, the food and grease promptly shoved in my mouth. Benny was back to arguing inflation and Selena pouted. It was supposed to be cute, but, to be honest, it just pissed me off. She had nothing to pout about. She had it good—family, money, education and a nice little job as a legal secretary. Sure, her mother and father were a little hard on her sometimes, pushed her, but she needed that push to even

44

attempt to do something with her life. She could do or be anything and I was pretty confident that without the nudge from her family she would be a professional shop-a-holic. A fucking spoiled brat.

I was in a mood today and if Selena wasn't careful, she would be on the receiving end of some serious man-grump.

"I thought we should catch up tonight. I could bring some Indian, wine, maybe a movie?" This was code for: I'll bring dinner and alcohol if you fuck me senseless. And usually I would be right on board. Not today though, and I hated Indian. I hated wine even more.

"I'm working tonight," I managed to say between mouthfuls.

"You don't do night shifts anymore," she grumbled.

"Volunteers are sick and Blue took a couple of days off." I kept shoveling food in my mouth in an attempt to not have to talk to her.

"Maybe I could stop by the warehouse?" Selena suggested. I clenched the fork with a little more gusto than needed. If she referred to Mercy's Shelter as 'the warehouse' one more time I would throw my greasy breakfast in her damned lap. Well, no I wouldn't, it tasted too good to waste like that. But I would definitely shout, then she would cry and I would feel like shit for yelling and making her cry.

"Sorry Selena, not tonight." This was code for fuck off and Selena didn't get it.

"Jax, I haven't seen you in over two weeks," she leaned in, her whispering voice a seductive breath in my ear. Okay, maybe that stirred something, but a moment later a girl walked up to the counter with long black hair and my thoughts suddenly detoured to another girl with long dark hair and beautiful brown eyes.

"I saw you out the front of your office last week. I can't tonight, I'm busy," I said with a little more force. Shit, now she was pouting again. I finished my breakfast; actually, I pretty much inhaled it without a thought other than this was the best greasy breakfast on the face of the earth. I threw some money on the counter, leaving a substantial tip and was surprised that I had all but forgotten Selena who still sat by my side. She looked a little taken back and I felt guilty.

"Sorry babe, maybe later in the week? Give me a call." This was code too. I really didn't want to catch up, but if she pushed, I might eventually give in. I gave her a quick peck on the cheek and left The Pit Stop. I had to drop into the office and make sure everything there was being handled and then I would go home for a couple of hours shut eye before heading back to Mercy's. And I had to admit, my heart did some crazy lurching shit at the thought of seeing Ella again.

CHAPTER 5

Ella

I had to get out of Mercy's. The moment I woke my eyes had darted around the room hoping to see Jax and when I hadn't been able to find him I was disappointed. I was angry at myself for wanting to see him, angry for caring. He was likely on his way home to see his wife and I was fawning over him like some naïve teenager. I needed to get my Claymont life together and first step was work. I had spoken to Rita a few months ago and when she realized the direction I seemed to be headed in she had mentioned an old friend who owned a florist in Claymont. She was apparently the type of employer who wouldn't ask questions and would pay me cash. I just hoped she was looking to put someone on.

The thick snow on the street outside had already been plowed. The snow fall had been substantial last night, but this morning the sun shone brightly melting the worst of it. I navigated the unfamiliar streets with ease. Claymont was a pretty town, small and nestled at the foot of some pretty impressive snowy mountains. The streets were quaint and tidy and even at this early hour there were people moving about with casual intent. I had read on a flyer at the bus depot that Claymont was home to a very large college , so no doubt the young faces passing me by were students getting ready for their day, filling the café's and moving about with a carefree ease that made me jealous. Perhaps that would have been me, planning a future, doing coffee with friends, laughing, smiling. Instead I had my usual sullen pout in place as I navigated the picturesque streets to the city's center searching for what I hoped would be a start for my uncertain future in Claymont. I easily found the little flower store and stood with my arms wrapped around me in the freezing morning air for almost an hour before I noticed a woman approaching the door searching through her bag like it was a bottomless abyss. She was startled when she looked up, but only for a moment.

"Ella?" she said with a little hesitation. I was surprised she knew my name. She was beautiful with platinum blonde hair styled into an elegant fifties style twist on top of her head. Her skin was alabaster white, the kind of white that could only be achieved with a healthy dose of makeup. Her full lips were painted a deep red shade that stood out in startling contrast to the rest of her pale features. Her eyes were a striking blue framed with heavy black mascara and eyeliner that was artfully applied to create an upswept look to her eyes. She wore a figure hugging red knee length skirt with a stunning white coat lined with fur over the top. She pulled off the pinup girl look with glamorous ease. I was jealous, she looked sensational. Rebecca was much younger than I had imagined. When Rita had mentioned she was a friend, I immediately thought of someone older, more Rita's age. But Rebecca couldn't have been much more than twenty-five. Rebecca smiled, eyes were full of fun and mischief, I liked her immediately.

"I spoke to Rita a couple of months ago. She told me you might be passing through Claymont and you might need some work. It's nice to meet you, I'm Rebecca. Come on in out of the cold." As I followed her through the entrance I was instantly hit by a wall of warmth.

"I have to keep the temperature up to stop the flowers from dying," she explained. "And to keep my fingers and toes from freezing off," she added with a smile. I didn't care what her motivation was, it beat the freezing chill outside hands down. The shop smelled amazing, just like spring. Flowers in buckets and vases filled the floor and shelves and a large table sat at the back of the shop. "Would you like a cup of coffee?" Rebecca asked, shrugging off her coat to reveal a tight fitting black top over ample breasts. I found myself glancing down at my flat chest with disappointment.

"Sure, do you have milk and sugar?" I asked silently chastising myself. I had bigger things to worry about than the size of my breasts.

"Absolutely, I also have caramel. Please tell me you will let me put caramel in your coffee, or a shot of whiskey?" How could I say no to caramel? Sugar and sweets were my favorite food group.

"Yes to the caramel, it's a bit early for the whiskey."

"It is, but I had a shitty night last night and this morning I've got Mrs. Beaumont coming in first thing to order flowers for the Thanksgiving Ball and she is one grade A bitch, so I am going to need the shot of whiskey." I smiled at Rebecca's casual and easy potty mouth. At least she wouldn't be offended by my constant and uncontrollable cussing.

The shop was small and full to the brim. She had a few knick-knacks for sale amongst the flowers, likely to be locally crafted trinkets. I liked it here. It was warm, smelled good and had a cozy feel. I really didn't care if she had me sweeping all day, I wanted to work here.

"Okay." Rebecca handed me a steaming mug of coffee. After taking a sip I had to admit the caramel was a welcome addition. "If Rita vouches for you that's good enough for me. I pay $9.50 an hour, cash. The store is open six days a week, but we won't jump in and work you straight into a grave. How about Tuesday to Saturday, eight to five?" I nodded. It was more hours than I anticipated and it meant I wouldn't have to find a second job. Rebecca smiled. "I always allow room for mistakes, but I expect you to learn from them. Me, I will never learn from my mistakes, I'm a glutton for punishment who needs my damn head examined, but hell, I'm the boss so I'm allowed." At that moment I wondered if she was talking about mistakes in the shop or life in general. Her eyes became a little distant and cloudy and she seemed somewhat sad.

"So, one mistake, we deal, two we get pissed, third time, you're out." She shook off her dejected moment, her carefree smile back in place.

"What would I be doing?" I wondered aloud. It really didn't matter, I wanted the job, but it seemed appropriate to ask.

"Oh, you know, the usual, shining my shoes, giving me hourly massages, pressing my linen." I stared at her skeptically.

"Will I be feeding your horses as well, my lady?" I joked and Rebecca laughed loudly.

"Oh Ella, we are going to get along just fine. My servant boy will attend to the horses, you can clean, serve customers, answer the phone, normal stuff. It would be nice if you could help me with some arrangements. Nothing too tricky to begin with, maybe some pruning and binding bouquets." I couldn't dance for shit, but at that moment I wanted to boogie around the store like an adolescent fool screaming hallelujah! Instead I settled for a more reserved nod and asked, "When can I start?"

Rebecca put me to work immediately and by five o'clock I was exhausted. I'd woken before five a.m. and I had worked without a break. My own fault, I was told to take two breaks, but I was too nervous to eat. Rebecca locked the door behind us and smiled.

"I don't really care what you wear to work; you will always have an apron on over it anyway, but make sure you wear your hair back tomorrow. You will be working with some pretty sharp scissors and pruning clippers. We don't want you accidentally cutting any of that beautiful hair off."

I nodded, but the thought of wearing my hair up kind of unnerved me a little. It had become an important part of concealing the 'real' Ella. If I was to wear it up, I might as well have been strolling down the street naked.

The thought terrified me, but I really wanted this job. It was such a good job.

"No problem," I murmured.

"You want a lift anywhere?" No way in hell was I going to ask my new boss to drop me off at a shelter for abused women.

"No, I'm good. I'm not far from here and I like to walk. I'll see you tomorrow." Rebecca jumped in her car and disappeared down the street. I pulled on my beanie and began the walk back to the shelter. It was an easy fifteen minute stroll at most, but I was tired. I hadn't eaten more than a chocolate bar all day and my stomach growled angrily for food. I even felt a little light headed. The closer I got to the shelter, the dizzier I became and as I reached the front door, I faltered as the world around me swooped and spun.

"Angel?" I don't know if it was the shock of his voice or the fact that I was dead on my feet, but everything promptly went black. The first thing I realized was I was on the ground, no mistaking the cold, icy pavement under my back. My body automatically tensed. Had I been hit? Had Marcus found me; was he here to finish me off? Was he waiting for my eyes to open, waiting for me to find consciousness so that I would not miss the next blow? I couldn't stop the shiver that racked my body and it had nothing to do with the seeping cold radiating from under me. Then three simple words brought me back, three simple words penetrated the cold and chased away the ghosts.

"You're safe, Ella." It was Jax, his voice firm but at the same time gentle, reassuring. "Come on Angel, open those pretty brown eyes for me." Somewhere in the deep recesses of my mind I didn't want to. I was afraid, embarrassed. But that soothing voice demanded my compliance and slowly I opened my eyes. For a moment the world spun and I thought it might go dark again.

Then I saw Jax, kneeling above me, a grin pulling the corner of his mouth into a cheeky smile. "There we go. And don't worry, you're not the first woman around here to faint on me. Usually they're screaming bloody murder for me to get the fuck away though." I didn't want him away. I wanted him closer. It had been a long time since I had let a man that close. In fact, it was before I had run from Marcus and you could hardly have called him a man. He had really been a boy at seventeen years old, very drunk and highly inexperienced, who definitely gave me no pleasure, or even cuddle once it was over. I wondered if Jax could give me what those boys had been unable to. I wondered if he could give me the care my life had long missed; I wondered if he could give me the safety I had been unable to find. But what frightened me even more was the sudden craving for the type of connection you could only get with an emotional and physical joining. Love, the deep, happily ever after, you are mine and I am yours kind of love. It was something I had been denied, it was something I continued to deny myself. But lying here now with Jax by my side, I wanted all that and I wanted it badly.

"Does your wife know you make women faint?" I wondered out loud. Where the hell had that come from? I was mortified and Jax grinned, a big grin, dimples and all.

"No doubt, if I had a wife she would be most impressed. Fortunately I am not married." Oh God, I almost sighed out loud. "Do you think you can sit up?" I didn't want to, but I tried. Whoa, quit with the spinning already. Jax chuckled. "Okay, take it easy." His hands pulled me back down again. "When was the last time you ate?"

"I had a chocolate bar at ten this morning." Jax just stared at me.

"That was it?" he almost yelled and I winced. Yelling was a trigger.

His big hands soothed my hair back from my face. Shit, my hair. I froze, unable to move or speak. I knew he had seen it when his thumb gently traced the small scar. "Angel, you need more food than a chocolate bar. You should have stayed for breakfast at least." Before I had time to realize what was happening, Jax had my backpack slung over his shoulder and he was lifting me from the ground. I tensed but held on to him none-the-less. His body was hard and warm and he smelled freakin' amazing. With every ounce of stealth I possessed I leaned in a little closer and took a deep whiff, hoping to God he didn't notice the crazy girl in his arms sniffing him like a damned dog. His arms felt like a cradle of comfort and protection as Jax carried me through the doorway into Mercy's Shelter.

"What happened?" came the same steady sure voice I had met this morning. A small blonde woman with pretty gray eyes strolled towards us and I could see she was worried. She had a comfortable confidence in her movements, I envied that.

"She fainted. She hasn't eaten today." Jax sounded slightly pissed and the woman gave me a frown that told me she wasn't happy either.

"I had a chocolate bar," I quietly argued.

"While I understand the importance of chocolates and sweets in a diet, it's not enough Angel. Ella, this is Mercy, my mother." he introduced me to the concerned tiny woman who stood before us. Jax had her eyes and when she smiled I noticed the dimples, one and the same. Lord only knows where he got his height from, no doubt his father.

"Well as much as I'm sure you would like to stand there all day holding her, go get her fed." Mercy chuckled. "I'm on my way out, perhaps we'll talk tomorrow Ella?" she said to me and winked at Jax. I wasn't sure I wanted to talk.

Talking usually meant revealing things that I tried hard to keep to myself. Jax was now carrying me through the shelter and gaining the much unwelcome attention of the few women who still occupied Mercy's during the day. Once we reached the kitchen, he carefully lowered me to a stool.

"You're not going to fall down again are you?" I shook my head. I still felt light headed, but I was fairly confident I was not about to faint again. Jax dropped my backpack at my feet and quickly turned to busy himself at the fridge. "Where've you been today?" he asked. I pulled my hair back over my face, hiding.

"I had to go see someone about a job. She wanted me to start right away." Jax stopped what he was doing and turned to face me, curiosity carved into his handsome features. "You got a job?" His words rubbed me the wrong way. Did I look so helpless that I couldn't get a job? Perhaps he thought I was stupid or something. I hadn't graduated school, I had missed too much in my final few years to warrant a graduation, but when I was there, when I cared, I did well. I also read a lot. I loved books almost as much as I loved sketching. I could have been or done anything with my life, before he stole my dreams.

"Yes, I got a job. I am capable of taking care of myself as much as having to find refuge in a shelter contradicts that idea. Now that I'm working I will be able to concentrate on finding an apartment. I haven't really spent that much time living in shelters. The lack of privacy kinda pisses me off." Jax chuckled.

"Sorry Angel, I didn't mean any disrespect. I'm sure you're more than capable of taking care of yourself. I just know there isn't a lot of work around at the moment. A few of the women who have been living here of late have had trouble finding a job." His words were not said with mockery.

"Well, I've never really had any trouble finding work. Washing dishes, sweeping floors, packing shelves. I'm not afraid of hard work or taking the dirty jobs that other people don't want. But this time I had a friend who knew someone here. They put in a word for me." Jax nodded and resumed to fixing me what looked like a sandwich. He brought it to the counter and placed it down in front of me.

"Mary gets in soon. When she does she will start fixing dinner. Have this now though, you need something in your system so you don't faint on me again." He grinned and grabbed two cans of Coke from the fridge pushing one towards me. "So, where are you working?" He sat directly across from me and I found I couldn't hide from his penetrating gaze. I was nervous under his scrutiny.

"Bouquets, downtown." Jax smiled.

"Rebecca Donovan, she's a good person. She donates to the shelter yearly. You will be the envy of all the women in here. Her store is warm and apparently it smells good." I couldn't help but smile at the memory. Yes, it did. Jax's smile turned into a slight frown. "Perhaps you shouldn't tell any of the other women just yet. They might get a little jealous." I nodded. I had no intention of telling any of them anyway. I rarely made friends in the shelters. I never stuck around long enough to make friends.

"I just need to stay a couple more nights and then I will get out of your hair. I get my first paycheck at the end of week and I will look for an apartment right away." Jax shook his head.

"Stay as long as you need angel. We have the room. Like I told you last night, today we've got two spare beds. Annie and Eli will be out of here in another week." I was glad they were getting out of here. No child should have to live in a shelter, regardless of how nice it was.

"They've been here nearly a month now. Eli's a good kid, he will do well in his own space," said Jax. I agreed, kids needed a space of their own, a place that didn't comprise of thirteen homeless women plus staff.

"You know, I'd like to earn my keep while I am here. I can't cook but I can clean. Maybe I could help around the shelter for a few hours at night?" Jax shook his head.

"You don't need to do that." I had almost finished the sandwich and I was feeling much better, stronger, more determined.

"Clearly, but I want to. I am more than capable of pulling my own weight and, to be honest, I like to keep busy." Jax considered that for a moment then nodded.

"Alright, I know Mercy would be grateful for the help. Mary did most of the laundry last night, so there is a ton of linen to fold and put away. You can help me clean up the kitchen. I can't cook for shit either so I always get clean up duty. I would appreciate the help." I finished the sandwich and rinsed my plate.

"If you point me in the direction of that laundry I will get it sorted before dinner." Jax showed me to the laundry room and soon after disappeared, leaving me to the large pile of towels and sheets.

Later that night, after my belly was full and I was feeling more alive than I had felt in the last four years, I helped Jax tidy the kitchen. The dishwasher was full and the few pots and pans left over I washed and Jax dried. I had carefully slipped on the gloves over my scarred arms, hoping, praying that he didn't notice.

"You know, you look like you've done that before," Jax teased as I scrubbed a pan, suds up to my elbows. His grin was mischievous and I found myself flicking the scrubbing brush in his direction. White suds landed on his shirt and for a heartbeat I panicked. What the hell had I done? Jax's eyes sparkled when he scooped up a handful of bubbles and flicked them back at me. He grinned, that big honest grin that made his dimples show. His playful nature was far too addictive and I found myself flinging more suds on him and soon we had abandoned the dishes and we were both sopping wet. I laughed loudly and the sound shocked me. Jax lost some of his smile, a thoughtful reflection replacing it.

"I like that sound, it suits you. You should use it more." I blushed, the usual response around Jax now and I let my hair fall forward over my face. That was my answer for everything. Run and hide. It pissed me off that I did it because I was better than that, stronger than that, but for some reason I couldn't seem to stop myself. Jax brushed my hair over my shoulder so he could see my face.

"What happened here?" he gently asked, his thumb tracing my scar again. His touch could not be ignored and the only thing I found frightening about it was the fact I wanted it more. I also found myself wanting to confide, wanting to unburden myself of the secrets that poisoned my soul. "You don't have to tell me if you would prefer not to. No pressure." Little did he know that in that moment I did want to tell him. My secrets had been my own for so long, maybe it was time to let them go.

"I hit the corner of a table," I offered. Of course it wasn't the whole story. Jax nodded.

"Was that before or after he hit you," he asked me matter-of-factly. I hesitated and finally cleared my throat to speak. "After," I murmured. Jax was silent while I finished the dishes. Quickly I pulled off the rubber gloves and tried to pull my long sleeves back into place.

Jax was too perceptive though, it seemed this guy heard, saw and knew everything. He carefully grabbed my hand and I flinched. His penetrating gaze observed me as he continued to hold my hand in a weak grip that I could easily break away from.

"I won't harm you, Angel. This?" His thumb traced the scar on my wrist. My heart hammered. I didn't want him to think I had tried to kill myself and I especially didn't want him to think of me as weak. His eyes held no pity, instead perhaps curiosity and something else. I was an expert at reading people, at seeing the truth in someone's eyes, but I couldn't make out what Jax was seeing and feeling right then. Horror? Fright? Guilt?

"It's not what you think," I snapped. Jax didn't react to my abrupt hostility. "I wouldn't do that to myself. I wouldn't give him the satisfaction." I was angry. Not at Jax, but Marcus. He did this to me, he's the one that ruined me. With blazing eyes of fury I turned to face Jax. I pulled my wrist out of his big warm hand and I angrily pulled my sleeves up and turned my arms over for Jax to see the marks in all their horrid glory. He looked at my scars and the playful joy in his eyes only moments before was completely and utterly gone. He looked at me with questions but did not voice them.

"These were mine." I pointed to the light scars that laced my forearms like a horrifying web of pain. "They were my lowest point. I did things, horrible things with the intention of pissing him off. I hated myself for the way I behaved. I had so much self-loathing that I did this to myself. But these," I pointed to the deep ugly scars on each wrist. "This was him. He drugged me and he cut me. He told me it was to prove that he owned me and controlled me." Jax's fingers lightly traced the scars, the gentle sweep of his fingers betraying the anger in his eyes.

"For a long time I hated myself, but I would not kill myself. I would not let him win the game." I didn't care if the scars repulsed him like they did me, I just had to be sure he knew I didn't try to commit suicide. Those warm grey eyes found mine and he nodded; he understood, he believed me.

"There you are." A woman's voice at the doorway interrupted us. I abruptly pulled my hands away and pulled my sleeves down, taking a hesitant step away from Jax. At the door stood a woman, long blonde hair styled perfectly. Her make up immaculate, dressed in an elegant pencil line skirt and fitted button down top. She looked like a model—glamorous, flawless.

"Selena, what the hell are you doing here?" Jax snapped. I winced at the callousness in his voice and was glad he didn't speak to me like that. The woman, Selena, didn't seem fazed though. Her eyes took me in, a touch of irritation behind them and a whole lot of repulsion. I instantly disliked her.

"I told you I wanted to see you tonight. Beth said I would find you out here. I brought a picnic; I thought we could spread it out in your office and have some alone time." There was no missing the meaning behind "alone time" and she made damn sure I was listening as she stared at me pointedly and spoke in a sing song voice that made me cringe.

"I already ate Selena and you know very well I don't have an office." She laughed, it was fake, horrible.

"You pay most the bills here so your mother's office is as good as yours." I could feel the tension rolling off Jax beside me. It made me restless and uncomfortable. This is what I hated—confrontation. This was a trigger and I had to get away from this uncomfortable lover's quarrel. I looked at Selena who was quite obviously a girlfriend and she was a bitch.

I felt like such an idiot. As if a man like Jax would truly care about a damaged little girl like me. He would want a real woman like Selena who looked perfect, no doubt not a scar would mar her beautiful body. I felt sick to my stomach.

"Excuse me, I'm just gonna leave you guys so you can have that alone time." I tried to offer Jax a smile, but I know it didn't reach my eyes. I snuck out of the kitchen and all but ran for the common room. I shook my head at my own stupidity. I had made a fool of myself, I almost allowed myself to care, to want. As if my battered soul could take that kind of risk.

CHAPTER 6

Jax

I still couldn't believe Selena was standing in front of me. I couldn't believe that she thought it would be cool to come here and the fact she had looked at Ella with such cold hostility was a reality bitch slap for me. I must have been stark raving mad to have been sleeping with this girl. What the hell was wrong with me? She was a heartless bitch and she just stood here in front of me now, smiling like an arrogant fool. I couldn't even pretend to contain the anger that boiled at the sight of her.

"You need to leave." I didn't move towards her. Her eyes flickered with uncertainty, but she quickly put that mask of confidence back on.

"Don't be silly. I came down all this way to see you, the least you can do is have a drink with me. I bought the red you like." I hated the red, I hated wine full stop. I was more of a beer kind of guy, but Selena liked me to look refined when we went out for dinner, which was rare. After all, our relationship had mostly been physical. We were not considered an exclusive couple which made me wonder why, all of a sudden, she seemed to be pushing for more.

"What are you doing Selena? We've always kept things casual. What's with the sudden clingy attitude?" She sighed and pouted that pout that was supposed to be cute, but it wasn't.

"Because Jax, casual doesn't work for me anymore. I'm not getting any younger, I will be twenty-five next month and it's time for me to settle down. You and I are perfect together. You could move into the apartment with me and sell your house; it is too far out of town anyway. "We can build up your business so that I can stop working. Don't freak out," she gave me a pointed look." Too late, I was already freaking out.
"Then we can think about kids. Maybe three, but in the future, like a year or two from now, once your construction company becomes sustainable and you can quit coming in here." I shook my head and laughed. Clearly Selena misunderstood my humor as she smiled back. The woman was certifiably delusional.

"Okay Selena, I normally wouldn't be so abrupt with a

woman, it's not my style, but clearly you are no ordinary woman." Her smile wavered. "You should not have come here tonight, not ever. The way you just glared at Ella with such bitterness was not only inappropriate but childish."

"She was touching you," Selena tried to intercede.

"Actually, I was touching her but that makes no difference to us or what I am about to say. I want you to leave. I want you to take your expensive wine that really does taste like piss and get the fuck out of here. I want you to delete my number from your cell and not call me again, ever." That got rid of her overachieving smile. Now she looked as pissed as I felt. "And this is a shelter. Mercy's Shelter for Abused Women. Not a fucking warehouse!" I felt better for adding that to my tirade.

"How dare you. After everything I have done for you." I laughed at that one.

"Seriously Selena, what the hell have you done for me, please enlighten me?" She hadn't done shit for me and she knew it as she stammered for words.

"I was there when you had your nightmares. When you had therapy, I was there for you." Woop-de-fuckin'-do. I had nightmares every fucking night and she thought having been witness to a couple granted her some sort of access to my head, to me? As for the therapy, she had absolutely nothing to do with that. That was on me. I dealt with my shit, Selena was nothing but an awkward and uncomfortable spectator in that part of my life.

"You know what Selena? I'm not interested in having this argument with you. Just do us both a favor and leave. We both knew what we were doing and it was nothing but an occasional fuck. I'm not at all what you need and lord knows you are definitely not what I need, or want." I knew that stung her like a bitch. She actually took a step away. Without a backward glance she pushed her shoulders back and left.

I threw the dishcloth across the room and took a few deep, calming breaths. I couldn't believe I had spoken to a woman like that and here of all places. I was pissed at myself for losing my cool, I was pissed at Selena for pushing me, but most of all, I was pissed that she had interrupted the moment between Ella and I. Ella had shown me her scars and it was a big deal. She hid them well, behind her clothing and hair and I wondered how much more of her body was covered in them. The scars up her arms were classic self-harm scars, small and pale. But the nasty rigid scars on her wrists, they had been deep and cut with purpose. They were meant for death and when I looked into Ella's pleading eyes I knew that she hadn't done that to herself which meant someone had hurt her, badly. She seemed too young to have been married, so most likely her father or another relative had harmed her, maybe even a boyfriend. I hoped Selena hadn't destroyed the small bond of trust I had managed to form with Ella. I needed to know more, I needed to know who had done this to her and if the bastard wasn't already dead or suffering in prison, he soon would be.

"So, what did you do? Run over her kitty cat? Spill coffee on her Louis Vuitton? Oh My God, please tell me you told her one of her boobs is bigger than the other?" Beth raised me from my thoughts and I couldn't help the smile that tugged at my lips.

"One of her breasts is bigger than the other?" I wondered out loud. I had honestly never noticed, never paid enough attention to those plastic monstrosities. I actually preferred more of a natural appearance and a little smaller. More like Ella and the thought made me internally groan. What was I thinking?

"Good lord, I don't know. But little Miss Perfect would be horrified. No doubt she would have scheduled an appointment with her plastic surgeon for first thing in the morning. That girl is more plastic than a Barbie doll." I laughed out loud at that one.

"I take it she's no longer on the premises?" I asked.

"Gone like yesterday's news. In fact, she left so fast I thought her panties might have been on fire." Damn, Beth had a way with words.

"Yeah, well, I have no idea what's going on with her panties nor will I in the future."

"Good to hear. Selena Liander is a bitch. You can do better than that." Beth picked up the dish rag I had thrown and tossed it on the bench. "Ella came out looking a little pale before, is she alright?"

"Yeah, she showed me some scars." I rubbed my hands over my face, trying to control the rage at seeing her body marked in such a way.

"Scars, as in plural?" I nodded and Beth's frown told me she was thinking the same thing I was, who the hell had hurt her?

"I want Dave to talk to her." Beth shook her head.

"She might not want to talk to Dave. She seems to have already established a connection with you. Maybe you should try talking to her again. See if you can get her to open up further. See if you can find out if the asshole who hurt her is in prison and if he's not we can try putting him there."

"I'm not trained for that kind of thing, Beth."
I could already feel the anger growing inside, I needed to go down into the basement for a round on the bag; I was far too tense. The women would see it and it would make them nervous.

"You don't have to be trained to lend an ear. You don't have to do anything different than what you've been doing. Show her she can trust you, let her lean on you." I nodded and suddenly felt tired. I had only a few hours' sleep the night before and this afternoon when I had finally gotten home all I wanted to do was come back to the shelter and check on Ella.

"I'll take first shift tonight. You go calm yourself down and get some shut eye." She didn't have to ask me twice.

"She opened up tonight; she could have flashbacks, nightmares."

"She had nightmares last night." Beth's frank admission shocked me. I hadn't heard a peep from Ella before my shift ended at two a.m.

"It was after you went to bed. She didn't scream out but she was unsettled, crying in her sleep.

"Fuck," I murmured. Many of the women had nightmares, but the fact that Ella was having them really bothered me in a way it shouldn't have. I was far too drawn to this girl.

"I'll keep an eye on her. Go get some sleep." I reluctantly left the kitchen and forced myself not to head for the common room. My brain screamed at me to keep a professional distance from Ella. Too bad my heart seemed to have a different plan entirely.

Ella

    The blonde bimbo left in an awful hurry and she didn't look happy and that made me happy. I couldn't believe I had shown Jax my scars, but a small part of me felt some resemblance to peace for having done so. I had shared something of myself with someone. Few people knew about my scars, and only two people knew the truth—me and Marcus. Fucking Marcus. Was he still looking for me? Surely after all these years he would had given up? Somehow I knew better, Marcus wasn't the giving up type. I knew he had searched for me in the beginning. Rita had told me that the police came looking for me at the bus station. Luckily for me I had not been there long enough for anyone to be able to make a positive I.D. That was when Rita earned my loyalty and trust; she didn't tell them a damn thing. I sighed. I really needed to call her. It had been three months since I had last spoken to her using the phone she had bought for me after dragging me out of the bus depot four years ago. She had earned the right to ask how I was and expect an honest reply.

    I settled at the table beside Eli who was again drawing. For a moment I wondered what had happened to the pictures I had sketched last night. Most likely in the trash, I thought. Annie sat beside me and ruffled Eli's curly brown locks.

    "Bed time, buddy," she said. Eli groaned. "Go brush your teeth please." Eli didn't argue, not once. He slipped off the chair and disappeared into the bathroom.

    "Jax tells me you will be leaving soon." Annie looked a little shocked, followed quickly with irritation, perhaps not impressed that Jax had been talking about her business. It was sort of an unspoken rule in the shelters, everyone minded their own business.

    "That's a good thing. It will be good for Eli to have his own place." I quickly tried to calm the anger that simmered in Annie's eyes. She took a deep breath and nodded. She was pretty in that girl-next-door kind of way. She had a light sprinkling of freckles across her nose that I had captured in the portrait I had drawn of her the previous night. Her hair wasn't really one shade in particular, but a combination of many shades—blonde, brown, red with all different hues in between. Her eyes were beautiful, a green that shimmered vividly between blue and emerald. She had the same look all battered women did—tired and betrayed. Women who had been hurt in such a way held their emotions close and in check. They didn't want others to see their pain, they didn't want others to see any weakness; the vulnerability that had been exposed by the man who had hurt them. Fine lines around Annie's eyes and mouth suggested she had at one time smiled, a lot.

"He's a good boy. He never once complained when I packed his bag and made him leave behind all his toys. He didn't deserve that." She looked so sad I wanted to give her a hug, but I held back and nodded, giving her the only thing I could, an ear to listen. I knew what it was like to leave behind a home, but leaving mine created a feeling of euphoria. For Eli it must have been confusing and frightening.

"Toys can be replaced. It's good you got him out, no toy is worth staying," I whispered.

"No, it isn't, but to a five year old, toys are special. They hold memories, they are important."

"He will have new toys, new memories; perhaps better memories." Annie smiled, but it was a smile full of regret and bitter memories.

"He never saw anything. He heard my husband yell and that frightened him, but I made sure he never saw him hit me. He saw my bruises later of course. I told him I fell or something incredibly ridiculous and he always believed me."

She sighed as she gathered the crayons and paper into a neat pile. "He hasn't asked about his father once. It's as if he has accepted, without argument, that he is no longer a part of our lives."

"Children are far more perceptive than we give them credit for." When Annie smiled this time it was real, full of hope.

"You are very wise for someone so young." I laughed at that. Annie looked barely a few years older than me. Perhaps she thought I was a child myself. People often assumed I was younger than I was; I was small, my features petite. I guess it was easy to misjudge my age.

"Well, I'm twenty-two but I feel a lot older. I guess this sort of life makes us grow up much faster than we are supposed to," I wondered out loud. Annie quietly slipped away and I grabbed some of Eli's crayons and began sketching a picture of my new boss, Rebecca. Perhaps if I could save enough money for a sketch book and charcoal I could put some pictures up for sale in the store. Dream on, Ella. Stop trying to recapture something that is long gone. I threw the crayon down with a little too much force. Beth reappeared in the common room and I wondered where Jax was. It was confusing to feel like this about a guy. My mission had always been to avoid men altogether, they frightened me, even the ones whose eyes were filled with care and understanding. Men were bigger than me, well, everyone was bigger than me, but men were more powerful. No boy or man had ever captured my attention in the way Jax had and I hadn't even kissed him. The fact I found myself wanting to was even more of a shock. Perhaps his honest desire to help me, to 'rescue' me is what drew me to him. All girls wanted to feel cherished and wanted, but I knew Jax didn't want me like that. God I was such a fool.

Shaking my head I grabbed my backpack and made my way to one of the spare beds at the furthest end of the room. The bathrooms were not handy at this end, but there appeared to be no one in the two beds beside me, which meant if I had nightmares, I would hopefully not disturb anyone else. My nights were still haunted with visions of Marcus. I occasionally woke screaming, sometimes crying. I didn't want these women, who were battling their own demons, to be witness to mine. I didn't wish my nightmares on anyone, not even the blonde bimbo, Selena. She didn't realize how lucky she was. The fact she had looked at me with, what I can only assume was, jealousy was ridiculous. She certainly had nothing to be jealous about. No one wanted my life, not even me. She looked like one of those girls who had it all and it seemed as though she had Jax too. Though he certainly didn't seem happy with her tonight; his tone icy cold, his eyes looked at her with frustration and anger. Not the same kind of anger Marcus was consumed with, just irritation. It's all in the eyes. No one can hide what lies there, but it takes someone special to be able to see it. Most people look at the face as a whole, body language, or gauge the voice, the words. I blank all that out and concentrate on eyes and Selena's eyes were fake. She was fake and I couldn't understand why Jax would want a girl like that. Sighing, I pulled the blanket over my head and closed my eyes, waiting for the inevitable tug into exhaustion, where images of Marcus continued to haunt me.

CHAPTER 7

Jax

Once my shift began, I found myself sitting by a dim lamp in the common room, watching Ella. If it didn't feel so right I might actually feel like some sick crazy perv. This tiny little girl had somehow become an important part of my life. I tried to examine it, look at the situation objectively, compare my need to help her to the need I had to help the other women, the need I had felt to save Sarah. At the end of a long hour of consideration, I decided my want for Ella must be simple, primitive male lust. Yeah, even that didn't feel right. Sure I wanted her, but not just that delectable little body, I wanted all of her—heart and soul included—and I had never felt that way about any of the other women who came to Mercy's, especially not Sarah. Shit, this is what the guys I served with called 'pussy whipped'.

With the sun up again I found myself in the kitchen getting breakfast ready. Mary would be in soon but I thought I'd surprise her and take the initiative to get the ball rolling. Porridge, toast, cereal and fruit; I couldn't screw that up. The wafting arrival of coconut filled my senses. Ella stood beside me, tousled hair and rumpled clothes, reaching for the freshly brewed coffee.

"Porridge, cereal or toast?" I asked. She grumbled and shook her head, taking a long sip of her coffee. She sighed. My girl wasn't a morning person. My girl? I was not renowned for my possessive tendencies towards women so this 'claiming' confused the hell out of me. Furthermore, Ella was not mine. "You're not leaving without eating and you're taking that when you go." I nodded toward a brown paper bag sitting on the counter. I had made her up some lunch a short while ago. It was the first time I had ever made lunch for someone other than myself. I remembered Mercy making lunches for me as a kid—a sandwich, piece of fruit and a muffin packed in the same style paper bag. Admittedly, Ella was no kid, but I liked the thought of personally taking care of her, feeding her. She peeked in the bag and then looked at me confused.

"You made me lunch?" She was completely and utterly

bewildered. Her mouth hung open in astonishment. She looked adorable.

"You're acting like no one ever made you lunch before." Her head slowly shook.

"Not since I was ten." I glanced at her. She looked sad, another glimpse at the real Ella.

"Your mother?" I gently nudged her into conversation. Her eyes flared for a moment with silent fury. Interesting.

"No. My mother didn't do things like that." Had her mother been the one to hurt her? I knew not to push, she needed to tell me things in her own time.

"Well, if it makes you feel any better, it's been a long time since someone made me lunch too. And it's nothing to get excited over. It's just a sandwich, muffin and an apple. I didn't have to cook a single thing, so you should be safe." Her frown disappeared with a shy smile as she leaned against the counter, holding her mug of coffee in a death grip as if worried someone might try and take it from her.

"Toast, with jam," she muttered. I quickly put two pieces of bread in the toaster. I thought it best to keep the conversation light, easy.

"You are quite an artist. Ever think about doing something more with that?" She got that whimsical faraway look and smiled. This was good, a topic she liked to talk about.

"I love to sketch; portraits and landscapes especially." She blushed at her confession.

"You've never thought about going to college to study, maybe trying to pick up work in a gallery?" She looked at me like I'd grown an extra head. "It's not impossible, you do have options." She shook her head.

"It's not in my future anymore. In fact, I am very careful not to think about the future at all. My plans usually don't stretch beyond a few days—what I need to do to stay safe, have somewhere to sleep. My life is about survival now, not fancy dreams of art." She was so matter of fact about it but there was no missing the disappointment in her words.

"You're not safe here in Claymont?" I asked. She shrugged and emptied what was left in her mug into the sink and washed her plate.

"Thanks for this." She held up the last bite of her toast. "And this." She grabbed the lunch I had prepared for her and pushed it into her backpack.

"Not a problem, just make sure you eat it. You don't need to faint to get me to fuss over you." She blushed and I pretended not to notice as she quietly snuck away.

***

"Jax, come take a look at this," Mercy called from the doorway a few minutes later. I followed her down the hallway and into her office where she promptly shoved a piece of paper in my face. It was a receipt for the electric bill I had paid two days earlier. I shrugged.

"Uh-huh. And?" I knew she would be pissed that I had paid the bill, but I also knew the shelter struggled to make ends meet and relied heavily on donations.

"Jax, I don't need handouts." I laughed and threw the bill back down on top of the crazy-ass clutter that Mercy called an organized mess.

"Mercy's Shelter survives on handouts, don't be petty." She scoffed and looked away.

"My son shouldn't be paying my bills. The shelter is mine. I started it; it's my job to keep it running." Stubborn woman.

"Yeah well, consider it a donation from Carter Constructions."

"Carter Constructions has already given several hefty donations this year. It's a small company and I'm sure they can't afford to make another one." I shook my head. My company was doing more than alright. It was making a comfortable profit and I hardly had to stick my head in the door. I could knock together bits and pieces in my shed and drop them in to the shop as I pleased. Charlie and the boys kept the place running while I was on missions and now when I am busy at Mercy's. Then there was the money I had accumulated in the army. I hadn't had much cause to spend it, other than to buy the few acres of land I owned just out of town and the small but comfortable house I had built on it. The shit I did and saw in Afghanistan might give me nightmares for the rest of my life, but it certainly left me comfortably financed.

"You know what, Mom, I love this place just as much as

69

you do. I want to be a part of it and I can afford to pay some of the bills and if you don't like it then tough titties." Mercy just stared at me. She knew I meant business when I called her mom, it was like playing the guilt card.

"Did you just say tough titties?" she stammered and I almost burst out laughing. Mercy was a good girl, even heck was a swear word coming out of her mouth. A small smile crept into her stubbornly pissed features.

"I did. So suck it up and take my money or I'll open my own damn shelter." Her face broke into a full blown grin and I couldn't help but smile back. My mom was so beautiful when she smiled.

"So, tell me all about your Ella." My Ella? I sighed and rubbed my stiff neck.

"I don't know. She seems different, special. I feel somehow drawn to her and she seems to trust me. She has scars, she showed me."

Mercy nodded, eyes solemn and understanding. Mercy was acquainted with this sort of story personally. My dad had been one grade A asshole.

"They're all special Jax and they all have scars; some are worn on their skin, some deeper. I know you feel as though you let Sarah down but you didn't, Jax. You don't need to use Ella to make amends with Sarah's death. Sarah was well beyond our reach when she came to us."

"For starters, none of them are beyond our reach. Secondly, I'm not using Ella to make amends. I'm just trying to do what I am meant to do and be there for her, help her, like all the women." I hesitated a moment. "Actually, she kind of reminds me of you. I mean, not in a motherly kind of way, she's just tiny like you. And she has so many scars all over her arms and wrists and God knows where else. No doubt plenty of the psychological kind too." I knew Mercy immediately thought the same thing I did when I first saw the scars on Ella's wrists.

"She didn't try and kill herself. She was a self-harmer at some point, most of her scars are faint and thin, classic self-harm cuts. But the scars on her wrist were forced. Someone gave her those scars, most likely her father. She mentioned a 'him'. She said she didn't try to commit suicide because she didn't want to give him that satisfaction. Apparently she sees this as some sort of a game and she doesn't want him to win." Mercy considered that for a moment.

"She's confiding in you, that's good Jax. She needs someone she can trust, someone who will do the right thing by her." I nodded, secretly pleased that Ella might trust me enough to let me in but also noting the hidden meaning behind Mercy's words. My relationship with Ella needed to remain professional. Ella needed that, she deserved that.

"I heard Selena dropped by last night," Mercy said, changing the subject. I groaned, loudly.

"I also heard she left pretty soon after looking pretty angry." Mercy sighed. "Jax, the women and children who stay here don't need your personal life played out before them like a bad soap opera." I couldn't agree more.

"Yeah, sorry 'bout that. I didn't invite her to drop by last night and I made sure she knew it wasn't cool. She won't be dropping by anymore, ever."

"It wouldn't be a problem if she had some interest in the shelter, in the people who come here for help. I get the feeling that little tramp would only drop by for one thing and it would more than likely include this desk and her back on it." My mouth dropped open at my mother's crude description. Her furious blush confirmed she felt just as awkward saying it as I felt hearing it. I couldn't believe my mother was talking so frankly about my sex life. It was completely and utterly uncool.

"Don't say another word. You, me and my sex life is totally off limits. But just so we are clear Selena's back has never graced this desk or any other piece of furniture in this shelter, nor will it. Not just because that is completely unprofessional and yes, I know there might have been a time when old Jax thought differently, but new Jax doesn't behave like that. And I called it quits with Selena, for good." I took a deep breath. God this conversation was almost as uncomfortable as the sex talk she had forced me to have with her when I was fourteen.

"Good, on all counts. And Jax, I'm proud of you, always have been, even when you were old Jax. Though I do like new Jax much better. Go home and get some sleep. Or better yet, go do some real work and make up that money your company 'donated' to our shelter." I didn't miss the 'our shelter' bit. My heart swelled just slightly at her words.

"Thanks Mercy," I said quietly as I stood and wrapped my arms around her shoulders.

"You're a good son, Jax. I love you more than you'll ever know." She hugged me back, her little arms holding me tight.

"I love you too, Mom. And, if this chick flick moment is over, I'm going to The Pit Stop to have Benny serve my heart an unhealthy dose of grease."

"Oh, that sounds good. It's been too long since I've had a Pit Stop breakfast. Dave and I might stop in after our shift tomorrow for one." Mercy was suddenly captured in a greasy breakfast fantasy as I snuck out of the shelter.

CHAPTER 8

Ella

I couldn't believe Jax had made me lunch. As I walked to Bouquets I stared at the brown paper bag in my hand, my surroundings and walk was a complete blur. Once at work I sat trimming thorns from rose stems and couldn't help but cast curious glances at the innocuous bag. I barely remembered my daddy making me lunch for school. Such an innocent harmless gesture, but I found myself wanting to save that simple brown paper bag and tuck it away in the bottom of my backpack with my most prized possessions—the sketches of my daddy and the phone Rita had bought me. It was a paper bag for goodness sake!

"You hiding the crown jewels in that bag?" Rebecca teased. Her hair was in another difficult looking twist inspired by the fifties and she was dressed in a figure hugging dress with a skinny belt sitting high on her waist. The black apron with the word 'Bouquets' in a stylish yellow cursive across the front didn't detract from the sexy look she was rocking today. I, on the other hand, had donned my best pair of khaki cargo's, the only pair that didn't have a single stain on them, a grey long sleeved thermal with my best blue t-shirt pulled over the top and black Converse sneakers. I too wore the mandatory black apron and today, my hair was neatly held back with a blue scarf. Rebecca was all class and I felt like a homeless woman standing beside her. I smirked at the ridiculous revelation. And now I was looking at the damn brown paper bag again.

"No, just lunch," I murmured. Rebecca was great with the customers. She smiled and laughed like she was old friends with everyone who walked through her door. When an elderly gentleman came in to order flowers for his wife's funeral, Rebecca slipped effortlessly into compassionate mode. She helped the man plan a simple arrangement of lilies, his wife's favorites, and held him in a warm tight embrace before he left. I blinked away the stubborn tears that threatened to spill at the sight of the old man's own grateful weeping. The shrill of the phone woke me from my daze.

"For you," said Rebecca with a mischievous smile handing

me the cordless handset. It took me a moment to move, I was stunned into an imbecilic trance. I never got calls, I only made them once every couple of months to Rita. "Don't worry, it won't bite," She laughed.

"Hello," I whispered.

"I couldn't wait until you called, I had to call and check in. How are you?" Rita's cheerful voice eased any trace of apprehension from my body. I couldn't help the small laugh that escaped my lips as I moved to the back of the store.

"You scared the shit out of me," I muttered.

"Sorry, honey. Rebecca called me last night and said you were working for her. I'm glad, she is a good person, hun, and you'll be safe there."

"I like it here. The store is so warm, it smells pretty damn good and she puts caramel in her coffee, or whiskey depending on who she's expecting in the store. Oh God, Rita, caramel and coffee it tastes like heaven." Rita laughed.

"You and that darn sweet tooth. You should be the size of a house!"

"Hows BJ and Larry?"

"There both fine, honey. My little girl is home from college for the weekend and we've declared war on BJ. He refuses to wear his hearing aide so Renee and I are not speaking to him as punishment. He can't hear a bloody word we say anyway. God it must be freezing there, please tell me you have somewhere warm to stay?"

"I stumbled across a shelter. It's the cleanest I've ever been in and they serve meals with real meat," I whispered.
I never hid the truth from Rita. She had earned my trust and honesty.

"You shouldn't be living in a shelter, Ella," moaned Rita. I knew she wanted better for me.

"It's okay, Rita, honestly. It's warm and clean. The owner, Mercy, is amazing and I've been helping out around the place. Jax even made me lunch today." I chuckled at the memory of that little brown bag.

"Jax?" Oh wow, had I actually said his name out loud? "Who's Jax?"

"His mother owns the shelter and he works there. He

seems like a good person Rita, they all are. I have to get back to work but I'll call before Christmas, I promise." I tried not to think about Christmas which was now less than two months away. Holidays and birthdays had lost their joy when Daddy had died.

"About Christmas, sweetheart. I don't want you to be alone this year and I know you don't want to come back to Dunston, so why don't we meet at Larry's. I'll give you a bus ticket as your Christmas gift." Larry's place was only a nine hour drive from Marcus, still too close. And I had never really spent a Christmas alone since leaving that hell hole called home anyway. There was no end of volunteer work during the holidays; I always managed to keep busy.

"I can't, Rita," I finally confessed, not wanting to disappoint her but knowing I just couldn't turn myself around and head back toward Marcus. The closer I got to home the worse the panic attacks became. Rita sighed.

"I know honey, I just thought maybe over the years things might have gotten a little easier for you. Maybe BJ, Renee and I could meet you somewhere? Renee would love to finally meet you." I knew Rita couldn't afford a trip like that for all of them at this time of the year.

"Honestly Rita, I just want to help out at the shelter. It makes me feel good to be helping somewhere. And I've got Rebecca, so it's not like I'll be completely alone."

"Okay, sweetheart. I'm not going to push but I would really love to see you again one of these days. Maybe once Renee is back at college I could come down to Clayton and visit you and Rebecca. I've got a free trip up my sleeve with work." The thought of seeing Rita again actually made me smile. I really did love her, she had saved my life. Oh boy, those damn infuriating tears were threatening me again. I swallowed hard, pushing the lump of emotion back down my throat.

"I'd love that. We'll talk again when it gets closer. Give my love to BJ and Larry and Renee of course."

"You take care, Ella. Be smart and keep safe."

I disconnected the call and took a moment to compose myself before heading back into the front of the shop. Rebecca was busy taking an order as I resumed the thorn pruning, a tedious though somewhat rewarding job. It felt like I was ridding something beautiful of something ugly. I wish it were that easy with life. Simply cut away all the nasty, ugly parts of ourselves and leave behind the beauty. Life would be so much easier.

***

When I got back to the shelter today, there was no fainting. Instead I felt lighter than normal, carefree, even excited. Talking with Rita always infused me with energy and hope and the thought of seeing her after the holidays made me ridiculously happy. My thoughts quickly swung to a certain blonde haired giant with steel gray eyes. My brain was screaming all sorts of profanities about how stupid I was behaving, but my heart was skipping around like a school girl in piggy tails, all full of hope and innocent anticipation. Two more women had left the shelter today, supposedly for good. Well, they had said for good but apparently they bounced back and forth between their violent home and the safety of Mercy's regularly. Jax was nowhere to be found and once again I was confused by the relief and disappointment that racked my heart. All this inner turmoil was making my head hurt and my body crazy; I needed a break from it. I sat in the middle of my bed and folded laundry. My mind drifted with the monotonous task as my eyes wandered to the long, clean walls of the shelter. They were painted blue like the sky and I suddenly wished I had some paint. I could add big fluffy white clouds and a bright yellow sun, maybe some children playing around a big old oak tree. Better yet I could sketch or paint pictures of all the staff and have them framed and mounted along the wall, maybe even some of the women who passed through the shelter. I snorted loudly and most unlady like. My fanciful thoughts and dreams would never be anything more than that—dreams. "Idiot," I snarled quietly to myself.

"Who are you talking too?" I jumped so high I nearly fell off the side of my bed grappling with the sheet to keep myself from falling. Jax stood over me with a cheeky grin on his face.

"Fuck, you scared the shit out of me," I yelled.

"And you've got a dirty mouth." He smirked. "What if Eli had of been with me?" I looked around feeling a little guilty and Jax chuckled.

"Don't worry, he's down in the laundry room with Mary. And anyway, all those years in the army have turned me into quite the swearing machine so, if you ever need pointers, feel free to ask." He just stood there, his hands shoved deep into his pockets suddenly looking like a tall awkward boy. No words were exchanged, the moment full of unease and uncertainties. Jax boasted confidence and arrogance but underneath all that big strong handsome man were insecurities, just like the rest of us.

"You want to help?" I offered. Part of me hoped he'd say no, the weak part, the scared part. Another part of me prayed he'd say yes and I was assuming this part of me was all lustful woman. He grinned and promptly sat at the end of the bed and began folding towels.

"Looks like you've done that before," I teased, throwing his own words back at him from the previous night. He chuckled and nodded his head.

"There was a time when I was referred to as the Laundry King 'round here. People had respected and worshipped my skills." It was my turn to laugh at his mocking arrogance.

"So, what made you decide to become a soldier?" I asked after a short silence. Jax shrugged as he set a pile of clean towels to one side and began folding pillow cases.

"Laundry expertise only gets you so far," he winked at me, "and I always considered myself as some sort of defender of the human race. For a short while I considered being a superhero, but I had no special powers or cool costume, so military it was." I folded my legs in front of me Indian style, a grin stretching from ear to ear. I liked his playful nature; it helped me to relax. "I thought about becoming a police officer or even a fireman, but one day, a few weeks before graduation, this guy turned up at school to talk to some of us about the military— the opportunity to travel, learn skills, make a difference—it was everything I needed to hear. I signed up the next day. You already know how the story ends."

"Do you regret it, being a soldier, going to war?" Jax shook his head, his eyes serious.

"Not at all. I learned skills—how to build, fix things, shoot a gun." His grin was cheeky. "Every boy's dream is to play with a gun. When I was a boy, I had so many damn toy guns I could have started my own neighborhood armory."

As for me, guns made me nervous.

Sure, I had handled one, clicked off the safety and pointed it directly into the heart of a demon, but I know if I had of pulled that trigger, it would have changed me for the worse. Jax watched the play of emotions on my face.

"Don't get me wrong, Angel, I'm not some crazy hillbilly weapons freak. I have a gun and I have a license to carry it but it stays locked up at home and it's only taken out to be cleaned or for the firing range now and again. I got my gun play out of my system in the army." I nodded and found myself paying far too much attention to the folded towel before me.

"What about you, Angel, any regrets?" I laughed but it wasn't a laugh filled with humor, more like a noise filled with shame.

"Much of my life is regret." I sighed and unconsciously rubbed my arms. "I do wish I had graduated high school though," I quietly added, locked in memories of the few times I actually enjoyed school, before hate caught me in its ugly grasp.

"Why don't you then?" I looked at Jax and saw the sincerity in his words. I knew he was right, I could take night classes and graduate but then what? I couldn't plan beyond a few days let alone my entire future.

"Thanks for helping." I quickly stood, abruptly ending the conversation and gathered the laundry as Jax slowly stood with me.

"I'm off tonight," he said. I hated myself at that moment, the panic and disappointment that blindsided me. I nodded sharply and turned to leave.

"I've got the day off tomorrow but I thought I'd drop by and say hello anyway," he called out at my departure. I stopped and glanced back over my shoulder, my heart flipping wildly at just the sight of him.

"I'd like that," I confessed, before quickly running away.

☐

CHAPTER 9

Jax

The next afternoon I dropped by the office of my construction company to take care of a couple of things and ended up giving Charlie, my best friend and manager, a ride home. He jumped into the passenger seat of my pickup, pushing the package that had been sitting on the seat to the floor.

"Shit, take it easy," I growled, reaching down to pick it back up and securing it safely between us. Charlie couldn't help himself as I drove off down the street, peeking in the package like the nosy prick he was prone to being.

"You heading back to kindergarten?" He smirked, waving a box of pencils about like a complete child. I grabbed the box and stuffed it back in the bag.

"It's a gift," was all I offered. But Charlie never gave up that easily.

"Uh-huh, for a kindergartener? I shook my head. He patiently sat and stared and I knew if I didn't give him something else he would continue to harass me.

"For a girl," I mumbled.

"A girl girl?" he said with a light innocent voice, "or a girl girl?" His voice deepened and his eye brows wiggled in an attempt to look and sound like a seductive deviant, but he couldn't pull it off; he was too much of a douche to look seductive.

"A girl, as in a member of the opposite sex, I'm sure you remember them." Charlie laughed.

"I do, in fact I enjoyed the company of one last weekend." My eyebrows rose in surprise. Charlie had been going through somewhat of a dry spell for a month or two now. I had never pried before, but I got the feeling he was into someone and taking things slow.

"Who?" I demanded.

"No one you know, now back to your girl. I'm assuming your elusive answers mean it's a girl girl," he wiggled his eyebrows again and I laughed. "And knowing you, she is sex on a stick; so spill." I rubbed the back of my neck as we drove and shuffled in my seat nervously. I never had trouble telling Charlie about girls in the past, shit, he seemed to enjoy living vicariously through me so I was happy to divulge all the nasty details. With Ella, there were no nasty details and even if there were I didn't want to share them with Charlie.

"Fuck me, it is a girl girl and you fucking like like her." I laughed at Charlie's childlike words. In all the years I had known him he hadn't changed. He was all about goofing off and pissing people off. He was the exact opposite of his strict Catholic parents. When we were in school, Charlie gained a reputation for being somewhat of a badass. He started training with a local kickboxing school and was pretty fucking good at it too; unfortunately Charlie knew it. His arrogance rubbed plenty of kids the wrong way and he began getting into fights; his temper unhinged and fragile. His parents were at a loss, which only spurred Charlie on—anything to ruffle his parent's feathers. It took Mercy dragging him into the shelter one summer to adjust his attitude. Charlie bitched and moaned for weeks about having to work his summer vacation, but it wasn't long before he saw the future that might lie ahead of him if he continued down the path he was on. With a little help from Mercy he whipped himself into shape quick. Today, Charlie could still kickass with the best of them. In fact, he still trained regularly at Lee's Gym but street violence and bullying was no longer a part of his life. He had embraced his calling—Charlie was all about protecting and defending now.

He hated the brutality that Mercy's Shelter protected women from and he was more than happy to put in shifts whenever my construction company wasn't demanding his time. His cocky and smartass attitude obviously still thrived though.

"So, what does she look like?" He started with the basics and for Charlie this was the most important part.

"She's a woman, a beautiful, tiny, perfect woman and she's living at the shelter." That shut him up. His playful and flippant remarks stopped and he looked at me with a troubled wrinkle in his brow.

"You're hooking up with a homeless girl?" My angry eyes stopped him immediately.

"Fuck no, I'm not. I'm buying her fucking paper and

pencils. She likes to sketch." I was way too defensive and not fooling anyone, especially Charlie. He nodded and shrugged.

"Okay, whatever. I guess it won't bother you to hear that I saw Selena out last night." I shook my head. No it didn't bother me at all. Other than the fact her name reminded me of too many wasted nights. "She was fussing all over Daniel White like he's her new fucking Ken doll."

"I feel sorry for Daniel, but they do make a perfect couple, I mean, he does look like Ken and all." I mused and Charlie laughed.

"Yeah, he's got that plastic hair thing going on. If I hadn't heard first hand from you how much of a sex pot Selena was I'd accuse him of having the whole asexual Ken doll package going on."

"Okay, we are definitely not talking about Daniel's junk." I finally pulled my truck into the parking garage at Mercy's.

"What we doing here?" asked Charlie.

"Dropping off the gift." Charlie's eyes lit up. "And you're waiting here. The ladies don't need another intimidating male walking around in there."

And Charlie was definitely intimidating. He wasn't as tall as me, but he was just over six foot two and he wasn't small either; there wasn't an ounce of fat on him. He was all lean muscle with tattoos to finish the bad-ass look. Charlie gave me a pretty impressive scowl as I left him sitting in my pickup.

I found Ella sitting quietly on the floor of the laundry room, her head buried in a book.

"Hey," I said as I entered, not wanting to catch her unaware.

"Hey." She smiled. She looked so young and innocent in that moment, her smile genuine and at ease. She was happy to see me and that sure as hell made me happy.

"What you reading?" I tilted her book forward to catch the title. I knew it well, Great Expectations.

"I always thought Pip was a chump." I sat down beside her and she cast me a nervous yet surprised smile. I shrugged. "It's Mercy's favorite book. Whenever I was deployed overseas I took a copy, it was kind of like I was taking a piece of her away with me. I read it a couple of times but usually just stuffed it in the bottom of my pack and stared at it like some sort of crazy fool when I was homesick." I held out the package I had bought for her. She simply stared at it like it might bite her or something. "Don't worry it's nothing nasty, just a gift," I explained.

"Why?" she blurted out.

"Just call me the giver who keeps on giving. I like to give presents, ask anyone. Hell, I bought Eli a noisy little truck yesterday and he didn't get all stiff and suspicious when I gave it to him." She hesitantly took the parcel.

"But I'm not a kid," she whispered.

"No, you are definitely not." It was pretty hard not to notice those enchanting eyes, perfect curves and lips that begged to be nibble on.

She was most definitely a woman. She wiped her palms on her thighs like she was about to dismantle a bomb or something and carefully peeked inside.

"Holy Shit." She breathed in as she tugged out the sketch book. I knew it was the good kind too, I had asked for the best. There was a box of pencils and a carton of charcoal.

"The guy at the store said if you sketch portraits one of these would most likely be your medium. I wasn't sure which so I bought both." Her fingers touched the packet of charcoal with reverence. "So charcoal it is," I observed. She looked up at me anxiously and I could see the tears threatening to fall. I smiled and stood, allowing her the space I knew she would prefer. "So, draw me something tonight." She nodded and let her hair fall forward, hiding her face, hiding the tears in her eyes that would no doubt escape as soon as I was gone. I turned to leave. "On the inside of the sketch book I wrote my phone number. If you need anything call me. Like anything, a ride, someone to talk to, anything, okay?" She nodded again woodenly, but clutched the charcoal to her like she was holding a baby. I left her sitting on the floor of the laundry room, her eyes wide and full of unshed tears, with a gift she had looked at with such reverence. It almost made me lose my shit.

CHAPTER 10

Ella

It took me a long time to get off the laundry room floor. I just sat there like a stunned fool, tears falling down my cheeks over a damn gift, but oh what a gift. Some girls might prefer jewelry, some clothes, but for me this was the top shelf stuff. Jax, a man who barely knew me, who didn't really know my secrets, none of my dirty awful past, he had bought me a gift that pierced right through all the bullshit and wrapped itself right around my heart. I wondered if he knew everything I've done—the alcohol, the drugs, how much of a whore I was—would he still want to buy me gifts? I doubt he would want to come anywhere near me. While my hand twitched with the anticipation of drawing again, a small part of me was reluctant. Indulging in my art meant indulging in my dreams and indulging in my dreams would only result in disappointment. My life had been filled with so much disappointment I didn't know if I could take much more. Sketching had been the only constant in my life, the only thing that had always been there— before, during and after Marcus—regardless of how rarely I picked up the charcoal now, it was still there. By the time I dragged myself from the laundry room floor, I had missed dinner, but still managed to scrounge up some left overs before helping Mary clean the kitchen. Eventually I found myself in a big comfy rocker with the sketch book from Jax in my lap. After some time I sat with a single piece of charcoal, hovering nervously over the page and after even more time, I placed that single piece of charcoal to the page. My hand danced with familiarity across the sheet of paper leaving dark black lines plain and bold against the white backdrop, but with a simple brush of my finger, those blunt lines softened and grayed to create shadows. My portraits were black and white, but it was the monochrome shades of gray in between that make them seem so alive.

I drew a portrait of Mercy. She was beautiful to draw, her face classically beautiful with tired lines but eyes filled with steel and determination. Jax had asked me to draw for him then draw for him I would. This would be my gift to him in return for his kindness. A portrait would usually take me anywhere from twenty minutes to an hour, but I wanted this to be perfect and an hour and a half later my finger blended the last shadow across the elegant arch of Mercy's neck.

Then, without hesitating, I carefully turned the page to find a fresh white sheet of paper just begging to be brought to life.

"You are very talented," said Mercy as she sat down on the couch before me, curling her feet under herself, her small hands wrapped around a steaming mug of coffee. She looked so childlike and innocent that I found myself wanting to sketch her again just as she looked right now.

"Thank you."

"How are you doing today, Ella?" Her smile was warm, welcome. She was one of those women who just drew you in, her soul so bright that you couldn't refuse but return her joy.

"I'm okay. I've got a job and soon I'll have enough money for an apartment; I'm really pretty lucky. Many of the women here don't have a job and still carry bruises. They're the ones that need your kindness." My honesty seemed to surprise her.

"That's very noble of you to put the problems of others before your own. Just because you can see one person's pain doesn't mean that it doesn't exist on people who don't show the physical abuse."

"True, but really, I'm doing alright." I was drawing a portrait of Jax and Mercy leaned forward to check it out.

"You seem to be comfortable with Jax, you're not afraid of him." It wasn't a question.

"No, he doesn't scare me. He may be the size of a giant, which was very intimidating at first, but I knew he wouldn't hurt me. I could see that in his eyes."

"He is kind of tall." Mercy laughed. "You can read people so easily, just by looking at their eyes?" I nodded.

"My dad always encouraged me to watch people closely, especially their eyes. People can't easily hide the truth from their eyes. It was supposed to help me with my art but I found myself learning to read people and their intentions. I knew the man who hurt me was going to hurt me from the moment I saw him. That was perhaps, in some ways, scarier than him actually hurting me. Just watching, waiting. His eyes were pure evil." I shivered with the memory. Mercy sat and watched me thoughtfully.

"It has helped you to stay safe though, your ability to see people for who they really are." I nodded.

"Mercy, can I ask you something about Jax?"

"Of course, but I might not be able to answer. Sometimes our stories are our own to tell." I took a deep breath and looked her in the eye.

"While Jax is busy trying to help everyone else, who's helping him?" I wondered out loud. Mercy's smile faltered and she stared at me with some confusion. I held up my sketch.

"Don't you see what's in his eyes?" I asked her. My picture wasn't finished, but I had captured his eyes perfectly. It was an image in my mind from when he had sat quietly in this very chair the prior night. He obviously thought I was asleep but I was awake long enough to see his eyes slip into a familiar place. Pain, hatred, guilt. I had seen them all at one time or another in the eyes of one person or another. I had seen the look in my own eyes too many times to recount. Mercy's smile was completely gone now as she reached out for my sketch.

"This is how you see Jax?" she asked, surprised.

"Not all the time, but it's there." Jax was good at hiding his own hurt and suffering.

"Like I said, I watch people closely and sometimes it means I catch a glimpse of something that nobody else sees. I don't know Jax's story but he kind of looks like he needs saving too." Mercy nodded thoughtfully, handing the sketch book back. I could tell my picture had upset her.

"Jax has demons, like all of us. He has talked to someone about them and is doing much better, perhaps not as well as I thought, but definitely better. Your very astute Ella, you have an extraordinary gift and I don't just mean the art. Perhaps it was something other than sheer luck that brought you to us the night of the storm."

"Like fate?" I wondered. Mercy smiled.

"Maybe…maybe you will be as good for him as he is for you," she murmured, leaving me alone in the big living area.

Jax

I had somehow managed to keep Ella from myself and my thoughts most of the day, keeping myself completely immersed in work, but now that I was home, alone and quiet, she was all I could think about. Her grateful, shaken expression when she had seen the sketch book and charcoal I had bought for her the day before was playing back through my mind like an endless loop. I squeezed my eyes shut willing my mind to find darkness and yet she was all I saw. That fall of waist long hair as smooth as silk, those dark eyes so dark they were almost black, her full lips, soft milky skin. I groaned. I couldn't stop thinking about her and the thoughts were making my jeans rather uncomfortable. A cold shower was what I needed, a cold shower and a lobotomy.

One cold shower and an inevitable jerk off later I still felt like a wound up, irritable and very horny adolescent. Resorting to a glass of whiskey and some AC/DC, I lay back in the recliner and studiously took in my surroundings. I loved my house, built with my own two hands. It was a two bedroom loft style home, with a high roof, thick exposed beams and polished hardwood floor. An enormous shag pile rug that Mercy had convinced me I needed for winter sat in front of a large open fire place. My TV sat virtually unused on the wall; my pride and joy, my stereo was housed in a large wooden cabinet under it. My guitar lay on the couch like an abandoned old friend following a lonely jam session from a few nights ago and my bookshelf was now full of CD's—the books I had donated to the shelter. The living area opened out into a combined dining room and kitchen, also with hardwood floors. A large study come guest room, a laundry room and a bathroom occupied the other end of the house.

The master bedroom occupied the upstairs loft, along with an impressive bathroom with a huge double shower stall big enough for me to spend hours of heated bliss under. My king sized bed sat against the wall with matching bedside tables and my walk in closet was full of jeans and t-shirts. One brand new Hugo Boss suit that I had spent far too much money on sat in a garment bag at the back of the closet along with my military formal wear. I was lucky, I had a good life considering the shit I had seen and done. I had all this—a nice home, a good job, family. Things could have gone differently for me if Mercy hadn't of had the guts to leave my dad. If she had of stayed with the abusive alcoholic bastard, Ella's life could have been mine. It never ceased to astound me the people who found themselves on the streets, homeless, abused. A fucked up life was not discriminatory. Young, old, rich, poor, plain or beautiful—bad shit could happen to anyone. I hated that my world was full of women who had been harmed by men. I knew it was a power thing and that most of those men would never pick on someone their equal. What I would give for time alone with the assholes who hit these women. Mercy told me to let go of that attitude. The women didn't need a violent man to deal with their violent men. It took every ounce of self-control I possessed to keep my shit together sometimes, the urge to lash out at the fuckers who hurt these women was almost debilitating. But I couldn't help them by scaring the shit out of them. Mercy was right. One act of violence does not fix another. Finally the whiskey began to work its way into my body and mind and I somehow stumbled my way to bed where I sank into blissful darkness.

***

The air is thick with smoke and hot, so hot I can barely breathe. I glance down and notice I'm in my army fatigues, rifle cocked and steady at my shoulder. I know I am dreaming, but I can't wake and I can't stop the infernal nightmare from playing out before me. We had good Intel, the terrorist extremists were supposed to have been living here in this hell hole for two weeks now. We were doing a sweep of the dilapidated building, bricks and fixtures falling apart around us, suffering the explosive power of war.

The door at the end of the hallway is closed and I move silently to it. With a hard shove, the door swings open and the stench of burnt flesh and blood makes my stomach roll. My teeth are clenched shut to try and stop the rising bile. With my gun held high I allow my eyes to sweep the room. Blood, so much blood. You can barely make out the bodies, they are blown into bits. Just random chunks of human remains scatter the room. I slip on the grizzly remains under my feet and as I scramble up off the ground, the room suddenly changes and I know immediately where I am now. The bright white tiles and smell of bleach fill my senses. It should comfort me after the blood and death of the desert I just left, but it doesn't. I know what awaits me here. My eyes are squeezed shut and I turn, open them. There she lies like a broken doll, her small body slumped against the wall, a pool of blood a stark contrast against the white tiles. "Sarah," I whisper. Her eyes are closed and she could be sleeping if it weren't for the deathly pale look in her face and the blood. Fuck I'm sick of the sight of blood. Falling to my knees in despair I lurch forward and throw up.

I woke with a strangled roar, sweat drenching my naked body, the sheets thrown to the floor. The fear, the horror consumes me for a moment until I realize I am home, in my room, in my big ass comfortable bed. My heart eventually steadies but I still tremble. This nightmare is like an old enemy, familiar and unwanted. It soaked its way into my darkened dreams after finding Sarah and obviously the many therapy sessions I had endured following that were only a temporary solution. Fuck how I wish I could scrub the bloodied images from my mind.

I glance at my digital clock, four a.m. Not a chance in hell that I'm going back to sleep after that. I pull myself from my bed and put on my clothes from the night before still lying in a discarded heap on the floor. The shed in the back of my home is immaculate and made simply for building furniture. Here I find my solitude, I can allow myself to be absorbed by my work and I can leave the vicious memories for a short while. This is how I understand Ella's need to sketch, the need for her mind to simply stop and escape. I wonder how she slept last night. I had left her my phone number nearly two days ago now and she hadn't used it, but that didn't surprised me. I wanted her to, hoped she would, but it was too soon. Girls like Ella are strong and resilient and fiercely independent. I was also well aware that girls like Ella just wanted to be loved and desired, they wanted to feel safe. I wanted all that for Ella, I wanted to be all that for her even though I knew it was wrong. Shit, she didn't need my nightmares on top of her own. But right now I couldn't think of a way to stop myself from pulling her in. I wanted her, I needed her.

CHAPTER 11

Jax

When I strolled into the shelter early Sunday morning the place was quiet. Mercy met me at the foyer, she was far more subdued than normal and it wasn't just from the night shift. I could tell something was up. She moved towards me and wrapped her arms around my waist hugging me close. "What's wrong?" I asked, hugging her back. She scoffed and pushed me away.

"It's called a hug you big oaf, deal with it." Okay, she was snappy. Perhaps some of her mood was attributed to the night shift after all. I chuckled.

"Don't get your panties in a twist, I'm cool with the hug but you seem sad." She plastered a big bright smile on her face and I could tell there was sorrow beneath it.

"I'm just tired, honey. Dave is taking me to The Pit Stop for a greasy breakfast and then home to sleep the day away like a lazy sloth." I groaned. I hadn't had time for a Pit Stop breakfast and now I knew it would be all I could think about. Perhaps I would sneak out at lunch. Benny's special breakfast was an all-day affair and the thought had me almost drooling all over myself. David came up and pulled Mercy into his arms, placing a chaste kiss on her forehead.

"Come on woman. Benny's is calling you and bed is calling me." He pulled my mom towards the front door.

"Jax." I turned back to face her before entering the rec room. "Maybe you were right; Ella is special...she's different. Take good care of her." Okay, now I felt like I had stepped into a cheesy chick flick. Mercy smiled at the apparent look of shock on my face.

"Don't be afraid to be what she needs. You could both be good for each other." I tilted my head considering her words.

"Did Beth bring in some of her 'special' cookies this morning?" I asked, my hands putting 'special' in the appropriate air quotations. Mercy laughed and shook her head, leaving me standing there with no doubt a dumbfounded expression on my face. Yep, I was looking for Beth's cookies the moment I had a chance. I moved through the shelter with a little too much excitement; I was dying to see Ella and make sure she was alright. When I discovered she had already left my mood quickly dropped to below freezing and Beth of course was quick to take note.

"What, didn't you get lucky last night?" she snapped throwing another fuse at me. The damned thermostat was screwing up again.

"Where are your cookies and I mean the good ones not the plain ol' boring ones sitting in that container on the kitchen bench?" I demanded. Beth snickered as she leaned against the door frame.

"They're the only cookies I brought in and because you seem not to have noticed I haven't brought the good kind in for over a year now. All my baking is clean as a whistle these days."

"Mercy was acting weird this morning, I assumed you snuck her one," I rubbed my eyes and grabbed the fuse. "I'll fix this, might work the bag for a bit too."

"Good idea," Beth murmured as I stalked past her.
I was punching all of my frustration into that damned bag and it still didn't help my mood. With every hit I imagined it was one of the men who had hit the women who came to Mercy's. I wished I knew what Ella's abuser looked like, it would have made the whole exercise more worthwhile. My fists connecting with the bag were the only sound in the damp basement and I soon shed my shirt and worked up a sweat. A gentle cough behind me had me snap around surprised.
No one ever came down here, especially not Beth, she was too damn scared of the ghost that she was convinced lived among the boxes and crates, so no one ever snuck up on me. I was shocked to see Ella sitting half way down the staircase. Her eyes were glued to my chest, her cheeks flushed.

"You have a tattoo," she noted a little breathlessly. I nodded. I had a tattoo. Selena was the only person, other than the tattoo artist, who knew about it. But I was the only person who knew what it meant. It was personal, not something I wanted to share. But I found myself wanting Ella to know about it and sharing something personal like this would help with the trust we were developing. It wasn't a small tattoo and how I had managed to keep it a secret was beyond me. It took up almost my entire back and I endured many hours of mind numbing pain just to cover it and keep it a secret. I knew Ella would appreciate it from an artistic perspective. The entire tattoo was in shades of gray; a large crucifix, drawn in such a way to give it a worn, weathered wooden look, sat between my shoulder blades and below it in an elegant scroll was a quote. Ella stood and carefully descended the few remaining steps, walking cautiously towards me. I stood perfectly still as she moved to my back.

"He will wipe every tear from their eyes and there will be no more death, or sorrow, or crying, or pain."
The silence grew almost uncomfortable before she circled to stand back before me once more. Her head was tilted in thought and she watched me carefully. Then, like turning off a switch her eyes brightened and she looked at the punching bag.

"Would you teach me?" she asked. I was thrown for a moment. I was positive she would ask about my tattoo, about what it meant and represented.
I was prepared to tell her, a little of I I'll-show-you-mine-you-show-me-yours. But I was also relieved I didn't have to explain. I guess I wasn't as ready as I thought I was and perhaps Ella realized that. Or perhaps, like everyone else in this shelter, we would tell our own stories once we were ready without pressure or expectation.

"There's not much to teach about punching a bag of sand." I grinned.

"I want to know how to punch a man, properly." she explained.

"You live on the streets and never took a self-defense class? Many shelters hold them for free you know." She stiffened at my words, her lips pursed and ready to argue. I was pretty sure it was the 'free' comment that had her spine stiffen. Ella didn't seem like the sort of girl to take handouts if she could avoid it. She was a proud little spitfire my angel.
"The first time I saw you, I walked you through the doors of this shelter and you stood with your fists clenched ready to sock

me one if I so much as breathed wrong. I'm sure you're more than capable of taking care of yourself but I'd be happy to show you a few self-defense moves." I reached out and took her wrist, feeling the ridges of her scars under my fingers. She flinched and I ignored it. "Clench your fist, like you did that night." She was tense and as nervous as a rabbit but she obeyed, clenching her fists. I positioned them appropriately in front of her, one hand a little lower protecting her torso the other higher protecting her face. She looked so damn cute and mad as hell. "If you thought I was suggesting you couldn't afford to pay for self-defense classes, I'm sorry. Many people attend those classes, they aren't just for people who can't afford them. They are put on to be made available and accessible to everyone." She seemed to relax a little and when I say a little I mean the most minuscule, tiny of fragments.

"Now, let's get one thing straight. You're not weak." I looked her right in the eye so she could see that I believed that was the God honest truth. "But," I went on, "you're tiny, like a doll. Hell, I have no doubt I could wrap you up and put you in my pocket." Her brow furrowed.

"You could damn well try," she snarled. I tried to hide my smile behind my hand as I continued on.

"Most men will have the upper hand over you because of size alone." She nodded. "There are advantages to being small though. It puts you in a position to attack down here a little easier." I pointed to my groin. Her eyes dropped and I tried hard not to think of the fact she was looking at my dick. "With your hands up like this, your attacker immediately thinks you're stupid enough to try and hit him in the face."

"I'm not going to?" she asked, looking a little disappointed. I laughed.

"Not yet, Angel. First of all, you are going to either knee or kick the fucker in the nuts." She blushed. "Give it a try." Ella's eyes widened.

"I'm not going to kick you in the nuts," she said shocked.

"I'd actually prefer you didn't as well. Use your knee to attack my boys, just go slow." With great hesitation and blushing furiously she finally, slowly raised her knee. "After you attack from below, punch hard and aim for the throat or face."

She moved her fist forward, slowly. "Good girl. Now try it faster, put some effort behind it." She didn't look so sure. "Come on Angel, show me what you've got." She did. A sharp kick to the groin which I blocked followed by a quick jab to the face which almost connected. She had quick reflexes. She looked a little worried; actually, she looked a lot worried.

"That's the girl, go again." Some of the worry faded as she went through the maneuver again. We practiced the move a few more times and I corrected her stance, her fist.
"Turn around," I finally prompted. She hesitated. This maneuver would bring me closer, she would feel more defenseless at being attacked from behind. "You can trust me Angel, I promise." She turned, slowly. "If someone comes at you from behind there are things you can do to get free." I moved closer; damn she smelled good.
"I'm going to put my arms around you, okay? If you want me to stop, you just say so." I approached her like you would a frightened puppy. Slow and steady, whispering words of encouragement. As I wrapped my arms around her shoulders I felt how rigid she was under me. Her breathing had accelerated and her eyes were squeezed shut. "Good girl, now you can break away from me easily. If you can get at the fucker's hands, you grab a finger and pull back, hard. Or you can raise your foot and stomp hard on his foot. With a bit of luck the grip will loosen enough for you to pull free. Try and grab for one of my fingers." Her breathing was too fast. "Angel?" She didn't respond. I immediately dropped my arms and moved in front of her. Her eyes were wide, her face pale. She looked completely and utterly terrified.

CHAPTER 12

Ella

I hadn't had a panic attack in months. It wasn't a fear of Jax that had actually triggered the attack. It had been the way he stood behind me, the feel of his chest against my back. Flashback. Marcus had approached me like this when he was going to rape me. Somewhere deep inside my brain I knew Jax wouldn't hurt me; I even recognized how different he felt compared to Marcus, but my mind still short circuited and I lost it. I was back at home and Marcus held me breathing in my ear. I knew I was gasping for breath—my chest felt tight, my lungs screamed for air. Black spots danced before my eyes and I knew I was going to lose consciousness. Then his words cut a path to my mind, I heard Jax and gradually his calm, assuring voice brought me back.

"Deep breaths Angel, breathe with me baby. You're safe here. It's just you and me and you know I won't hurt you." I opened my eyes and concentrated on Jax, focusing on his eyes that were so gentle and honest. I finally got control of my breathing and my body slowly became mine again, under my control, away from the memories. "That's it Angel. You're safe." His hands cupped my face and he kept watching me, breathing with me. "What frightened you?" he asked, his grey eyes searching mine. Thought eluded me and the words started gushing out without censor.

"When y-you were behind m-me," I whispered. "It reminded m-me of h-him." He nodded with understanding. Jax pulled me closer and folded me into his arms, my cheek pressed against his chest, absorbing his warmth, his strength. My throat ached with the effort it took not to cry. My tears weren't trying to escape for Marcus or because of the panic attack, but for Jax's kindness. His tenderness was what did me in.

"He hit you, he cut you; did he hurt you in any other way?" I knew what Jax meant, he was wondering if I had been raped. I was fortunate and glad to be able to shake my head in the negative. Gradually Jax's heat poured into my body and I was thankful he didn't ask me any more questions. I really didn't think I could hold my shit together if he did. When I was back in control, I reluctantly pulled away from him.

"You have triggers that start these panic attacks?" he cautiously asked and I gave a short nod. "There are ways to help stop the attacks, breathing techniques. If you are aware of the triggers you can work on preventing future attacks." I shifted uncomfortably before him, embarrassed that he had seen the attack and nervous at having exposed a weakness.

"You hungry?" He deftly changed the subject. A moment ago I was ready to throw up, but now, yep, I was starving. I nodded, feeling a little empty and tired.

"I've got to pick up some supplies, thought I'd drop by The Pit Stop for one of Benny's famous all day breakfasts. You wanna come?" I couldn't really afford to eat out but I really wanted to; I wasn't ready to put distance between Jax and I yet. What can I say? I was a glutton for punishment. A little numbly I nodded again. Jax pulled his shirt on and I was disappointed that his rippling hard stomach was covered.

"Come on, Angel." He grabbed my hand and led me up the steep staircase. At the top, he stopped and glanced over his shoulder at me.

"Not many people know about my tattoo. In fact, pretty much no one does, especially Mercy. I'd appreciate it if you didn't say anything."

"I didn't expect Mercy to be the sort who wouldn't approve of tattoos. You were a soldier. I thought it was pretty much mandatory for soldiers to have tattoos." Jax laughed and the sound helped me to relax a little more.

"True, but it's not so much the tattoo itself that I prefer to keep to myself. It's the content, the meaning."
Jax had demons too and he was good at hiding them.

"Jax, I am the queen of secrets. Yours are more than safe with me." He nodded satisfied and led me through Mercy's and out a back door.

Jax drove a big, black, luxurious Dodge Ram. It was the nicest vehicle I had ever been in, much nicer than Marcus's pussy Beamer M3. The Dodge was a working man's truck. A man who was proud of who he was and not interested in slick speed but perhaps more safety and comfort. Shit, even the seats were warmed. The panic attack that had gripped me less than fifteen minutes ago was all but a distant memory as I sunk into the tan leather seat. I groaned, out loud.

"Comfortable?" Jax asked grinning.

"Please tell me The Pit Stop is like hours away," I moaned. Jax laughed loudly.

"Sorry Angel, only a few minutes." My eyes slipped closed as I enjoyed the short ride. "You know, I'm finding myself more than a little jealous of this car right now. You've never had such a contented look on your face with me." Jax's smile was sly and knowing and suddenly I had images of him doing things to me that might just put that look of content on my face. I blushed and his grin was shit eating proud, almost as if he knew what I was thinking. We pulled up in front of a tidy little diner that I realize was less than a block from Bouquets. As I reached for the handle the door opened and Jax stood on the icy footpath before me, his hand outstretched. I didn't hesitate when I took it, feeling completely safe by his side, my hand in his. Jax let go all too soon and I was quietly disappointed. The sunshine that had started the day had disappeared behind a blanket of thick grey cloud. It would snow again tonight. I reached back to grab my backpack and Jax stopped me.

"It will be safe here; you can leave it in my truck if you like." I hesitated. I never left my backpack behind. It was always with me, it was all I had. "You can bring it in if you want. It doesn't bother me one way or another. I just thought you might like to leave it here, it looks heavy." I stood for a moment conflicted. To leave my bag or not leave my bag, that was the question. "You're thinking too hard Ella. Come on Angel, let's just eat before I pass out this time, I'm starving." I could do this, I could leave it there. The truck was right outside the diner. I stepped away from the Dodge and before I could change my mind, Jax slammed the door shut and locked it. "And just so you know, I invited you to lunch which means my treat. When you invite me out it can be your treat." I didn't really know how to respond to that, so rather than address it I pretended to ignore it.

The Pit Stop was warm and cozy and thankfully not too

crowded. We sat at the counter alongside two old men who appeared to be in a deep and meaningful conversation with the man behind the counter; something about the cost of meat and export tax.

"Jax!" the man behind the counter bellowed. His loud voice made me wince, but I knew it wasn't spoken in anger but shouting kind of made me nervous. He was huge and round with a thick tangled beard and warm friendly eyes that were watching me curiously.

"Benny," Jax said, his voice much more calm and soothing. "This is Ella, Ella this is Benny. This is his fine establishment and he is the genius behind the all-day breakfast." Benny reached out his hand to shake mine. Jax looked concerned for a moment, but I didn't hesitate to reach out and take Benny's hand. Although I had always kept my distance from men, even the ones with friendly eyes, having Jax beside me made me feel safe.

"Pretty Ella," sighed Benny. "Please tell me I can get you something other than a salad." I hated salad.

"No salad, meat for me thanks. I prefer it soaking in grease with some bread to mop up the mess." Benny looked at me like he was in love.

"Thank God, a real woman. Jax, hold on to this one, she is a rare commodity." I blushed as Benny turned to the kitchen.

"That she is," Jax murmured. I wasn't sure if I was meant to hear it but I did and my heart pitched dangerously. Coffee with cream and sugar was slid towards us and Jax prepared mine just the way I liked it, though a dash of caramel would make it perfect. Benny practically ignored us as his argument continued on with the old timers. Jax told me about his best friend Charlie who also worked for him and went on to tell me about the town, the College that fed the businesses and the shelter. Basically anything that wasn't too personal. I felt comfortable, happy. I found myself thinking about Claymont in a more permanent way. Could I stay here permanently? I could get my own apartment, maybe sell some of my portraits to make more money? There was no reason Marcus would find me here, as long as I stayed off the grid. Thinking of my future was a strange concept and frightening. To want something like that and have it taken away from me would be devastating. I knew it was easier not to want, not to plan, but not even a ten foot solid brick wall in my mind could stop the dreams that were beginning to churn away.

As I mopped up the last of the grease off my plate with a slice of bread, I discovered the diner had become quiet. I glanced up to see Jax, Benny and the two old timers watching me, waiting. I grinned. "I think you've spoiled me for all future breakfasts, Benny," I admitted. It was obviously the right response, as Benny beamed with pride.

"Sorry, that wasn't exactly lady like," I groaned with embarrassment, wiping my grease covered fingers on a napkin. I had all but devoured the meal without a pause and finished it by dumping my fork and promptly using Jax's last piece of toast to mop up every last drop. I might as well have picked up the plate and licked it clean. Hell, I still might. Jax chuckled.

"Screw lady like, Angel, you have no idea how fuckin' hot that was. We're gonna have to sit here a few minutes longer so I can get myself under control. There is no way I can concentrate on driving after watching you eat. It was sexy as hell." Sexy? How in the hell could someone hoovering their meal like a starved beast be sexy? I'm sure at one point I even grunted. I was mortified and Jax was in a lust crazed fog. I guess that was just one prime example of the very vast and extensive differences between men and women.

Eventually we left The Pit Stop and Jax had two errands to make before heading back to Mercy's. I tagged along at each stop and left my backpack in the car each time. The second time wasn't quite as difficult as the first and the third time was a breeze. I trusted Jax to keep me and my things safe. By the time we got back to the shelter it was getting dark. I helped Jax unload the boxes he had put in the back of the Dodge and settled into what had quickly become my evening routine—helping with the laundry, giving the bathrooms a quick check and finally helping Mary in the kitchen. I liked Mary, she actually reminded me of the female version of Benny. If Mary wasn't already married I would have suggested to Jax that we try and set the two up. Finally I found myself in my new favorite chair, bright lamp at my side and sketch book open in my lap. I was sketching a portrait of Benny tonight. He was fun to draw with his larger than life eyes and big bushy beard.

I didn't see Jax settle down beside me, but I smelled him, clean and fresh. It reminded me of the woods. Damn he smelt good.

"I'm about to head off," he said with a little reluctance in his voice. I didn't want him to go, I had enjoyed his company today, panic attack and all. But I nodded before flicking back a couple of pages in my sketch book and carefully tore the picture along the perforated edge. It was the portrait I had drawn of Mercy. I handed it to him and waited nervously. It was a long time before he said anything; he just stared at it, taking in every shadow, every sweeping bold line. Mercy looked tired in the portrait, but at the same time determined. It was how I saw her. Finally, Jax moved. He placed the picture carefully aside and slid out of his chair, kneeling before me. All I could do was sit and stare with my heart racing, my eyes not willing to blink in case I missed something. Jax's rigid stomach pushed against my knees, his hands rested on the arms of the chair. I was caged in but didn't feel threatened. In fact, I think the only thing I was in threat of was being kissed and that didn't seem to frighten me nearly as much as it should have.

"Damn Angel. Seldom am I speechless." He shook his head, no doubt watching me carefully to see if I would panic over his closeness. He carefully reached for my hand. My finger-tips were blackened with charcoal, but Jax didn't seem to care. He held my hand tenderly in his. "This," he whispered, squeezing my hand. "This is a gift." His fingers then touched my face with reverence, running tenderly down my temples, tracing my scar and finally sweeping around my eyes which fluttered closed. "These," he brushed his thumbs gently over my eyelashes, his face so close I could feel his breath on my skin. "These see more truth than anyone I have ever known." His hands left my face and I opened my eyes again as his hand very slowly dropped to my neck, his fingers following the line of my collarbone, then his palm opened. "And this," he pressed his hand over my chest, right over my heart, "this is the most beautiful thing in existence." I was stunned. My breathing was now embarrassingly fast and I'm sure he could feel my heart pounding frantically under his hand. Please kiss me, I silently begged. He did, but not at all how I expected it. Jax took my hand once more and placed his warm soft lips to the center of my palm. No one had ever kissed me in such a way. The kiss vanquished all ugliness and left me feeling raw, naked and beautiful. This kiss rocked my world like no other touch could. When Jax finally stood and simply walked away with Mercy's portrait in hand I almost wept at the loss of his body so close to mine. It was in that moment I realized I could easily love Jax Carter.

CHAPTER 13

Jax

I had to get out of Mercy's and fast. If I didn't I was going to start mauling Ella like a sex crazed fool. Fuck she was simply beautiful, inside and out. She was perfect and there was absolutely no way I was going to be able to keep a professional distance. As far as I was concerned, she was mine. I glanced down at the picture of Mercy. It was flawlessly stunning. Ella got it right in one simple elegant sketch. She had the weary look in her face that Mercy always wore, but the strong determined eyes that made her who she was. Ella seemed to be able to sketch people honestly, seeing in their eyes and faces what most others would likely miss. I ran a hand through my tangled mess of hair. Shit, my memory was burned with the scent and feel of Ella. As my fingers had touched her face I had almost trembled with the exquisite hunger that surged through my body for this woman. When I placed my palm over her chest, right over the delectable rise of her breast, I thought my body would explode. There was no fear in her eyes, she was not scared of me. What I did see there floored me though, trust. How, in such a short amount of time, had I gained this angel's trust? One thing I knew for sure, I would not betray it and I would not fail her like I had Sarah. It was in that moment, on my knees before Ella that I realized something monumental. Something that I felt needed to be marked in my life permanently in the form of a picture, a song, another tattoo maybe? This was the moment I realized I was in love with Ella. Fuck, I loved her. I had never loved a girl before. Not like this. I loved Mercy, I adored women. I spent a good portion of my life showing women just how much I adored them. But this was different. Sure I wanted her just like any red blooded male would, but I could see Ella as my forever girl. I could picture her in my home, in my bed all tussled and cute.
I could picture her with a ring on her finger and a baby in her belly. I groaned loudly. I was done for, Ella owned me and I would likely do anything for her. A sucker punch to the head wouldn't have floored me any less.

The next morning when I arrived back at Mercy's I kept a

careful distance from Ella, I didn't want to overwhelm her. Thankfully she left for work soon after I arrived which gave me a little room to actually get my body under control and use my brain for longer than a few minutes. She had seemed quietly happy before she left, casting shy glances my way every now and again. It made me wonder what experience she had had with men. She didn't flirt and act like other girls her age did, but having been hurt by a man would certainly dampen any desire to try and attract members of the opposite sex. She blushed so easily though and I had caught her more than once watching my body carefully, as if seeing a man for the first time. She was an artist so perhaps it was simply attention to detail. Hey eyes were filled with a familiar look that wasn't at all clinical, the raging blush in her cheeks told me that much. She was young, Annie had admitted that she thought she was a teenager but Ella had confessed to her that she was twenty-two. Twenty-two was too old to be a virgin, surely. Damn, I was now imagining myself sinking into that beautiful little body and my raging dick was demanding attention, right in the middle of Mercy's fucking kitchen!

"Are you reading tea leaves or something?" Her voice was so familiar and welcome I couldn't stop the stupid grin that crept over my face. I was man enough to admit I had missed her today and man enough to admit I knew she finished work at five and it was now a little after seven. My shift had been over an hour ago but I refused to leave until I knew Ella was back and safe. Where had she been the last two hours? I made sure to keep my front to the sink when she entered the kitchen, I didn't want to scare her with the bulge in my jeans.

"Good evening, Angel. Where've you been?"

"I went with Annie to look at apartments."

"And?"

"And they found a really nice place downtown. It has two bedrooms so Eli can have his own room. It's clean and the super said he hasn't seen a rat in months." Ella chuckled and I couldn't help but smile along with her. "They move in on Sunday and Annie invited me over for pizza that night to celebrate." She looked wistful. "I've never been invited to someone's place for dinner before." Her voice was so low I almost missed her confession.

"Really?" I tried not to sound surprised, but hell, I was and I guess I couldn't help but sound it. Ella nodded.

"How old were you when you left home?"

"Seventeen, almost eighteen."

"Before that, you never went out with your parents, maybe to their friends' place for dinner?" She shook her head.

"My mom was kind of embarrassed of me. I was sort of rebellious as a teenager and she was embarrassed by some of the things I did. She was also a bit of a perfectionist, she liked everything to be orderly, tidy, I wasn't. I liked jeans, she liked dresses. I liked my hair messy, hers was perfectly tidy. I liked boy shorts and sports bras, she had to have Victoria's Secret. I wasn't the daughter she had hoped for." I was pissed; her mom sounded like a fucking bitch. Shit, her mom sounded like Selena.

"What about your dad?" Now I was pushing. I wanted to know more and I knew I should just let her offer the information when she was ready, but screw that. She trusted me, I knew she did. Time for a bit of Ella's history, as painful as I knew it would be to hear, I needed to know. Ella fiddled with the cup, examining it like it was a fine work of art.

"My dad died when I was thirteen. He didn't really have friends; he had work colleagues—he worked a lot. He had to keep Mother happy and financed. We ate in, always. He at least made sure he and I sat down to dinner every night; Mother was out a lot." I leaned against the bench, settling in for what I hoped was a long and thorough discussion. She had my full undivided attention.

"I'm sorry he died, he sounded like a good man, someone who would have protected you." Ella's breath seemed to hitch and she tried not to look at me. I placed my finger under her chin and turned her to face me. "How did your dad die?"

"Heart attack." Two simple words that obviously tore a little girl's life apart. "In our kitchen. We were home alone, as usual Mother was away. I called the ambulance and he was taken to the hospital. I sat there alone until midnight when mother finally stumbled in, tipsy from too many cocktails. She had promised to be home for dinner but obviously she was late.

I didn't get to see my dad. She took me home and we buried him a week later." Her voice was emotionless and it broke my heart. We were on a roll and I had no intention of stopping now.

"Who hurt you, Ella?" She breathed deeply and seemed to be finding the strength to continue. Her thumb began to trace the scar on her opposite wrist in a methodical motion. Clearly she was oblivious to what she was actually doing. It was a habit, something she did when this man came into her thoughts.

"Marcus, my step-father." I held back my sneer, I wanted to kill this man. "Mom married six months after Daddy died. I knew Marcus would hurt me—I saw it in his eyes." Even at thirteen she was far too perceptive.

"Did you ask for help? Go to the police?" I knew she would bristle at my questions but I had to know. I needed to know who had failed her so I could bring a world of hurt into their lives. She did indeed stiffen at my words and her sharp eyes focused on me.

"I was a mess, Jax. I did stupid things after my dad died and Marcus came into our lives. First it was just to embarrass him and my mom, but later it was a way to escape. I used drugs, drank, slept around." She was watching me closely to gauge my response and I was careful to keep the look on my face neutral. I had no doubt she expected me to dislike what she was saying and I did, though not likely for the reasons she would assume. I hated that she was thrust into that life, that she did those things to escape someone who had betrayed her, who was supposed to protect her regardless of whether he was her biological father or not. "I was in trouble with the police more than once, I couldn't go to them; they thought I was your typical delinquent teenager and Marcus had a friend on the force anyway. He always made sure I was found, dealt with and placed back into the hands of my step-father. After I was hospitalized for my apparent suicide attempt there was no way any one would ever believe me." I hated hearing the mess her life had become. Her dad had loved her, made a good start for her then between her selfish mother and abusive step-father, it had all fallen down around her.

"What about the bruises. Surely people saw them, asked questions?"

"If they were on my face Marcus kept me home. He's a pretty successful businessman, he had an office at home so he didn't need to leave the house and he could make sure I stayed put. I tried to escape once, but the police found me and delivered me back to him with a bow and all. That's when he did this." She rubbed her wrists. I shook my head in frustration. "I was biding my time, waiting until I turned eighteen so I could leave without having to worry about being returned, but that's when he tried to rape me. That's when I left." Mother fucker! "I knew Marcus had a gun in his office and I was able to get the drawer open and grab the gun. I wanted to kill him so bad, but I couldn't do it. He hit me like my life was nothing to him—he cut my wrists and let me bleed to within an inch of my life just to prove he could do whatever the fuck he wanted with me and I couldn't hurt him. What does that say about me?"

"It says that you are more human than he is, Angel. It says that you realize how precious life is and you aren't as willing to take it as he is. It means you're nothing like that sick fuck." I couldn't maintain the distance between us anymore. I reached forward and pulled her hand away from her wrist and held it tightly in mine.

"Well, I ran. That's what I've been doing for the last four years. That's my story, Jax. The whole ugly fucked up game between my step-father and I." My hands were trembling and I couldn't stop them. My heart was pounding in anger. This asshole had beaten her, cut her, manipulated her and tried to rape her. I could hardly believe this tiny little angel was still alive after everything she had been through. I should have expected it though, she was a defiant little spitfire and there was no way she was going to let this fucker ruin her.

"I didn't go to the police because of this," she turned over her arm showing me her scars again, "I was in the system and I had a therapist. It was my word against his." Son of a bitch knew what he was doing.

"Your mother?" I somehow managed to spit out even though my jaw was locked shut with anger.

"She couldn't care less. She either turned a blind eye or

believed Marcus. He was good at pretending and faking it. She was away a lot, traveling. I was in therapy and that was good enough for her." I would never hit a woman, but right now, I might just make an exception.

Ella's mother was a first class royal bitch. I would like to say she didn't deserve to be a mother, but then there would be no Ella and if I was to be honest, I don't think my life would be complete without Ella in it. Funny how after only a few days I could happily accept that notion.

"What's his full name, Marcus what?" She blinked those beautiful brown eyes, calm and steady.

"Why?"

"I need to know where the fucker is, Angel. I need to know if he is still a threat to you." She simply stared at me, no tears in her eyes, only determination.

"He will always be a threat to me; he is a successful business man and I am the only one that knows the truth about who he really is." I shook my head.

"As you said, it's your word against his. He's not stupid, he's wrangled your life in such a way that he never has to look bad. He probably couldn't care less where you are right now, but I need to check it out. I have to know you are safe, Angel. Anyway, living like you have been, running, hiding, that's him still controlling you." She didn't answer me, chewing her bottom lip as she thought, looking far too sexy for the vulnerable woman she was right now.

"I don't know, Jax. I've kept myself safe by running, staying out of the system. If you start looking into him, it might alert him. He has friends in the police force." I shook my head, still holding her wrist, my thumb running comforting circles over her scars.

"I know people too, Ella. I'm military—I have connections. I can do this so no one but you and I will ever know. Please, let me protect you." I could see her mind working over my words, considering them.

"I need control, Jax. He took that away from me; I can't give that up, not for anybody."

"I know, Angel. I don't want to control you I just want to make sure you're safe."

She sighed and I could see the defeat in her body as she slumped forward a little.

"Fairmont, Marcus Fairmont, of Pitcher & Fairmont Advertising in Dunston." Definitely not close by, in fact over fifteen hundred beautiful miles away.

"I won't fail you, Ella. You have my word." She nodded looking a little overwhelmed.

"I never considered the way I was living was still giving him control, I never thought of it like that. I want my life back, Jax." And she would have it back, if it was the last thing I did.

CHAPTER 14

Ella

It seemed I had suddenly developed a chronic case of verbal diarrhea or the content control portion of my brain was on the fritz. Once the words started coming out, they didn't stop, like a train master who was simply unable to pull the train up in time, I just motored on. What would Jax think of me now, his little drug addicted whoring angel? God, I was as pathetic as Marcus told me. The disrespect I had shown myself, my body, it was shameful. Now, to top it off I was running like a scared little rabbit, still allowing Marcus to control my life. I was living every second of every day with Marcus on my mind and it had to stop. Regardless of what Jax now thought of me, he said he would find out if Marcus was still searching for me, so that was a start. I could only hope that he had moved on to bigger and better things and if so, maybe I could have a future here in Claymont, anywhere for that matter. If I didn't have to live in fear of Marcus I could go anywhere or be anything. I rubbed my head which thundered like a jackhammer. I felt ill for having spilled my guts, old memories had been cracked open and I just wanted to curl up somewhere and forget. It was at times like this I could understand how easily I had fallen into the deep abyss of escape. Drugs and alcohol gave me that escape but there was no way I would allow myself to travel that path again. It would only lead to self-loathing, to self-harm. The occasional fruity cocktail was as far as I would drive that train—I was a reformed addict who needed to finally get a grip on my life. I needed to make changes and plan for a future. Jax had left, he said he needed to make some phone calls and now I stood in the middle of the common room, my head spinning with thoughts of past, present and a possible future. I noticed Annie by her and Eli's bed.

She looked so happy and she had every right to be. She had her own apartment, she would be leaving soon. I watched her for a moment as my mind recognized a crazy idea beginning to take shape. If I were to be honest, it had been gradually taking shape since I'd gone to see the apartment with Annie this evening. My feet began moving towards her before I had even realized what I was going to do and say.

I stood before Annie, watching her as she carefully folded clothes, tucking them away in her suitcase. She glanced at me and smiled.

"Penny for your thoughts, Ella?" she asked as she continued to tidy up the small area she had tried to make somewhat homely with a few toys and a small framed picture of her and Eli.

"You look happy," I noted. She finally shut the suitcase and sat on the edge of the squeaky bed.

"Less than a week and we're out of here. I've never had my own place. My husband and I were together in high school, then college. We always lived together. I am excited about having something that's my own." I understood wanting your own things, your own space and it made me think what I was about to ask was simply selfish. But the quote 'nothing ventured nothing gained' rang over and over in my splitting head. I shuffled from one foot to the other nervously, playing with the imaginary dirt on the floor before me.

"What's on your mind, Ella?" Annie asked again, patiently watching me.

"Umm, I was hoping to ask you a favor." Annie patted the space beside her, suggesting I should sit. I did but instead of nervously shifting on my feet I now nervously fiddled with the drawstring on my hoodie.

"I know you're just getting on your feet and the fact you just said you were looking forward to having your own place kind of makes me reluctant to ask you this now. So you can say no and I would prefer you did rather than take pity on me, I don't need pity." I was blabbering.

"Ella, if you need somewhere to stay for a while, you're more than welcome to stay with us. As long as you're happy with sleeping on a couch, which to be honest can't be any worse than the beds here, I'd love to have you stay with us." I stared at her, surprised. I really had talked myself into expecting a resounding no. "Are you sure?"

"Actually I sort of hoped that by taking you with me tonight you might have thought of coming to stay for a while. Can you pay a little towards expenses?" She asked, as if an afterthought.

"Of course, I'll pay my way—I'll give you money towards rent and food. And if you need me to watch Eli, I can do that too." Annie smiled.

"Excellent. Then you will be helping me out. I've been offered a couple of dinner shifts at the diner and I would like to take them but I need someone to watch Eli. It would be Friday and Saturday nights, so it might cramp your social life a little." I laughed loudly.

"I barely have a life, let alone a social life. It's fine, really. I work Tuesday to Saturday until five each day, so I'm completely free for babysitting duty in the evenings." Annie clapped her hands together with excitement.

"Perfect." I still wasn't sure if she might regret this sooner rather than later.

"It won't be for too long, just until I get on my feet with enough money to get a small apartment. And you can ask me to leave at any time; I can always come back here." Annie smiled and took my hand in hers.

"Honey, you shouldn't be here. None of us should be here. If I can help you get out, then I would feel like I am somehow paying back Mercy's Shelter for taking care of Eli and me." I was no longer completely homeless. I had moved from an uncomfortable lumpy bed in a homeless shelter to a couch. I had lived in crowded conditions before, never any less than four people in the one place at a time. It was cramped and the complete lack of privacy was downright uncomfortable. Living with Annie and Eli would be the closest I had come in four years to something that would almost resemble a normal family living situation. I smiled, suddenly feeling a little giddy, excited and nauseous all at the same time.

"Thank you, Annie." I breathed with relief and she squeezed my hand and smiled back at me.

"Us girls have to stick together." She smiled before I slipped away to my own bed.

***

My sleep that night was restless, filled with horrifying visions of Marcus. I vaguely remember Mercy brushing my hair tenderly and whispering words to help soothe me back to sleep.

When I finally woke, instead of feeling refreshed and wakeful, I felt exhausted and emotional. I needed to keep myself busy, completely immerse my brain with something other than the bitter memories. Work was a great distraction. Rebecca excelled in keeping me on my toes and smiling. She had a sharp wit and humor that had us both laughing all day long. Once back at the shelter the snow had begun to fall and I was starting to feel a little trapped in the warehouse. Annie was working and Eli was off playing with Dave. I was still restless, my memories having been cracked open the night before were obviously affecting me more than I thought they would. I walked aimlessly around the shelter. There really wasn't much to do.

Even the bathrooms were clean as a whistle, but eventually my edgy temperament got the better of me and I decided to clean them again. When I finally reached the last bathroom, the smallest cubicle, I noticed a shiny bronze plaque at the bottom of one wall. I knelt down and gave it a rub with the rag, running my fingers over the words inscribed into the shiny metal.

Rest now sweet Sarah in contented silence with no more yesterdays or tomorrows to trouble you. Now is a time to forgive life and be at peace.

I sat for the longest time reading and re-reading the quote, wondering who Sarah was. How did she die and why was the plaque here, in a bathroom of all places? Eventually I moved out of the small bleach filled room and found myself descending the stairs to the basement. The punching bag hung innocuously in the center of the room. A pair of training gloves sat on a bench and I thumbed them nervously. They were definitely going to be a little big, but I slipped them on anyway; a small part of me reveling in the fact that they belonged to Jax. I approached the bag nervously and gave it a small nudge. Then I fell into the stance Jax had shown me and gently began tapping the bag. After a while I picked up my thrusts and put a little more force behind each punch, imagining this was Marcus's body I was attacking, slamming my fist into him as he had slammed his fists into me. Strangely it didn't bring me the contentment I hoped it would. Sweat fell from my brow, my hair clung to my skin and I pulled off my t-shirt and long sleeved thermal, leaving me in a sports bra and cargos. I swept my hair into a messy knot on my head, slipped the gloves back on and resumed my relentless attack on the inoffensive punching bad, releasing all the energy and rage that had been building inside. Finally my arms gave out, aching with fatigue and I leaned against the bag, allowing the cool touch of the canvas to seep into my skin.

"You're a natural." Jax's voice startled me and I spun around to face him. He was standing at the bottom of the staircase watching me carefully. I somehow stopped myself from wrapping my arms around the bare skin of my stomach, but his eyes didn't stray below my face and for some reason I was disappointed. Why would he want to look at my body? I was just a scarred, broken, used girl that no real man would ever want.

"I've spoken to an old friend who was in the army with me. He works security now and is going to look into Marcus for us. He'll be discreet. You have nothing to worry about, he won't slip up. Hopefully it won't take more than a week or two to find out where Marcus is and if he's still trying to find you." I had no idea how anyone could find out such information but I didn't question it. I had to try and put trust in Jax. If he said he could do this and keep me safe, then perhaps he could. Right now, with dreams beginning to form and take shape in my life, I needed to believe he could.

"Do you feel up to working on those triggers and breathing techniques I told you about?" The night before had been rough and the day not much better. I wasn't sure if I was up to it but, for some reason, I didn't want to disappoint Jax, so I nodded. He walked cautiously forward, his eyes on mine, ignoring my scars and my body. Perhaps he found my scars as ugly as I did. "I want to know how you're handling the fear today. You will be facing away from me, so I won't be able see your face. We'll use a number system, okay?" I nodded as he stood facing me.

"One is perfectly fine, ten is shit has hit the fan." A small grin tugged one corner of his mouth and I managed a small smile in return. He motioned with his hand for me to turn around and reluctantly I did. My eyes were closed and my back prickled with awareness waiting for his heat to whisper across my skin.

My body was tense with nervous anticipation.

"What number, Angel?" I thought about it for a moment. I was fine, a little nervous, but definitely a long way from a panic attack.

"Three."

"Okay. A panic attack is a reaction to fear, so recognizing it and managing it is your first step. I'm going to touch you now, Angel." As promised, his hand rested on my shoulder. My heart stuttered, curiously though it wasn't with fear, it was with something else entirely that pulsed from his touch right through to the junction between my thighs. Then his other hand was gently rested on my other shoulder. Still no fear but perhaps something akin to desire caused my nipples to harden. Oh God, I hoped he didn't notice.

"Angel, number," Jax murmured.

"Um, four maybe?" Jax then stepped in closer and I could feel the length of him down my back, his body was rigid and swamped with a delicious heat that soaked into my skin. I felt his breath on my neck then ever so slowly his arms wrapped around my shoulders and chest, holding me close. And there was the panic, floating through my body like an ugly spirit. My breath sped up and I fought the inevitable attack.

"Control your breathing. Take long deep breaths and then you're going to count them. You breathe in for five through your nose and then out for five through your mouth." I obeyed, counting a little too quick but counting never-the-less. "Now I want you to curl your toes and squeeze the muscles in your feet, count to five then relax, then do the same with your legs, thighs, stomach, all the way up to your eyes." I did while Jax continued to hold me close, still taking breaths that were too shallow and quick through my nose and out through my mouth. After a few minutes Jax finally spoke.

"Number?" It took me a moment to realize what he was asking. I tried to answer, my mouth opened and shut several times. Number? I couldn't think past 'stay conscious'. "Angel, it's me and you know I won't hurt you. He's not here with you anymore and he hasn't been for a long time. Think about that, think of where you are." I did. I thought about

Mercy's Shelter, I thought about my bed upstairs, my backpack stashed safely under it, Mary most likely in the kitchen and Eli demanding attention from anyone who would glance his way. "Breathe with me, Angel. In through your nose, one, two, three, four, five, now out through your mouth, one, two, three, four, five." My breathing began to even out as I followed Jax's lead, breathing with him, listening to his voice, feeling the rhythmic rise and fall of his chest at my back. "You're doing beautifully, Angel," Jax whispered encouragement in my ear, his lips close. I melted under his praise. "You're going to let go of this fear. I'm going to help you beat it, beat him." It was a promise and it was the best promise anyone could have ever offered me.

CHAPTER 15

Jax

If I didn't let go of Ella soon, I was going to embarrass myself. My hardened member was pounding against the zipper of my jeans, begging to be released. Well, he was just going to have to calm the fuck down because until I was home in the privacy of my own bedroom, or bathroom, maybe I'd relent and give in to his demands in the truck, but until then, he was going to remain safely behind the layer of denim. I was trying hard to keep the lower half of me away from Ella. All she needed while I was helping her prevent a panic attack was my dick shoved in her back. I had learned a long time ago that this particular part of my anatomy functioned quite well without the use of a brain and right now it was only emphasizing that fact. Ella thankfully moved away, slipping off the gloves that were way too big and quickly putting her thermal and shirt back on. Her scars bothered me. They weren't ugly, they didn't diminish the fact she was beautiful, but they represented a pain she should never have had to endure. I wanted to kiss every one and make it all better for her.

"Who's Sarah?" The name startled me. I blinked, once, twice, my brain wrapping itself around her question. How did she know that name? "There's a small plaque in one of the bathrooms." Of course, dumb shit. I'd arranged the damn thing.

"She was a girl who came to Mercy's for help." Just the mention of her name caused me to sweat, my body to tense. No matter how long I talked to Dave about this, it was obviously something I could never move past. My eyes avoided Ella's. She saw too much when she looked into them.

"Why is there a plaque in the bathroom?"

"That is where she died—she committed suicide. It's small, out of the way. Most people don't notice it." Ella nodded.

"I cleaned in there today. If I hadn't, I wouldn't have seen it. It's personal, she meant something to you." I knew what she was thinking.

"Not in the way that you think. Yes, I cared about her

professionally and I let her down. I didn't see her pain for what it truly was, I wasn't able to save her."

"That's what your tattoo represents, isn't it? At first I thought it referred to war and you being a soldier, but it's not about that at all. It's about Sarah. 'He will wipe every tear from their eyes and there will be no more death, or sorrow, or crying, or pain.' It's for Sarah right?" My nod was restrained.

"Am I a project for you, Jax? Are you trying to find repentance in me? Because you won't find it here, you won't find it anywhere, Jax because you don't need forgiveness; you did nothing wrong." I shook my head slowly.

"First of all, you are not a project for me. I want to protect you because I like you, in the famous words of my best friend Charlie, I like like you. I want you to be safe, I want you to be happy and some primitive part of me wants to be the one that brings you that. Fuck knows if I want forgiveness for Sarah. My mind is all kinds of fucked up over that and a whole truck load of other shit. Dave has done his best to help me work through it but maybe it's something only I can work through, on my own."

She stood before me, her eyes searching mine, her brow furrowed looking perfectly beautiful and angelic. I ran my hands through my hair in frustration. "I care about you, probably too much and in a completely unprofessional way. I want you so bad and it's unfair to you. I've been unprofessional with you, Angel. I want you to be safe, I want you to have a future, here, in Claymont and I want to be a part of it. I'm a selfish son-of-bitch for wanting that but I can't seem to fucking help it." She just kept on staring at me, shocked to her core no doubt, perhaps even repulsed and more than a little freaked out.

"You want me?" she asked a little dumbstruck.

"Yes, Angel, I want you. You're beautiful, sexy, smart, funny and strong. I've never wanted anyone quite the way I want you." Yep, she was stunned into silence. We stood and stared at each other for what felt like fucking hours. Finally she looked down at her arms.

"This doesn't repulse you, the things I've done, that doesn't bother you?" she asked, bewildered. What the fuck? She thought I was repulsed by her scars? Her past? I stepped forward but stopped short of touching her.

"There isn't a damn thing about you that repulses me. I adore every inch of you, scars, nightmares, demons and all." She shook her head and slowly a smile crept into her features.

"I would prefer you lived in a nice big warm cozy house but not because I pity you or am embarrassed by your living arrangements. I want you to have things, nice things. I want you to be warm and safe." She sighed and shook her head in what appeared like disbelief, like it was so implausible that someone might care about her or think of her as beautiful and sexy.

"Well then, you might be happy to know that I am moving in with Annie and Eli on Sunday." It was now my turn to stare. I knew my smile had dropped and Ella looked suddenly nervous and worried.

"That's a good thing, Angel. If I seem disappointed it's only because I've kind of gotten used to you being here, near me." She still looked nervous. "Don't worry, I'll be dropping by regularly to check on the three of you and I hope you want to drop in here to check on me occasionally. You know, make sure I'm eating my Wheaties and all." Ella laughed.

"You eat Wheaties?" I laughed and shook my head. "Never."

"Maybe I'll drop by and make sure you're not threatening the health of the girls here by attempting to cook."

"Very little chance of that, Mary would slice my fingers off if I tried to mess with her kitchen. Since I have this incapacity to cook and I tend to eat out a lot maybe I will ask you to join me sometime, for dinner?" Fuck, did my brain and mouth even work together? Ella looked a little taken a back, but finally she composed herself as she walked towards the staircase.

"As in a date?" she asked suspiciously. I rubbed the back of my neck nervously.

"I guess me asking you out to dinner, just the two of us would fall under the premise of a date. But if you think you might say no, I might revise the invitation and make it breakfast or lunch, that's less date like."

"I've never been on a date before."

"Is that a yes?" She left me hanging for the longest time. I'd never been turned down by a girl before and if this particular one said no I think I might just turn celibate and give up women altogether.

"Maybe." Her smile was a little seductive as she looked back over her shoulder at me and slowly climbed the stairs out of the basement. Holy shit, I had just asked her on a date and she had said yes. Well, maybe, but that was good enough for me. I rubbed my eyes and looked around the dimly lit basement. I wanted to dance a little, perhaps strut a quick M.J. Moonwalk across the grubby floor. I rubbed my tired neck. Since when did I get all goofy over a date? I guess since meeting Ella.

The next week crept by far too slowly. I didn't see much of Ella, not more than a quick hello in the morning and occasionally a goodbye in the afternoon if she made it back to the shelter before I left.

Carter Constructions was pretty busy. With the holidays approaching, everyone wanted everything finished yesterday and Charlie was working a sixty hour week just to keep on top of things. I found myself leaving Mercy's to put in another four hours at my own office. Moving day for Annie, Eli and Ella came and went in a flurry of action. Between Dave, Charlie and me, we got all the furniture and boxes up into Annie's apartment in a couple of hours. They didn't really have much. Dave and I managed to track down some Goodwill furniture and between all of us we were able to find plenty of people willing to donate necessities like plates, dishes and cutlery. Charlie was most impressed with Ella. The little spitfire gave Charlie as much grief as he gave her.

Charlie liked to torment, he prided himself in it. In fact, I wondered if he had attended a school I didn't know about in torment, mockery and practical jokes. But Ella handled him like a pro and she had Charlie practically eating out of the palm of her hand. I had to give him a number of stern back-the-fuck off looks before he finally dragged my lovesick ass down the stairs as the sun finally disappeared for the day.

Now, it was Wednesday and I hadn't seen Ella for three

days. I was surly and irritated as I beat the shit out of the bag in the basement trying to blow off steam, wishing like fuck that Ella was here. The unforgiving beep of my phone caught my attention and I glanced at it sitting on the table behind me curious who the message was from. It was a number that I didn't recognize. I pulled off my gloves and checked the message.

UNKNOWN: Hi

I stared at the innocuous word for a moment wondering who the hell it was from before finally sending a quick message back.

JAX: hi, who's this?

The next message came back quick.

UNKNOWN: Ella

And just like that I was grinning like an idiot.

JAX: Angel! Saving ur number now. Are u ok?

ELLA: I'm fine. I wasn't sure about txting protocol, but just wanted to say hi.

JAX: Txting protocol requires no less than 2 txts a day. Ur behind

ELLA: Hmmmm, then so r u

JAX: But I didn't have ur number, otherwise ur phone would be full of messages from me. U free tomorrow night?

ELLA: Yes, why?

JAX: Movie?

ELLA: Ok

JAX: I'll pick u up, 6pm? Dinner first at Pit Stop? My treat cause I'm inviting. That's the dating protocol.

ELLA: Ok, but I get to choose the movie. That's dating protocol too, so I've heard…

I'd watch a five hour operetta if it meant hanging out with Ella. She could choose whatever the hell she wanted.

JAX: Deal. See u tomorrow angel X

Tomorrow night couldn't come quick enough and when it finally did I raced home from Mercy's and dressed like a man possessed before returning back into town. I was standing on the doorstep of Annie and Eli's apartment at five minutes to six. The door opened before I even had a chance to knock and Eli pummeled into me. I grabbed him and swung him over my shoulder fireman style.

"Totally uncool little man. What if it had of been Megatron at your door? You'd be captured and I'd have to dig out my damn cape to rescue you and I have no idea where it is right now." Eli giggled out loud as I deposited him on the couch. Annie appeared from down the small narrow hallway, still in her uniform from Danny's Diner.

"Hi Annie, you look tired." She nodded and I suddenly felt like an impolite prick for pointing out the obvious. "But you look happy too. You look good, apart from the big dark rings under your eyes, but otherwise perfect. And the dark rings are barely noticeable." Annie burst out laughing.

"Smooth, Casanova," she teased. "I've worked every day this week and I'm working the next two nights. I'm kind of beat. Ella has been a God send. I don't know how I would do this without her here. She was even able to get off work early to pick Eli up from school today and Rebecca let Eli hang out at Bouquets. Apparently, my boy is very good with roses."

"I helped Ella cut the thorns off!" Eli said proudly.

"Good stuff little man. Did you bring a flower home for your mom?" Eli looked a little guilty and shook his head.

"I'm sure if you ask Rebecca nicely she will let you bring one home." He jumped up and ran to Annie, wrapping his arms around her waist.

"Maybe next time, Mom, but only if you're good," he giggled. The apartment looked cozy. It looked lived in, like a real family's apartment should look.
Ella's backpack sat neatly beside the couch, apart from that you wouldn't have even known she was living there.

"Where's Ella?" I asked just as she appeared in the hallway and nervously entered the small living room. I was reduced to a speechless lump within seconds. She wore a pair of jeans that hugged her body like a second skin. An equally tight fitting long sleeved top in a radiant shade of red, scalloped at the neckline and giving a teasing glimpse of the swell of her breasts. Her long hair hung loosely over her shoulders. She looked stunning, glowing, a far turn from the tired looking girl who had slipped across the shelter's doorway over two weeks ago.

"Wow, Angel," I finally exclaimed.

"Momma reckons you will think she's hot," said Eli in childlike innocence. Ella blushed and I couldn't help but laugh.

"Yeah, hot is one word for it." Ella still looked uncomfortable. Annie cast me a knowing look.

"Well, the sooner you two get out of here, the sooner I can get this little man with the uncontrolled mouth off to bed and I can enjoy having the TV to myself." Ella reached for her coat and I snapped it up holding it out for her to slide her delectable little body into. Once we were comfortably in my pickup, Ella cast me a nervous glance and cleared her throat.

"You look nice," she noted shyly. I was wearing a pair of old frayed jeans, a long sleeved black shirt and my favorite black all-weather jacket. Not really much different to what I wore to work each day. "You look more relaxed than usual. I guess this is how you look when you're not working." I did feel a little more laid back than usual. The constant underlying layer of death that followed my memories, for some reason, felt a little more distant tonight.

"I guess. I haven't been out in a while; it feels good to do something normal." Ella's head tilted in thought.

☐ "I don't really know what normal is," she whispered.

"Well Angel, it's about time you learned."

CHAPTER 16

Ella

I was on a date with Jax, my first date ever, and I curiously didn't feel nervous. I was worried about what Jax would think when he first saw me. I had borrowed some of Annie's clothes and she had even insisted I wear some mascara and lip gloss. She had given me a tiny bit of foundation to help cover the scar by my eye and for the first time ever I had looked in the mirror and felt attractive. My eyes were bright and clear, my pale cheeks had a slight flush to them. I felt like a woman, a woman about to go on a date with Jax Carter. Oh who was I kidding, I was nervous as hell. I was glad Jax was taking me back to The Pit Stop. I knew that place now, it was familiar, safe and most importantly it wasn't fancy. I didn't do fancy; I didn't even own a dress and I wondered if Jax liked that sort of thing—women in sexy dresses looking all seductive and beautiful. Selena was definitely the type of woman who liked to dress up. I couldn't be more further from that if I tried.

"Benny." Jax smiled in greeting as we entered The Pit Stop.

"Jax, Ella. You two look like you need a table tonight."

"Candle lit table with your best view," Jax joked. Benny scoffed.

"Blah, you don't need candles, the ambience in here is perfect for romance." Jax chuckled as he led me to a table by the front window. The snow had begun to fall outside and the streets were dark and empty. I was warm and safe. I was on a date about to enjoy a hearty meal, not completely homeless and pathetic and not at all scared. How could my life take such a drastic turn after so many years of indifference and fear? Where would I be now if I hadn't of run? How ruined would I be? I shivered at the thought.

"Where are you right now, Angel?" Jax asked. It brought my thoughts back to here and now, back to warm and safe.

"Sorry, sometimes I just kind of…fade out."

"I've noticed. Tonight you stay with me though, okay. I'm your typical male, easily emasculated when the girl he's having dinner with loses interest and starts thinking about other things." I wasn't sure what to say so I just nodded. A woman saved me from any embarrassment by sliding up to our table to take our orders. She took in Jax with appreciative eyes and she looked at me with all out hostility. Jax ignored her though, his eyes on me only.

"What will you have, Angel?" I quickly glanced at the menu. The butterflies in my stomach had caused my appetite to retreat but thinking about the breakfast I had enjoyed with Jax a week ago made me salivate.

"I don't suppose we could have the same as last time we were here?" Jax grinned.

"Two all-day-breakfast's with everything, a chocolate shake and orange juice." I almost moaned at the thought. I was suddenly starving.

"Not a problem Jax," beamed the waitress. "How's Selena, I haven't seen her in a few weeks?" The waitress's eyes cut to me with a sly grin. Then I was assaulted with a horrifying thought. Was Jax still supposed to be dating Selena? I had assumed it was over, but what if it wasn't? This girl probably thought they were still together and wondered what he was doing out with me. My stomach had gone from starving to nauseous in seconds.

"I have no idea, Lisa. I haven't seen Selena in a while either. Could you bring the drinks out first please?" I could tell Jax was irritated, I could see it in his eyes, but he didn't give Lisa the benefit of knowing she had rattled him.

"Sorry," he offered once Lisa had moved away from the table. I shrugged feigning, nonchalance.

"I guess if you're seen out with me instead of your girlfriend people are going to wonder." Jax looked a little pissed at that comment.

"Angel, Selena is not my girlfriend nor was she. We were just friends, who...," Jax seemed to be trying to find the words, "you know, barely friends, just a guy and a girl who..." He was stuck again. Friends who what? Had snacks and wine in his mother's office? My blank face made him chuckle. "Shit, Angel. We slept together sometimes. But we weren't exclusively dating, it was simply I'll scratch your back if you'll scratch mine." First I was mortified. I didn't like thinking of Jax with other women, but I couldn't really talk, I was definitely no saint. Then my mortification was replaced with anger. I knew I wasn't experienced when it came to men and dating but I knew I wasn't interested in that sort of relationship with anyone, especially Jax and if he assumed that I was that kind of girl he was wrong.

"She was your fuck buddy?" I gasped with indignation that I wished I didn't have. Jax grimaced.

"Not anymore. I wish I could tell you that I've had deep and meaningful relationships with maybe one or two girls. The truth is I've had exactly zero deep and meaningful relationships and way too many girls. I've got a history here in Claymont and I'm not proud of it. Not that it is an excuse, but coming home from Afghanistan, seeing the shit I saw, doing the shit I did—I was a loose cannon and I did a lot of things I was not proud of. I've changed. I didn't want to be that person anymore so I cleaned up my act. I've been in and out of therapy dealing with my shit. Selena was something I clung on to and I have no idea why, but she is out of my life permanently now. She's not the kind of girl I see myself with; she is not my forever girl, never was and I wish I had of realized it a long time ago."
I stared at him, opened my mouth to speak and was stopped by the unpleasant Lisa who brought our meals over and dumped them before us with absolutely no grace or care.

"Anything else I can get you kids?" she asked, in a voice laced with false enthusiasm. Jax said nothing. We just simply stared at each other as if the world around us no longer existed.

"Oooookay, holler if you need me?" She left, thank God.

"Are you going to say anything? If you don't want to do this we can eat and I'll take you right home. I'd be lying if I said I was okay with that but I want you to know you can trust me. I won't do anything to hurt you and if dealing with my shit on top of your own is too much, I understand. I'll back off." I shook my head, shaking free the confusion and shock that had settled there. I didn't picture Jax as the type of guy who slept around and used women. He fought for women, protected them, he didn't use them. I guess sometimes when fighting for your sanity and happiness you can easily end up caught in a vortex that can get completely out of hand and you end up doing a lot of things you wouldn't normally do. I, of all people, knew that lesson well. It was obvious Jax had used sex to suppress his nightmares and escape. Who was I to talk? I had done the exact same thing.

"The women you were with, did you hurt them?" I found myself whispering.

"Fuck, Angel. Not ever not once. As much as it shames me to say it, I never spent the night with a girl who expected more than just a night. Mine and Selena's relationship was always clear. Recently she decided she wanted more and I stopped it right then for two reasons." Jax stared at me, making sure I was listening. "One, I didn't want that with her, a future. For the first time I actually saw her for who she really was and, to be honest, she's a bitch. Second, I find myself wanting a future with someone else." I wasn't breathing, I wanted to, but couldn't. I was terrified of what Jax might say next.

"I find myself attracted to a particularly beautiful brunette with exquisite chocolate eyes and a smile filled with sunshine and yes I am aware I sound like a pussy right now, but it's the truth. And I don't want you freaking out. We will take things slowly, one day at a time. I plan to woo the heck out of you, Angel."

"Woo me?" I grinned, caught somewhere between thrilled and stunned.

"Woo, as in date, as in force you to see what a catch I am and make you want me so bad I will consume your every thought. One day at a time Ella, I'm going to give you a future and you're going to trust me with your heart." Holy shit, I couldn't tell Jax Carter this but he already owned my heart. "But before we can continue this," he stuck a piece of egg in his mouth and chewed thoughtfully before continuing, "I need something from you." He didn't elaborate and I grew frustrated.

"What?" I asked him suspiciously.

"I need to know your last name? I can't be dating someone whose name I don't even know." He smirked. A small laugh escaped my lips. I was expecting him to ask for something deep and emotional, maybe even life changing.

"Munroe. Actually, it's Munroe-Spencer. My mom hated

Munroe, she said it sounded common and boring so her maiden name was thrown in. I always found it a little ironic because there is nothing uncommon about Spencer."

"Ella Munroe, I like it."

"Ella Mai Munroe, my dad always called me Ella Mai. He allowed mom to have the hyphenated surname if she allowed my middle name to be Mai. Dad said it was some sort of spin-off of that girl in that old black and white show, about the hillbillies that struck oil and moved to Beverly Hills and it pissed my mom off." Jax laughed loudly.

"Elly May, The Beverly Hillbilles." Just like that, the tension that had filled the air disappeared and my appetite had returned with a vengeance. I inhaled my meal, just like the last time Jax had brought me here and just like last time Jax seemed genuinely turned on by the gusto way with which I enjoyed my dinner.

"You don't have some sort of weirdo food fetish?" I found myself teasing him.

"Only when watching you eat, Angel. Don't worry though, for the most part I don't want to do anything particularly kinky or weird with the food, though chocolate sauce and whipped cream could prove entertaining." His grin was wicked and teasing, but his eyes did not betray his desire. Just like that, I was blushing again.

My memory of the movie following dinner was vague. It was a comedy and I remember people laughing around me. I spent the hour and a half completely and utterly conscious of the fact that Jax had discretely worked his arm over my shoulder. Every now and again he would whisper something in my ear and the feeling of his breath and lips so close would spend my head into a spin. I was as smitten as a school girl as I sat there silently squealing in my mind how the sex god beside me, for some bizarre reason, wanted me. Jax was replacing all my missed opportunities and experiences with new ones and I cherished every single moment.

CHAPTER 17

Jax

Thursday evening with Ella had been deeply satisfying. She was relaxed, she joked and laughed, she blushed, often. I loved making her blush and it was done so easily. Any touch was innocent and gentle and I had never felt more satisfied. Sure, I wanted her, all of her, but a night of virtuous attention came with its own fulfillment. I was continuing to gain Ella's trust and inevitably her heart and the journey would be an exploration of learning each other in the most important and simplistic of ways. A part of me still felt as though I was betraying Ella, taking advantage of her. No matter what I told myself though, I could not deny the pull to this angel any longer. I would take things slowly, enjoying the smallest, though possibly the most magical of moments. Holding hands, laughing, teasing, sharing a meal, a movie, Ella seemed enthralled with the most humble of daily activities, perhaps from having been denied so many of them for so long. It was helping me to find a new appreciation for my life as it was now. It almost felt as if every touch from Ella, every smile, every shy glance, was washing away my troubles and making me whole again. I was beginning to feel a resemblance to the man I used to be, happy and carefree.

Saturday was supposed to be my day off. My first day off in over three weeks, but somehow I found myself in the office of Carter Constructions with a thundering head ache, helping Charlie fix up one hell of a screw-up. I had woken up in a cold sweat on the tail end of a grisly nightmare. My day had started badly and proceeded to get worse.

"How the fuck did she order the wrong lumber?" Charlie roared. His hair was a mess. It looked as though he had run his hands through it in frustration for the last twenty-four hours solid, which he most likely had done.

His eyes were blood shot; he obviously hadn't slept much last night. Our secretary, Belinda, had ordered several thousand dollars' worth of lumber for a special order and unfortunately, she had ordered the wrong product. That meant we had a shed full of useless lumber and we were officially behind on what had been a rush job to begin with. I shook my head as I glanced over the paperwork in front of me one more time, hoping the order might suddenly change. If it had of been our supplier in the wrong, then I could easily send the lumber back and refuse to pay, asking for a rush on the correct product. The order was still wrong though, in Belinda's incriminating and far too neat cursive print. Charlie continued to rant and rave and, to be honest, he was making my headache much worse than it needed to be. I grabbed the phone and called my supplier. Thankfully their office girl, Noelle, answered and I quickly began charming the panties off her. By the end of the conversation I was getting a supply on the correct lumber at half the normal price and Noelle was giving me her cell phone number. I hung up and looked to Charlie who watched me in awe.

"How the hell do you do that?" he asked and I shrugged.

"Guess I just have a gift." I handed Charlie Noelle's phone number. "Send her some flowers, from you, or the company. Don't put my name on it though, I don't want any confusion, I'm not interested." Charlie shook his head.

"That little girl has got you by the short and curlies, doesn't she?"

"Stop talking about my pubes, it's weird. Let's go get a drink, I need one after this shithole of a day."

We took my Dodge and headed to Andy's Office, Charlie's drinking hole of choice. It was close, only a block away, and I had to admit there was something about the old English style bar that was appealing, especially during winter. Andy had the place running like a dream, attractive friendly staff, good music, warm atmosphere. He had only had the bar for a little over a year and it was quickly becoming one of the most popular venues in Claymont. Charlie and I made sure we always got in early before the crowds and left as they started to trickle through the doors. Neither of us is really into the whole late night bar scene.

At the entrance we were greeted by Beef and Paris who gave us a friendly smile and stepped aside. Beef was called beef because, well, he looked like a great big slab of beef. He was huge, as tall as me, and a whole lot wider. He rarely smiled, with a shit scary glare permanently in place. Paris was tall and lithe, with short spiky blond hair and adorned with tattoos and piercings. She looked fierce as hell and I knew she was fierce as hell. She was also Andy's wife and she was witty, funny and smart. I liked her, I liked Andy, hell I even liked Beef. A few patrons who lingered outside were being given a hard time by Beef over their clothes and they barked obscenities at mine and Charlie's easy entrance. I chuckled, because, frankly, they were dressed a hell of a lot better than us. But we were regulars, had been since the first day and the thing about Andy, he looked after his regulars, especially those who spent big and didn't cause trouble. Charlie bought the first round and we escaped to a small 'L' shaped sofa in the back corner. In no time at all, I felt the drifting peace that the exact right amount of liquor can bring. I knew one drop more would cause me to stumble over that cliff, so I slowed down and grabbed a bottle of water much to Charlie's dismay.

"You're being stalked," Charlie murmured behind his long neck of beer. I groaned and sat back into the sofa.

"I'm not interested, you take it."

I knew Charlie was rolling his eyes. We had been friends since grade school so I didn't need to look to know what he was doing or thinking.

"She's fucking hot," he continued. I didn't care, unless of course she was a brunette with brown eyes named Ella. Suddenly, a tall leggy blonde strutted up in front of us, her dress might have been sprayed on it was that tight and short. She was beautiful, in that forged way that had some women pouting, smiling and laughing as if a camera were continually on them.

"Jax?" she carefully asked. Shit, was I supposed to know her? Perhaps she was a girl I once hooked up with. I looked at her face. Blue eyes, perfectly arched eye brows, bee stung lips. Nope, I'd remember her.

"Can I help you, darlin'?" I asked, trying to find a friendly smile when really I just wanted her to go away. She smiled and it was a killer smile, if you were into that kind of girl, and I wasn't anymore.

"I'm Noelle, from Tennison's Lumber." Oh fuck, the

Noelle from the phone call at my office only a couple of hours ago? What the hell was she doing here, now?

"I know we've never met in person, but one of the girls I was with recognized you." She settled down beside me and I moved along to make a clear space between us.

"Oh, I see," I said awkwardly. I wasn't used to being awkward with women. If I wanted in Noelle's panties I'd be fine. The fact I didn't though had me feeling like a bumbling fool. Charlie chuckled reminding me I wasn't alone in my awkwardness. "This is Charlie, you've probably spoken to him on the phone. He's my manager at Carter's." Noelle nodded, but her eyes did not leave me.

"Nice to meet you, Noelle," said Charlie ignoring her ignorance of him. "Can I get you a drink to say thank you for today?"

Noelle again nodded, her eyes still focused on me. I, on the other hand, had my eyes focused on anything but her.

"I'll get it," I interjected in a hurry.

"No boss, this one is on me." He winked at Noelle and he might have finally drawn some of the attention off me. "What will it be honey?" I had been assured by members of the opposite sex that Charlie was in fact easy on the eye and his flirty easy going attitude saw him rarely going home alone. But for some reason when I was there alongside him, the female eye seemed to draw my way. I personally had never found it a problem, until now.

"Merlot." Charlie disappeared into the crowd leaving behind an uncomfortable silence. It was Noelle who finally broke it.

"So, where is Selena tonight?" I was getting a little pissed with people asking about Selena. We may have had something going on for a while, but it certainly wasn't exclusive and we were rarely out together.

"You know Selena?"

"Not really. But I know a friend of hers. I was under the impression that you and Selena were together." I took a long drink and shook my head.

"Nope, not with Selena." Noelle smiled, her eyes alight with interest. How she wasn't picking up on my not-into-you vibes was beyond me. I decided a direct approached was needed.

"But I am kind of seeing someone, so sorry." Her smile fell.

"Very presumptuous to think I am interested in you," she recovered gracefully and I found myself smiling. Her fuck me eyes and pouty lips told me she was definitely into me.

"I don't think I formally thanked you for today, you helped us out of a tight spot." Diplomacy was on the agenda. She did help me out today and she did work for our biggest supplier, there was really no need for me to be a complete asshole. Noelle shrugged and brushed her hair back over her shoulder, her eyes lowered as she watched me through her thick false lashes. It was a seductive move to lure my attention to the graceful arch of her neck. I had seen it used hundreds of times before and, at one time it might have caught my interest. Here and now her seduction was wasted.

"You're a big client; it's in our best interest to help you out from time to time," she brushed my thanks off with nonchalance. Charlie saved the day by bringing back our drinks, water for me, thank fuck, but he soon disappeared again leaving me once more all alone with the temptress in the too tight dress.

"Your friends aren't looking for you?" I asked, hoping she would finally leave. She leaned in close and I could smell the subtle layer of perfume. It was nice, but I preferred Ella's fresh scent of ocean coconut.

"I don't want to hang out with them right now, Jax, I want to hang out with you." I felt the weight of her hand on my thigh and flinched as it began to make its way higher. My body responded appropriately but my mind was not into it. Her lips found my neck and for the briefest of moments my hand found her thigh. Feeling the soft warm flesh made my heart spike and dick jump, but I didn't want this. There would have once been a time when I would have grabbed this girl and dragged her to a back room for a quick fuck, no strings, just a few moments of freedom from my troubles. But I didn't need this kind of freedom anymore, this detachment and ugly wanton desire. My freedom, my desire was sitting in an apartment twenty minutes from here. As her hand inched higher, her wine laced breath on my neck I spotted Charlie and abruptly stood up from the sofa.

"Sorry, Noelle, I told you I'm seeing someone. I've gotta' go." My voice didn't hide the irritation I was feeling at that moment and I pushed my way through too many bodies, I'd been here too long and if Charlie wasn't so damned wasted he would realize that too. He was whispering something into the ear of a pretty blonde who blushed furiously and giggled.

"I'm going to leave you to it." I slapped him on the back to get his attention and he swung around to give me his best fucked up grin. "You wanna ride?" I asked. He shook his head and glanced back at the blonde who was now staring at me like dessert had just been served. I shook my head.

"Get out of here, you're stealing my thunder," Charlie groaned. I slipped out of the front doors of the bar and called out a quick goodbye to Andy who was talking with Beef and Paris. As I sat in my truck, I sent Ella a quick text message.

JAX: What you doing?

Less than a minute later her reply came through.

ELLA: Teaching Eli the importance of rock paper scissors. Want to join us?

JAX: Hell, that's an important lesson. I'm on my way. Pizza?

ELLA: No anchovies and Eli says no pineapple... & since I'm inviting you. I'll pay. Fix you up when u get here. ;-)

I couldn't remember a time when I was so excited to see a girl, particularly one who I wasn't going to be sleeping with. I needed to see Ella tonight, to wipe away the feeling of betrayal and cheapness Noelle's touch had made me feel. I needed to immerse myself in something good and Ella was my answer.

CHAPTER 18

Ella

Jax had been at a bar. He wasn't drunk though, but his clothes were smoky and there was the smell of beer on his breath. I hated bars, they were too crowded, men were too touchy feely in those situations and often mistook a no for a hell yes. I wondered who Jax had gone to the bar with and found a small ugly twinge of jealousy lacing my thoughts. Eli laughed as he and Jax played best out of five with rock-paper-scissors. It was an attempt to get Eli to go to bed. He was rather hyped up and it had been my fault. I had bought rocky road ice cream earlier today as a surprise and this was my first mistake in childcare—do not feed ice cream to kids half an hour before bed. Watching Jax play with Eli made me smile. He was so natural and carefree; you would never imagine the blood and death he had seen in his short life. A combination of being at war and Sarah had obviously left him with his own internal battle raging on but he hid it well. No wonder he had been concerned about the scars on my wrists the first time he had seen them. I sighed, wishing I could wipe away his bad memories. Life would be so much easier if we could just take a giant eraser and get rid of the things that bothered us. I guess we wouldn't be left with the memories of our mistakes, we would never learn, destined to commit the same fuckups over and over again. He glanced at me and winked. He had won and Eli was being marched off to bed.

I tucked Eli tightly under his blankets and put his night light on. He was afraid of the dark. I guess we all have our fears regardless of our age. I gave him a light kiss on his forehead and snuck out of the room, leaving the door slightly ajar so Eli knew we were close by. Jax lay back on the sofa, my bed, flicking through channels.

"You're good with him," he noted as I cleaned up the mess from dinner and rinsed our glasses. I was avoiding sitting down with Jax. We had been alone before but this somehow felt more intimate and I was nervous.

"Really? I'm fumbling with him. I've never had a younger

sibling or relative. I'm not sure what to do or say most the time." I folded the hand towel several different ways while Jax watched me curiously.

"What makes you more anxious, how devastatingly handsome I am or the fact that I am lying in your bed?" Jax grinned and I burst out laughing.

"Arrogant much?" I chuckled moving towards him. He held out his hand and with only a moment's hesitation I took it. Jax pulled me down beside him and continued to flick through the channels. He finally found a movie, a romantic comedy, which going by the actor's clothing was more than a few years old but I had never seen it. I had learned from our date a couple of nights ago that neither of us was into thrillers, action or horror and Jax wasn't big on war movies. Perhaps we both just needed to laugh a bit more. I wanted to ask Jax where he had been tonight; a small part of me needed the reassurance that it had not been with another girl. I fiddled with my fingers nervously, paying absolutely no attention to the movie. There had been a time when I was considered outspoken, even abrupt in the way I might confront someone about something that bothered me. He had put a stop to that, fucking Marcus. The hate for him had not dimmed in the slightest over the years. It burned inside me so fiercely some days I thought I might combust because of it. Just thinking about him enraged me, the life he had stolen from me, the girl he corrupted with his violence and domination. Who would I have been if my dad had never died? Would I be the confident fearless girl I was growing into?

"Angel?" My head whipped around to look at Jax, my eyes no doubt filled with the fire and revolt that had so quickly filled my head. "Deep breath, sweetheart." I hadn't even realized my breathing had become erratic and uncontrolled. Jax slid onto the floor in front of me and held my hands while I breathed my way back to composure just the way he had shown me. "Where did you go just now?" His thumb ran a calming circle on the back of my hand, centering me, helping me to feel safe, grounded. I didn't speak right away, I needed to collect my thoughts rather than blurt them all out in a hurried mess. With one final deep sigh I looked down at our joined hands then back up at Jax's patient face.

"I started wondering what you did before you came here tonight. I know you went to a bar and I wondered who you went there with. I know I have no right to question your activities, but I can't help it. I think it's a girl thing." I took a deep breath.

"You started going into a panic attack because you wondered who I was with tonight?" Jax asked with a cheeky grin.

"No, not exactly. I was having a hard time finding the courage to ask you and I remembered when I was younger I used to get into trouble from my dad for being too abrupt and upfront with people. He said I had to learn to be tactful. After my dad died and Marcus came along I was downright rude and disrespectful. I never feared speaking my mind, but after this," I glanced at my wrists. "I changed. I became withdrawn, shy, afraid of everything. I hate the person he made me and I wondered if my dad hadn't of died what I would be like now. That made me upset and I usually avoid thinking such things because I know it makes me upset. Once I got started though I just couldn't stop." I let my head fall forward, my hair surrounding my face like a curtain. Fuck, I was a mess. Why would anyone want to be around me, especially Jax? My body and my mind were ugly and scarred. Jax used his thumb and finger to gently lift my chin so that my eyes were level with his.

"Firstly, you can ask me anything, Angel. I don't care how stupid you think it is, or how much it frightens you to say it out loud, I want you to talk to me. It will help you get over the fears he put inside you. I will never be disappointed or angry with anything you ask me. Secondly, I believe the girl you were before Marcus is still here. You say you are afraid, but I've seen your strength and courage. You've survived more than any one person should ever have to endure, something like that takes incredible spirit. And shy?" Jax snorted. "Unlikely. You have no trouble making friends at Mercy's, confronting me, sassing Charlie. The real Ella is well and truly alive." Jax grinned and I ached to kiss his dimples. "We just need to work on destroying the shit that fucker Marcus has put in here." He tapped my head gently. "What counts is that he didn't break what's in here." He tapped the spot over my heart and took my hands again. I wanted to kiss him so bad. I couldn't stop my gaze from dropping to his full lips.

"What are you thinking now, Angel?" Jax whispered. My eyes shot back up to his.

"Did you go out to a bar tonight?" I blurted out. Jax chuckled and nodded.

"Who with?" I asked, feeling like a stereotypical control freak girlfriend.

"Charlie. We had a bad day at the office. My secretary screwed up an order and it took us a while to fix it. We went to Andy's Office, a bar on the other side of town, and Charlie snuck off with some woman and left me high and dry. Totally uncool on his part." The relief that flooded my body was ridiculously soothing.

"I had a drink with a woman." At his words my entire body became tense. "Charlie actually bought her the drink. She works for one of our suppliers and helped us out of a tight spot today. I had no desire to be with her, I did not want her in any way, shape, or form. I need you to know that up front. But she made it clear she wanted something with me. I said no, told her I was with someone and left. I won't ever lie to you, Angel, you can trust me." I sat quietly and processed his words. On one hand I was raging with jealousy over another woman wanting Jax, being out at a bar with him like a normal girl should. I couldn't do that. On the other hand, he had rejected her and told her he was seeing someone, me.

"Tell me what you're thinking," he encouraged. He was good at getting me to talk and express my thoughts and feelings aloud. It was something I needed to do to help understand the emotions that I was so unfamiliar with.

"I wish I could be that girl for you, the one who goes out to have a drink with you at a bar. I can't be that girl Jax. Bars freak me out—too many people, too many men." I shook my head in frustration.

"To be honest, Angel, I'm not into bars either. I sometimes drop into Andy's Office, usually during the afternoon, for a quick drink and then I'm off again. The fact that Charlie left me there with Noelle pissed me off and I intend to slap him a good one upside the head for it. I like you just the way you are, Angel. You don't need to be that girl cause I want this girl." Jax smiled as he raised my hand to his lips and chastely kissed the back of it. "The whole time I was there all I could think about was getting here to see you." Well, I was officially satisfied with his response and I guess I was grinning like an idiot now. "I love your hair, but you do like to hide behind it don't you?" He pushed my hair right back behind my shoulders and tucked it behind my ears.

"I guess I got used to hiding bruises, my scar. I don't like people seeing my eyes, my face. I don't like them seeing the truth there." He gazed into my eyes.

"I like what I see in your eyes, in your face. I would prefer it if you didn't hide it from me." His finger traced my scar, letting me know that didn't bother him and then my heart jumped as he very slowly and cautiously leaned forward.

"When I asked you what you were thinking about a moment ago I'm pretty sure you weren't thinking about where I had been tonight," he whispered. His breath was a light caress on my face that sent a spark of awareness from my lips to my stomach and eventually to the warm place between my thighs that Jax was currently knelt between.

"Maybe not," I breathed.

"What were you thinking, Angel?" he asked persistently. He wanted to hear me say it, he was going to make me say it. Fuck, I wanted to say it.

"I was wondering what it would be like if I kissed you." Jax's cheek gently brushed mine and I could feel him smile. His lips tenderly caressed my scar.

"You want to kiss me?" he asked. Oh good lord, he was really pressing his luck.

"Not anymore, with all this talking the moment has passed." His laugh was low and seductive and I knew the breathless tone of my voice betrayed my words.

"Really?" His lips tenderly kissed my brow and my hands gripped the edge of the couch on either side of my legs, perhaps hoping to keep me anchored to this world rather than the place of passion and seduction Jax was trying to take me.

"Really," I almost groaned as he kissed my other brow.

"Then, perhaps I should kiss you." There was no chance for rebuttal as Jax's lips pressed lightly to mine and my eye lids dropped closed, absorbing his touch, this moment. The kiss began soft and innocent, but when I opened my mouth in acceptance, Jax's tongue slid across my lower lip in a virtuous taste and then tentatively pressed forward to caress mine. Not a single thought could be processed. I was being kissed by Jax Carter and the moment outshone every single crucial little moment of my life thus far. In this man's arms, in this man's hands I was being reborn and restored into the woman I should have been. In this moment, I flew, captivated by the desire that inflamed my body.

CHAPTER 19
Jax

Ella's body trembled beneath mine, but the response to my touch, to our kiss wasn't fear. I'm sure if angels had a taste, Ella would be it. She was divine, sweet, perfect. There was no hesitation when she kissed me back and in that moment it took every ounce of strength I possessed not to lay her back and strip her body bare. I wanted her so badly it physically hurt and my brainless cock was suddenly trying to force its way through the brass zipper of my jeans. My hand held her neck, holding her to me and I knew I didn't need to pull her closer. Ella's hands had slipped from the almost unbreakable grip they had had on the couch to my arms, urging me forward. She wanted me as much as I wanted her. The vulnerability she had shared with me moments before was gone, she was a woman who knew what she wanted and I knew I could never deny her. The small taste of jealousy she had shown me made me want to beat my chest with pride. I loved it that Ella felt a sense of proprietary over me because hell, if another man so much as touched her I have no doubt I would roar like a wounded beast in anger. I finally let our lips reluctantly part, but I held her to me, my forehead resting on hers. I liked the breathless pant she had worked up, her chest rising and falling rapidly.

"You look smug." She rolled her eyes and I grinned. I was. I liked that I had this effect on her and wondered if she responded to anyone else like this. She had never been in a relationship before, but she was no stranger to being intimate with men. My body would have exploded under her lips if that were possible. Her kiss moved me like no one else's. In fact, kissing had never played a major part in my life. The women I had been with previously seemed more interested in achieving one thing and a kiss on the lips didn't really get them there. Kissing was intimate anyway, not something I really wanted to share before Ella. Selena's kisses had been more of a chastising sharp lipped sting to the brow or cheek, never anything passionate like what I just shared with Ella.

"You move me like no other," I found myself whispering. It was Ella's turn to look smug as she pulled away and searched my eyes, no doubt to confirm the truth in my words.

"Well, that was my first kiss so I have nothing to compare it to." Her words almost made me topple over with shock. Her first kiss? But she had been with guys before, how in the hell had she got to twenty-two without a kiss? I couldn't find a single word to ask her how, so I just stared at her like the curious treasure she was. She squirmed under my scrutiny, bashful eyes darting away from my questioning gaze.

"How?" I finally stammered. Ella shrugged.

"I just haven't done that before. It always seemed..." She was lost for words.

"Too intimate?" I suggested. Her face lit up, bingo!

"The boys I was with were only interested in one thing and never stayed the night, never cuddled, never kissed. It was actually more my rule then theirs but they certainly didn't object." She looked nervous. "I guess that makes me kind of a whore," she said reluctantly. Her words stung worse than a bitch slap.

"Fuck Ella, don't say things like that. You are not a whore, were not a whore. You were trying to survive, trying to escape a shitty life and you did what you had to do. You were looking for the love and attention you weren't getting at home. You were a confused little girl, not a whore and if I hear you say it again I will wash your mouth out with soap." She looked at me with those magical brown eyes then burst out laughing.

"My dad threatened to wash my mouth with soap when I called my mom a bitch—I was ten." She continued to laugh and it made me smile. "She was a bitch," she finally sighed. I climbed back onto the couch beside her, my hard-on still a force of nature in my jeans but I somehow managed to ignore it, dragging a pillow across my lap and encouraging Ella to snuggle closer.

"I've never met her, but I have to agree with you, Angel." There was no hesitation as she nuzzled in closer. As her breathing grew steady I thought she had maybe slipped into sleep.

"It's not forgiveness you need Jax, you just need to let go of your past. Now is what matters," she whispered on a yawn, her words so low I barely caught them.

"Maybe we both need to let our pasts go." I murmured

back. Ella yawned and I lay back letting her nestle further into my side, her head in the crook of my arm. She didn't answer me and I thought maybe she had gone off to sleep. I pressed a chaste kiss to the top of her head.

"I think you're right." Her words a final caress to my ears before she slipped into sleep. I didn't move as I lay there, listening to Ella's breathing even out to long, deep contented breaths of unconsciousness. Was it that easy though, just letting go? Memories just didn't disappear. Forcing my eyes shut, my thoughts were laced with blood, too much blood, like a lake pooling around her pale lifeless body. Fuck, I hated the vision of Sarah in that moment. If only I could let it go, if only I could wrap the present around me and forget the rest, then maybe the blood would disappear. Ella murmured in her sleep, shifting restlessly. My arm had long gone to sleep but I didn't dare try to move her. A rabid dog could chew the fucking thing off and, as long as it didn't disturb Ella, I wouldn't care. I pulled her closer to my chest, wanting to be closer to her, skin on skin, hell I'd crawl under her skin if it were possible.

Her hair fell through my fingers like water—it was beautiful, she was beautiful. I was freely able to admit I would likely never get enough of this girl and I was okay with that. Ella was in my keep now, it was my responsibility to protect her and I wouldn't fail again. This little angel had run long and hard; now it was time for her to settle down and have the future and dreams that every young woman deserved. Damn I was tired, bone tired. Too many years fighting, fighting for my country, fighting for my mom, fighting for strangers, a life filled with too much regret which I knew I shouldn't feel, because at the end of the day, it brought me to Ella. The same could be said for her. If her dad hadn't died, if her mother hadn't been a bitch, if Marcus hadn't come into her life, she wouldn't be here now, but I could never be grateful for the circumstances that had brought her to me. If I could give her back her dad, I would; if I could give her back the life she had lost, I would, even at the cost of losing her. I ran a calloused hand down my face and stifled a groan. I needed a few shots of whiskey to drown my thoughts. I should get up and go home but I couldn't bring myself to leave the warmth of her body. The sofa was too small or, more than likely, I was too big, my legs hung over the end awkwardly, my arm was dead, my neck at a painful angle and with Ella now draped pretty much over the top of me I had never been more comfortable in my life. I let my eyes fall closed and for just a minute, maybe a few minutes, I would enjoy the present.

CHAPTER 20

Ella

I woke to the sounds of muffled whispers and Eli's doleful attempt to be quiet. I didn't expect them to tiptoe around me, even though it was too early to be up on a Sunday. Annie had an early shift at the diner and as soon as Eli heard his mother's footsteps, he was wide awake and alert. After only a week we had settled into a comfortable household routine. The tranquil morning activities going on around me might have had a familiar feel about them, but the warm hard body pressed at my back was completely foreign. I knew immediately who it was, but it still shocked the hell out of me and my eyes sprang open in alarm. I glanced over my shoulder to be sure and found a beautiful pair of steel grey eyes staring back at me.

"Morning, Angel," he whispered, a smile tugging at his lips. Hell he looked gorgeous all sleep ruffled and messy.

"Hi," I managed, my eyes once again drifting to his lips remembering the earth shattering kiss from last night. He smiled that far too smug grin that I was coming to know well. His eyes drifted to my lips and in a sharp contradiction to the ever confident Jax, I blushed.

"Hi!" Eli's happy little voice came from beside the couch. Jax reached over and tousled his hair.

"What did you make me for breakfast little man?" Jax asked and just like that any awkwardness vanished.

"Eli, I told you to keep it down," hissed Annie.

"Don't be silly Annie, we're sleeping in his living room!" I grumped as I slid off the couch. I was not a morning person, I had never been a morning person and no amount of drop dead gorgeous man waking beside me would change that.

"What happened to your wrist?" Eli asked. All three adults in the room suddenly became motionless, stunned into an uneasy silence. My sleeve had slipped up, revealing the deep ugly scar across my wrist. Annie looked at me curiously, no doubt wondering what sort of an unstable girl she had sleeping on her couch and looking after her son. Eli's eyes were full of innocent curiosity and Jax, well I couldn't even bring myself to look at him.

"I…" I was lost for words. I couldn't even begin to explain my scars to a six year old.

"It was an accident, Eli." Jax grabbed my wrist, raising it to his mouth and placing a quick chaste kiss to my scar. "A terrible accident a long time ago, but Ella is fine now." Eli seemed more than content with that explanation but Annie's look told me she would be asking questions later. Annie and I hadn't told our stories yet, though if we were going to be living together, with me looking after her son from time to time, I think our demons needed to be laid on the table for both to see—no lies, no secrets. Honesty was an important part in building trust.

"Okay, I have to get going or I'll miss my bus." Annie wiped her hands on a kitchen towel as she put a bowl of hot porridge at the breakfast bar for Eli.

"Let me give you a lift Annie, I've got to go downtown and pick up some supplies for Mercy's. I'm supposed to be down there at seven, I'll have enough time to drop you off at the diner." I could see the relief in Annie's face, the bus sucked. It was warm, but it was often late and standing in the freezing cold by the side of the road waiting was a bitch made ten times worse if it started snowing.

"Are you sure?" Jax stood up, stretching and his hands almost brushed the ceiling. Damn he was huge.

"Absolutely, go grab your coat." Annie disappeared down the hall and Jax pulled on his own coat stuffing his skull cap in his pocket. I couldn't believe how sexy he was—his body was like a finely carved marble sculpture, his face crafted to perfection and he wanted me. Little, frightened, mutilated me. I still couldn't wrap my mind around that. Was the man crazy? He leaned forward and pressed his warm lips to mine. I immediately accepted the kiss, reaching to drag him forward, needing the safety and heat of his body. Jax pulled away though, his cheeks slightly flushed.

"Angel, if you keep kissing me like that I'll never be able to leave," he breathed in my ear. It gave me a small thrill to think I could affect him in that way.

"Eli, be good for Ella. If you act up, she will call me and then you'll have a real nasty auto robot on your case." Eli spluttered his porridge everywhere as he laughed at his mother.

"It's Autobot, Mom, not auto robot!"

"Or maybe Ella can just call me and I can take you back to Mercy's to do some laundry. I know how much you love that." Jax tickled Eli mercilessly before opening the door for Annie. Eli groaned at the thought of laundry. Jax glanced back in my direction.

"I'm sorry I have to run so early, but I promise to make it up to you." He winked. "Got your phone?" I looked about for the infernal device that was quickly coming to rule my life. I finally found it under a cushion by the couch and I waved it in the air like a miraculous discovery. Jax chuckled as he left the apartment and Eli looked over his spoon at me.

"What are we going to do today?" he asked. Looking after a six year old was still very new to me. I had no idea what I enjoyed as a kid, probably drawing. I thought for a moment as I cleaned up the kitchen.

"How about we go to the library?" I suggested. Apparently that was like the best idea in the world and as I watched Eli jump around the room like a little jumping bean I felt a small resemblance to the before Ella.
The carefree Ella who loved to sing out loud, dance in the rain and smile like there was nothing in this world to fear. Before Ella had been far too naïve.

I didn't see Jax again that day or the next. He was tied up with Mercy's and Carter Constructions but he sent me plenty of text messages confirming his thoughts were never far from me. Some of the messages made me laugh, some made me blush and some made me down right lustful.

"My vagina flowers came in," Rebecca sang from the front door, taking a bucket of flowers from a young delivery guy who seemed both mortified and intrigued by her words. I simply stared at her.

"You buy flowers for your vagina?" I finally managed to ask. Rebecca gave me a scheming wink.

"You don't think our vaginas are deserving of something special like flowers? In the wise words of Betty White, 'those things take a pounding'. First your period and all the equipment that goes with that business, then sex, which for the first time feels like you're being split in half, and then babies, God, child birth, that must be the death of our poor poonani." Rebecca sighed and I must have looked mortified.

"Poonani?" I squealed.

"Snatch?" she offered instead. I shrugged and grinned at her playful mood.

"Pootang?" I suggested and Rebecca snorted.

"Pink lips?" I laughed loudly at that one and it was a while before I had enough control to talk again.

"Beaver?" I shrugged. Now it was Rebecca's turn to laugh.

"Oh that's an oldie but a goodie. I think my sister used to call them beavers when she was eleven."

"We need our own name for it. What about central loving station?" Tears rolled freely down my face as Rebecca looked at me with an appreciative smile.

"I like it," I somehow managed to garble behind my shrieks of laughter.

"Me too, much better than coochie," Rebecca said thoughtfully.

"And you bought flowers for your central loving station?" We both erupted into laugher again and neither one of us noticed the chime above the front door.

"Looks like you ladies are having way too much fun to be working." Jax smirked from the doorway. Rebecca somehow found some composure and stared at him with a serious frown. "Actually, it began as a very serious conversation about buying our vaginas flowers and somehow turned into what I can only describe as blasphemy."

"Oh, you're going to have to explain yourselves now." Jax's look could only be described as enthusiastic.

"Rebecca bought flowers for her central loving station." Jax looked at me and blinked, once, twice.

"Central loving station?" he asked.

"Poonani," I explained and Jax nodded, caught somewhere between shock and amusement.

"Let's get some things straight. I did not buy my central loving station flowers. Yes Jax, we just made that up, sounds much better than poonani or beaver, much more grand. And my vagina flowers came in, Clitoria Ternatea, see?" She held up a small potted plant with a beautiful array of blue flowers that did look suspiciously like our central loving stations.

"Okay, I may have exaggerated my desire to know about your central love station discussion. Please, feel free to leave me out." Rebecca dusted off her hands and watched Jax with an appreciative eye. The unfamiliar sensation of jealousy rippled through my body and I squirmed uncomfortably. Rebecca was stunning, quirky, successful, confident, everything I wasn't. Jax would have to be crazy not to be interested in someone like Rebecca.

"So, to what do we owe the pleasure, Mr. Carter?" she asked in a purr that I knew was full of overt sexual interest. To my astonishment, Jax barely acknowledged Rebecca, his gaze was fixed right on me. My heart thumped hard and fast as those hungry gray eyes held mine captive in a blatantly possessive manner.

"I was hoping to take my angel to lunch." Rebecca turned slowly to look at me with eyes that screamed 'what the fuck'? She smirked.

"Huh, as it stands, your angel is due for a break and I need a moment with my clitoria. You know, to take in her grand beauty and all." I snorted, very unlady like, but I think in recent days I had proven the lady part of me had become a vague shadow that rarely came out to play.

"Off you go," Rebecca pulled at the back of my apron, releasing the knot and pushing me towards Jax. "Go, enjoy, take your time. You haven't had a break today, so take a long lunch." I gave Rebecca a suspicious frown.

"You keep your hands off the clitoria. The mood you're in you're likely to make it wilt." Jax tried in vain to muffle his surprised laugh and Rebecca smirked.

"You just leave me and my clitoria alone. I've been in the business long enough to know how to handle one." Jax groaned.

"Oh God. I think I need to clean out my ears. Or have a cold shower, maybe both." I followed Jax laughing into the street, leaving Rebecca and her latest Bouquets addition to some quality alone time.

CHAPTER 21

Jax

Over the past week I had observed Ella emerge into a somewhat confident woman with a somewhat tranquil joy. There was still a guarded presence in her eyes and she became nervous around strangers, especially men. I was pleased to note she would gravitate towards me in those situations, taking subtle steps into my body and accepting the simple safety of my arm around her shoulders. She was so tiny beside me and I liked that my size gave her comfort rather than fear. She had, in a short amount of time, been able to give me something invaluable, her trust. Tonight I was taking her into town, to the official lighting of the Claymont tree. The twenty foot Christmas tree was propped up every year in the center of town and laced with Christmas decorations and a week before Thanksgiving the lights were lit, accompanied with a live band, fireworks and food carts. It had taken a shit load of sweet talking and negotiating to get Ella to agree to come with me. She was not fond of large crowds and she was more than a little reluctant to partake in anything to do with the holidays. I was dying to take her out somewhere public and show the world that she was mine. Perhaps it was a little Neanderthal of me, but I wanted everyone to know that Ella Munroe was with me. Hell, I might as well lift my leg and pee on her.

As I pulled on my coat, the heavy riff from Highway to Hell broke my possessive thoughts. I glanced at my phone and felt my heart drop when I noticed it was Dillon finally calling in with information on Marcus Fairmont. I had been both eager for this call and dreading it at the same time.

"Dillon, tell me good news," I sighed, falling back into a chair.

"Hey man, how's things?" Dillon sounded tired as shit.

"Hopefully better in a few minutes, did you find him?" Dillon grunted and I could hear the distant shuffle of papers. He was calling from his office. I could imagine him with his military text book buzz cut he couldn't seem to leave behind, constantly worried brow and shit kicker boots no doubt kicked up on his desk. It was his business, he could put his feet on the desk if he wanted, but Dillon inside an office was an unusual combination. Dillon was made for the outdoors, his heart, soul and body created for action. His decision to take permanent leave when I did shocked the hell out of me. He said without me watching his six he was as good as dead. If the situation had been reversed, I would have felt the same. Dillon at your back in a sand filled cesspit full of untrained militants with itchy trigger fingers was about as safe as one could be.

"He's still in Dunston, hasn't moved. A missing persons file is still active and I have it on good authority that he hired a new PI twelve months ago, I'm still digging to see if that search is ongoing." I rubbed my pounding head as I absorbed the news. He was still looking for her.

"We need to make the missing person file disappear." It was easy enough to do; the file could be made inactive if the person was to be found not missing.

"Not a problem. Ella might have to make an appearance at the local police station to confirm her identity," Dillon confirmed.

"It needs to be somewhere else. Fairmont has friends on the police force and I don't want any reports leading anyone back to Claymont," I thought out loud.

"It can be done anywhere. Just take a road trip to Elkington, it's a solid nine hour drive. Police there will be able to get a copy of Ella's missing person file and confirm her identity. She's over eighteen, so if she wishes to maintain anonymity it won't be a problem."

"Thanks Dillon, not the greatest news but it's better than what I could have hoped for." Dillon sighed and it was a sound that made the hairs on the back of my neck stand up. He wasn't done.

"You have something else for me?" I asked.

"There was a reason he put a fresh PI on the case. I'm assuming since Ella is doing her damndest to avoid her family, she isn't aware that her mother died almost a year ago?" And there was our 'oh shit' moment. My mouth was so dry I could barely speak.

"How?"

"Suicide, got the report here." At the sound of paper

rustling and Dillon's muttered curse just beyond the phone, my stomach twisted into knots of nervous apprehension. I knew exactly what the report was going to say.

"Don't tell me she cut her wrists." Dillon paused at my words.

"Yeah, she did. Not a common suicide method, messy and most people hate the thought of cutting themselves. Drugs are preferred these days. How'd you know?" Fuck. Marcus killed Ella's mother.

"Was there anything to suggest foul play?"

"Not really, she had a heavy dose of sleeping pills in her system. Made me wonder just how she was able to make the incisions when she should have been passed out, but she had a small window of opportunity before the drugs took effect. Suzanna Fairmont had been in therapy for some time, apparently she harbored some pretty major guilt issues over her mothering skills and she still struggled with her former husband's death, according to one, hold on," more papers rustled, "Dr. Theo Stojanovic. Apparently Ella's father, Mr. Riley Munroe, died of a heart attack on November 25th, 2004, Thanksgiving Day, he was forty-one years old. Suzanna killed herself on the ninth anniversary of his death. Not to be a pessimist and not to refute the good doctor's ability, but from what I was able to garner, Suzanna Fairmont was your classic spoiled bitch who barely mourned her first husband's passing. In fact, all evidence suggests she was already sleeping with Fairmont when Riley died. She liked money—a lot—and it crossed my mind that she might have had something to do with his death, but I've checked out the autopsy report, seems a clean cut heart attack and there was no massive insurance payout to give her a real motive. Anyway, I dug a little and found a former friend of Suzanna's who was willing to discreetly talk. She claims Suzanna had changed over the last twelve months prior to her death. Stopped all travel, became less social, less shopping, generally withdrawn. What bothered me most though was this friend saw bruising on Suzanna. Said she hid it well but she saw marks on her arms and neck, seemed odd and Suzanna apparently didn't take well to being questioned about it."

"Fuck," I muttered.

"I've already emailed you copies of the reports," continued Dillon. I scrambled from my chair and made my way into the small room at the back of the house where my home office was set up. Sitting down at the computer I quickly fired it up.

"I'm going to send you some stuff too. I've made up a file for Ella, consider it classified Dillon. No one lays eyes on it except for you." The moment I had decided to make Ella mine, I had made notes on everything she had told me. Tried to memorize dates and create a time line. I don't know why exactly, it just seemed important to somehow document what she had been through.

"This Ella," Dillon paused, "she's special right?" I had only told Dillon the bare essentials where Ella was concerned and it wasn't the first time I had him help out a girl from Mercy's Shelter, but Dillon was observant.
He was the best at what he did because he had some sort of inexplicable sixth sense.

"Let me put it this way, if the fucker is able to still threaten her, I will gladly take up arms again." Dillon chuckled.

"Shit, sounds like love, Sarge." I couldn't help but smile. I wasn't about to admit that to Dillon, but he was pretty much spot on.

"Files are on their way now. Call me anytime, middle of the night if you have to. Let me know what you need in terms of money and I'll get it to you." Dillon scoffed at the suggestion.

"Don't be a dick. I don't need your money. You can build me a rocking chair or something." I couldn't help but laugh at the image of Dillon in a rocking chair.

"For my nan, you asshole!" he growled.

"Whatever you say," I chuckled. "Dillon, just be sure those files stay private and keep this quiet. If Fairmont catches wind that we are digging around, the shit will hit the fan." I ended my call to Dillon and stared at the computer a moment longer, briefly skimming the notes Dillon had sent me. I leaned back in my chair considering everything I had learned in just fifteen short minutes. Ella's father had died during the holidays, Thanksgiving Day of all days, no wonder she wasn't into Christmas. Marcus Fairmont was a bigger threat than I first perceived. He was definitely capable of murder and he had hired a new PI only twelve months ago in an attempt to find Ella. She had done a damn good job of staying hidden. All that running and living under the radar had paid off. For Ella to finally have her freedom I was going to have to take Marcus Fairmont out. If enough evidence could be compiled, I had no doubt we could take this to court. A man like Marcus Fairmont had shit in his closet, a truck load of it. He was well financed and a pro at hiding it, but nobody could bury their entire past. Dillon just needed to do what he did best, dig in deep and latch on. Dillon was like a bloodhound and once he caught wind of something there was no stopping him.

Abandoning the computer and heading out to pick up Ella, I tried to find the excitement I was savoring a short time ago, though I couldn't deny the heavy shadow that had fallen over my heart. I had no idea how I was going to tell Ella her mother had died, especially the way with which she died. Not tonight, I couldn't tell her tonight. Tonight was about making good memories. I rubbed at the knot in my neck and pushed the trouble away. Nothing could be done about it this minute, Dillon was working the case and I would do whatever necessary to keep Ella safe and happy.

CHAPTER 22

Ella

Eli bounced around excitedly in Annie's lap as we navigated the icy streets to the center of town. Annie seemed just as excited and she looked beautiful. She wore a vibrant red coat and matching hat and scarf. I glanced down at my own dark grey coat and the ratty old black skull cap that I twisted nervously in my hands. I looked ordinary, I looked less than ordinary—I looked homeless. Jax had been bugging me for days to come out to this town celebration with him. I, of course, was more than reluctant. Christmas just reminded me of my father's death and being in that frame of mind along with the embarrassment over my clothes and the fact that I was about to be tossed in with a large crowd, it was all making me feel a little ill. In fact, I was sure if I looked in the mirror I would be green. Oh God. I grabbed my stomach and twisted the center mirror away from Jax to look at my pale face. It wasn't green, but I definitely didn't have the cheerful glow and relaxed look like Annie.

"You look beautiful, Angel," Jax murmured.

"She's scared," Eli piped up. Damn kid didn't have an off switch. He was like beacon for truth which usually meant embarrassment for either one or all of the people surrounding him.

"From the mouths of babes," chuckled Annie.

"I feel sick. Do I look green?" I asked nobody in particular, pinching my cheeks in an effort to put some color into them. Jax pulled the mirror away from me and shook his head.

"You're not green, Angel."

"Come on Ella, if I can do this you can do it." I so easily forgot Annie's nightmares were still so fresh for her. She ran from the violence of her husband only four months ago.
Four short months and she managed to hold her head high and mask her face with an air of strength and resilience.
I knew she did it for Eli, she was as good for him as he was for her. Annie and I shared our nightmares only two nights ago. I told her my father died, but did not go into specifics. It was the wrong time of the year to be opening that wound. I told her

about Marcus, the beatings, the cutting and when I finally escaped. In exchange for the imparting of my demons, she told me about hers. Annie's husband, Phillip, was diagnosed with schizophrenia nearly five years ago and was refusing to take his medication. During episodes he became disorganized and frantic and eventually violent. It was hard for Annie to leave her husband because she loved him very much, but the degeneration of his behavior eventually began to wear their relationship thin. When Phillip began hitting Annie, she felt betrayed in the worst possible way. Annie had no family and their circle of friends had disappeared when Phillip's illness appeared. Looking over at her now, she looked so comfortable, so carefree. She hid her fear well, unlike me who felt like a fragile ice sculpture ready to fracture.

Jax had trouble finding somewhere to park his pickup and we ended up right outside Benny's. I looked longingly through the windows. It looked warm and quiet in there.

"Maybe I can just wait for you guys here," I suggested. Jax grabbed my hand and all but dragged me down the two blocks into town. As we drew closer, the crowds became thicker and my anxiety grew worse. I concentrated on Jax's big hand in mine. It was a lifeline that kept me connected to some resemblance of sanity. Large outdoor heaters scattered the footpaths of the short strip mall, along with country fair hot food. Music played from a make shift stage set up beside the very obvious and beautiful Christmas tree. It was enormous and the leaves were scattered with light flecks of snow.

Another dump of the white stuff like they had had the night I arrived in Claymont and the entire thing would disappear under it. Large gaudy decorations had been hung and on top sat a large gold star. I shivered as I stood and took it all in. It wasn't the cold that chilled me though, it was the memories that Christmas decorations brought with it. I tried to tell myself I hated them, but I didn't. I had always loved Christmas, the decorations, the music and goodwill that came with that time of the year. It just made me miss my dad more.

"Ahhhhh! Finally, I've been looking everywhere for you two," exclaimed Rebecca. I couldn't stop the laugh that escaped from my lips. Her hair and makeup was styled in her usual pinup girl façade, her legs encased in skin tight black lycra pants with a pair of sexy knee high boots. However, in a total contradiction to Rebecca's usual style, she was wearing the most hideous green knitted jersey with giant fluffy antlers attached to the front. A pair of gaudy dangling Santa earrings that flashed at regular intervals finished the ensemble. She shook her finger at me.

"Don't you dare laugh. I have one of these babies sitting at home with your name on it." She pointed at the sweater and I shook my head in mock horror.

"Over my dead body." Rebecca glanced at Jax who seemed as horrified as I was by Rebecca's festive attire.

"So, Jax," she sung. "Bet you've been wondering about my clitoria." Jax shook his head and laughed.

"Not even once." At that moment I was nudged sideways by a rowdy teen who appeared more than a little tanked. Jax pulled me in to the safety of his warm hard body. This is where I wanted to be, if I could live here I would. This is where I felt no fear, where my body responded to his in a most natural way. I wanted to wrap my arms around him and kiss him until the outside world disappeared.
I wanted, no, I needed him to kiss me again and touch me the way a woman was meant to be touched by a man and the fact that ever since the kiss on Annie's couch, he had handled me far too virtuously made me want to scream with frustration. I knew he was trying to do the honorable thing and take it slow, but something inside my body had been ignited by that kiss. Something inside me had been awakened and I suddenly felt like a starved woman craving a thirst for a tall, silver eyed blonde.

"Jesus Christ Rebecca, what the fuck are you wearing?" Charlie slapped Jax on the back and gave me a cheeky wink as he turned to take in Rebecca's loud outfit. Rebecca scowled and I was intrigued. Rebecca wasn't the type to care what others thought of her wardrobe, but the look she gave Charlie now could only be described as unfriendly, in fact it bordered on icy.

"I wonder if you've got those sexy little red panties on under that. You know, the one's with the little bows on the sides?" Charlie seemed to wonder out loud as his scorching gaze ran a path up and down Rebecca's body. A furious blush settled on Rebecca's cheeks and I was officially gob smacked. Jax's curious glance from Charlie to Rebecca confirmed he was just as surprised.

"Well, you'll just have to keep wondering because there is no way in hell you will ever get another sample," Rebecca said dismissively. Charlie grinned.

"Sample? Betty Boo, I did a whole lot more than sample." Rebecca's fists curled, her scowl deepened and Jax moved to intercede.

"You know kids, I'm not sure Annie's going to be able to comfortably explain this conversation to Eli and as intrigued as I am, perhaps now is not the time or the place."
Rebecca cast Eli a quick glance. His innocent little eyes watched her thoughtfully but then moved to something else happening over by the tree, dismissing the entire scene as easy as that.

"Well, that was unexpected." Jax chuckled as he moved back to my side while Rebecca and Charlie did their best to ignore each other.

"Hey, I need to find a bathroom for Eli," whispered Annie.

"Ohhhh, me too. You guys made me leave in such a hurry I didn't get a chance to go before we left." I was suddenly jumping around uncomfortably.

"If we didn't get you out the door that minute, you never would have left. You would have ended up locking yourself in the bathroom," Annie murmured. Yeah, she was right.

"I'll get the key to Bouquets, I'm sure Rebecca won't mind if we sneak in there." Jax was reluctant to let me go on my own, but at that moment I felt it was something I needed to do. No one else was out here having a panic attack about being in a crowd and I certainly didn't want to have to hold Jax's hand every time I needed to use a bathroom.

"It's nice in here," said Annie, inhaling the floral scent. "Warm."

"I think I could sleep in here," I admitted. I kept expecting Annie to ask me about Jax. We may have talked about our past, but for some reason I felt hesitant discussing my present and future. Annie had quickly adopted the rule of the street, your problems are your own and asking questions was a no-no. People talked when they were ready and I was glad for Annie's lack of questions and prying. We knew what we needed to know about each other, outside that we were just happy to have each other's friendship. Annie was sweet, kind and generous, a perfect mother. In that moment I found myself wishing my mother had of been more like her.

I wondered how Mom was doing, no doubt living the life she had always dreamed—money, diamonds, pretty clothes, first class flights to the most exotic locations. She had it all, but I wondered if she was truly happy.

"That blonde Barbie who was at the shelter a few weeks back is out there," murmured Annie from the window of the shop as I came out of the bathroom. I tiptoed my way through the dimly lit shop and glanced out the window, easily spotting Selena. She was, of course, the perfectly groomed, animated bombshell with a ridiculous entourage of friends following her around like lost sheep.

"She is the reason I hated school so much," Annie muttered. I quietly chuckled, observing Selena as she laughed her way amongst the crowd, completely carefree. School for me was like a vague blur. I know there were cliques—the jocks, the cheerleaders, the geeks, the drama club and the list went on. If anything, I probably floated between the stoners and the depressed emo crowd. I hated school too, but likely for different reasons then Annie. I was constantly hiding bruises and one very fragile heart. My stomach dropped when Selena seemed to turn and settle her ugly hostile eyes on me before glancing toward Jax who strolled with purpose towards Bouquets, Rebecca and Charlie at his back. Her snide and discreet smile in my direction confirmed she obviously remembered me from the shelter. It was like a car wreck that I just couldn't bring myself to look away from. Selena sang his name as she approached him and ran her hands up his arms in a familiar gesture that had my heart racing and stomach rolling. Annie cast me a nervous glance then scooped to pick Eli up.

"Come on, let's get out there," Annie suggested. I couldn't move though. I watched Jax like a hawk might watch its prey.

Watching every subtle movement, his hands, the tilt of his head. Most of all, I watched his eyes. Charlie and Rebecca looked nervous as they watched me watching him from outside the window. Jax took a hand from his pocket and rubbed his neck in agitation. He looked uncomfortable and pissed, I could deal with that.

He shook his head a couple of times and Selena seemed to be pleading with him, her hands rubbing his arms and eventually sitting restfully on his chest. Jax didn't try to move them and that fueled the jealousy that currently burned through my body. Jax shook his head again, irritated and then something changed. Selena's eyes were beseeching, her lips in a perfect ruby red pout; she mumbled a few more words and Jax listened. The change was immediate, acceptance and understanding bled through Jax's eyes, followed by a reluctant but firm nod. Selena reached up on her toes and he leaned forward allowing her to place a quick chaste kiss to his lips. It could have been a passionate affair of tongues as far as I was concerned, jealousy had reared its ugly head and was flowing through my veins with unexpected vehemence. Jax had leaned into this kiss, he had accepted her affection right in front of me, right in front of my friends. This I couldn't deal with, I was suddenly feeling ill again, but for a whole different reason.

CHAPTER 23

Jax

I had gotten tired of waiting for Ella to come back from Bouquets and I imagined her, Annie and Eli enjoying the spring time warmth of the shop. It was absolutely freezing and I was eager to find just a few minutes out of the icy chill in the air. What put a truly biting chill in me though was seeing Selena, standing but a few feet away from Bouquets. As soon as she saw me she pounced. She looked typical Selena, dressed to the nines, too much makeup, her following of Selena clones hanging off her every word.

"Jax!" she exclaimed, like we were the best of friends. She hadn't called me, just like I had asked, but seeing her here now, seeing her approach me like nothing had changed, pissed me off. "I need to speak to you about the Thanksgiving Ball next week. I told Daddy you were taking me, so I need to know what time you're picking me up." Her hands rubbed up and down my arms in what was supposed to be an innocent gesture, but I knew better. I was too stunned by her question to do anything about it though. I looked at her like she was speaking a foreign language and shook my head.

"I'm not going to the fucking ball with you, Selena." She pouted and fuck I hated her for it. I hated myself for putting up with it for so long.

"The event is sold out, Jax. There are no more tickets and you know it is where you do your thing and network for Mercy's Shelter." She spat the word shelter at me like it was a dirty word. And I shook my head again.

"We don't need the networking that bad," I smirked. Then she did what she knew would reel me in, she knew I would take the bait. Her eyes glistened with unshed tears, her pout now a solemn frown.

"Jax, my mother and father are going to be there and they will be so disappointed with me if I don't turn up with you. They will know I screwed this up, I always screw things up and they remind me of that every time I see them. I can't even get a job without Daddy's help. Please, surely after all these years the least you can do is pick me up, escort me in, be polite, have one dance with me then leave if you have to. Just don't make me walk in there alone. You secure donations for Mercy's next year and I get Mommy and Daddy off my back for another day." Her hands rested on my chest and I wanted to push her away but I also didn't want to create a scene in front of her friends. I rubbed a hand down my face groaning. Fuck, I couldn't believe I was giving in to her. But Mercy's needed the support and it was the biggest community event on the calendar—senators, wealthy business man, lawyers, doctors, the who's who of Claymont. It was worth a few hours of awkwardness with Selena. And her parents did give her a hard time, their love was harsh, no doubt the major contributing factor in molding Selena into the woman she is.

"Alright, I'll pick you up at seven but you'll need to find your own way home, I won't be staying long." Her eyes beamed with triumph and she raised herself to her toes. I knew she wanted to kiss me and for some reason, most likely habit, I leaned forward and allowed it. As I glanced up and saw Ella watching from inside Bouquets in mortified horror, I suddenly realized I had screwed up.

"You won't regret it," Selena sang as she walked away and I'm sure she cast Ella a quick grin. I was already filled with regret. Ella walked out of the florist, her face barely masking her rage. While Charlie helped Rebecca lock up I moved towards her.

"Everything okay?" she asked in a voice that contradicted the simmering anger.

"Just fine. You hungry?" I tried to move the conversation on to something else quickly.

I was too pissed off to answer any of her questions, I knew I'd lose my shit. She tilted her head to one side, as if looking at me from another angle might give her the answer she was searching for.

"You look guilty," she whispered. I hated that she could see me so easily.

"I haven't done anything wrong so I don't know why you would assume that I'm guilty," I growled.

"I don't assume, I know Jax, I can see it in your eyes. As far as I'm aware you haven't done anything to be guilty of either.

So maybe you can tell me why you feel that way."

"What do you want me to say, Angel? You want the truth?" She stared at me with those big beautiful eyes that were seething with frustration.

"You promised me that's all you would ever give me, remember? I can trust you, you told me that." I pulled the beanie from my head and ran my hand through my hair in frustration. Rebecca moved up to her side. I didn't want to do this here and now, but my night had started badly with Dillon's news then quickly descended into a cluster fuck with seeing Selena. Now Ella's questioning eyes were all I needed to nudge me into asshole mode.

"You wanna do this now? Fine, I'm taking Selena to the Thanksgiving Ball next week. I'd promised her a long time ago and it's important to her. We go every year together and we've been friends for a long time, I can't just let her down like that. It's a great opportunity to network for Mercy's too. There are no other tickets left and even if there were it's not like I can take you—it's crowded and glamorous, not really your kind of thing." I might as well have hit her. The pain in her eyes made me instantly regret my words. Even Annie, who stood behind her, took a short step back. Rebecca's eyes widened with shock and Charlie shook his head and groaned. I had to give it to Ella though. She recovered well. Her eyes glazed over with a look that broke my heart. Indifference and no doubt her life with Marcus had made her an expert at that look.

"Of course you have to go. Mercy's is everything, it's far more important than you and I." I went to interrupt her and tell her she was wrong, that she actually meant the world to me and I would happily give up Mercy's for her. Selena had wanted me to and of course I wouldn't. If Ella asked though, I'd give it up in a heartbeat. The thing is, I knew she would never ask that of me and that's why I loved her. Ella didn't give me a chance to speak though, her anger forcing words from her lips in quick succession. "Without Mercy's there would be no me, no Annie and Eli, no Sam, no Nancy. All those girls and women would be left out in the cold. Sarah would have died alone and cold rather than in a warm safe place. Finding money to keep Mercy's running is more important than anything, but the fact that the first thing that came out of your mouth was making Selena happy, that kind of pisses me off. Lord knows she would make the perfect date though. She loves the crowd and works it like a pro. I have no doubt she would do the full glamour thing too, beautiful dresses, hair, makeup the works. Fuck." Ella laughed but there was no humor in it, it was forced and a little bit manic. "Just like my mother, that's who she reminds me of you know, my exact opposite. No doubt Selena never flinched at your touch or went into a fucking panic attack. She is the better option, Jax, she is perfect for you. I hope the evening is profitable for Mercy's and knowing your past with Selena, I'm sure she'd be happy to scratch your back." I turned and walked away, somehow managing to hold my head high and shoulders back proudly. I didn't even notice Rebecca at my side till I reached the end of the mall and edged my way around the last of the crowd.

"My car's up here." She nodded down a side street and I hesitated at the darkness. She stopped and held out her hand. "Come on tiger, I know how to throw a punch, I'll keep you safe." I was furious that Jax hadn't even followed me, hadn't even attempted to reject what I had said. "You're coming to my place for a sleep over. You can borrow some of my clothes." I really just wanted to go back to the apartment and curl into a ball and cry. Who was I kidding? I knew I wouldn't cry. It took kindness to bring on my tears. What kind of a sicko was I?

"Annie will worry," I reasoned.

"I told her before I came after you that I would keep you at my place tonight and drop you home tomorrow. I thought you might prefer some space without the little critter under your feet."

"Little critter?" I wondered out loud.

"Eli." She winked playfully. "Cute critter that one, but perhaps not so much fun to have around when you feel like making a Jax voodoo doll." I felt so dejected and humiliated by Jax's words that I couldn't even force a smile. He thought I wasn't good enough for a ball. What pissed me off was that he was right.

"I'm homeless. Why would he want to take me to a ball? I don't even own a dress." I murmured, still angry. My eyes were fixed on the road ahead, but I still noticed Rebecca turn to glance at me as we drove out of the city.

"You met Jax at the shelter?" she asked. I nodded woodenly.

"If it bothers you having me in Bouquets, I'll leave without a fuss."

"Now why the hell would I want you to leave?" she snapped.

"Most people assume that a homeless employee would be more prone to theft." It was the honest truth. It's why I kept my home life, or lack thereof private.

"Well, that's just stupid. I trust you Ella, Rita vouched for you and Rita doesn't vouch for criminals, she's a good judge of character and I like to think I am too. Anyway, you live with Annie and Eli so you're not homeless you, douche." Her flippant regard of my living arrangements made me laugh.

"I sleep on their couch. I have four pairs of jeans, one pair of cargo's, five t-shirts, six thermals, one heavy winter jacket and a pair of all-star sneakers." Rebecca was quiet while she absorbed my far to short list of belongings.

"You don't own any underwear?" she finally gasped in mock horror and I couldn't help but laugh.

"I own underwear you dork, probably not as much as you and none of it has lace on it. I think I'm allergic to lace and frills."

Rebecca pulled into a small quaint looking cottage that looked perfectly adorable surrounded by a thin layer of snow. She only lived ten minutes from the city center, her home surrounded by other, much larger homes.

"Welcome to my matchbox. It pisses the neighbors off that this microscopic crib sits amongst their much more affluent and grand castles. It belonged to my grandma and she left it to me and my older sister, who escaped Claymont years ago, so it's really just mine now and I'm not changing it for anyone. It's awesome just the way it is." I nodded as she led me up the porch. As I wandered through the front door of Rebecca's house, I was instantly hit by the same humid warmth as her shop. The house was definitely small, but it was incredibly homely and neat and tidy. The furniture was scant which allowed the allusion of space. In front of the fireplace was a gorgeous cozy couch that was made for cuddling on. That's where I wanted to be right now, alone with my misery.

"Well tiger, what we are going to do is pull out a bottle of vodka, kick back some shots then go through my enormous closet that is full of clothes that haven't seen the light of day in several years. We are going to fix you up with some dresses and skirts, because apparently you need those." I stared at Rebecca's serious expression and began laughing.

"I don't think I would suit the sort of clothes you wear, Rebecca," I admitted. "No offense, of course. You look smokin' in those old style clothes, but it's just not me." Rebecca shook her head.

"Well don't freak out, but I didn't always dress this way. In fact, the clothes that are gathering moth balls are my pre-pin up girl clothes, all pretty dull and boring." She winked. "No offense, of course, I know you're not dull and boring at all." I smiled at that, Rebecca had no idea how dull and boring I wanted my life to be.

"If you try and give me anything that looks remotely like what you're wearing right now I will leave, and FYI, I'm not sure about the vodka. I've never drank that before and I don't drink very much anymore. It's likely to turn me into a blithering mess." Rebecca's jaw dropped open.

"You're shitting me! You've never tried vodka?" I shook my head as I wandered over to her clitoria that sat proudly in the center of a small dining table.

"I've had every other alcoholic drink under the moon and sun and a disturbingly large array of narcotics, which I haven't touched in a very long time," I glared at her pointedly, "but I've never had vodka." Rebecca shook her head.

"Vodka virgin." She sighed. "Well, we're popping that cherry tonight, so stop touching my clitoria, sit your ass down and get cozy. I'll get the shot glasses and bring the clothes out." She stopped on the way to the kitchen. "Fuck that, we'll drink in the bedroom, come on. And, FYI, you would look amazing in a fancy gown and you are definitely good enough to take to a ball. Oh, and screw you, this sweater is fabulous."

CHAPTER 24

Jax

I couldn't believe how badly I had fucked up with Ella. If I were able to separate myself from my body right now, I would literally turn and beat the shit out of whatever part remained. Charlie had forced me to stay in the city, he knew I needed to calm the fuck down and he was also well aware that Eli was wrapped timidly around Annie's legs watching the awkward scene unfold in confused innocence. I forced myself to stay and let the little man see the lights lit on the Christmas tree. Seeing the joyful glow in his eyes made staying with such an ache in my heart almost worth it. Eli fell asleep in the car as I drove him and Annie home. I helped her carry him up the two flights of stairs to their apartment and knew she would say something the moment I unloaded the sleeping babe into his bed.

"I didn't expect that of you, Jax." Her disappointment made the ache in my chest deepen. "What you said to Ella was hurtful. I don't know what is exactly going on with you two, or this other tramp, but to string them both along like that is really unfair, especially on Ella."

"I'm not stringing anyone along, Annie, I adore Ella. Fuck, I'd be lying if I said I didn't love her. Selena is nothing to me, I'm just helping her out of an awkward situation and it benefits Mercy's at the same time." I rubbed the knot that had taken up residence in my neck. "Perhaps I could have handled the situation a little better though. I've had a rough day and I just snapped." Annie shook her head as she leaned against the kitchen counter.

"Do you wonder if Ella's step-father used that excuse on her?" My eyes snapped to Annie's. "Do you think he hit her and told her it was because he had a bad day?"

"I didn't hit Ella, Annie," I growled.

"Of course you didn't, but you still hurt her. You basically told her she wasn't good enough to be seen at a fancy ball with you."

I groaned. "That's not what I meant. She hates crowds and this crowd is going to be full of women like Selena, fuck, like her mother and worse. I wouldn't put her through that."

Annie smiled. "And that's how you should have explained it to her." Annie sighed. "Don't push her too hard, Jax. She's fragile, she has trust issues, which she is completely entitled to. You need to do right by her, always, even after a bad day. If you don't think you can handle that then you need to back off now, before things go too far." Annie saw the situation for exactly what it was. I needed to be more for Ella, stronger and no excuse would pardon me.

"Thanks, Annie." I sighed. She gave me a quick hug before seeing me out the door.

Now I sat on my couch, a glass of whiskey hung precariously from my fingers, my head bowed in shame. I had let Ella down, I had broken a promise, again. In this moment, the tattoo at my back carried the heavy burden of shame and truth. Redemption was not for me, I had failed Sarah and now Ella. As that thought crossed my mind, Ella's words echoed in my ears. "Sarah would have died alone and cold rather than in a warm safe place." The truth in her words stung me. I couldn't save Sarah, but I gave her all I could and that was more than anyone had ever given her. I swallowed down my whiskey and quickly poured another. I needed the detachment tonight, I needed to escape. Thoughts of Ella would either drive me to call her or worse yet, drive me to Rebecca's to confront her. She didn't need that bullshit right now. I would explain myself, make this right somehow, but I knew she needed some space to see and think clearly. Remembering Selena's pleading eyes made me shudder; the girl knew how to play with the best of them. She knew exactly what she had to say to get what she wanted. I was taking her to this stupid fucking ball and I wasn't looking forward to it. It wasn't at all how I expected Thanksgiving to go. In fact, I had already spoken to Annie about having them all come out to my place for the night, perhaps Charlie and Rebecca too. Of course Annie had offered to cook, which was a good thing, considering my inability to boil so much as water. Then another memory consumed me. Fuck, Ella's dad had died on Thanksgiving. How the fuck could I have let that gold nugget of information slip? I stood angrily and picked up the closest thing to me, which happened to be my guitar. I swung it

hard against the brick fireplace and it shattered just as my
conscience did. I was taking Selena to the Thanksgiving Ball
on the anniversary of Ella's father's death. I roared with anger
at my own stupidity. Gripping the ledge of the fireplace until
my knuckles turned white, all the hate, guilt and anger inside of
me simmered dangerously close to the surface. With a long
breath I spun around and grabbed the bottle of whiskey,
gulping with furious impatience straight from the bottle.

No, redemption wasn't for me. If God was looking down
on me right now, his head would be hanging in shame, his
heart would be broken, just like Sarah's, just like Ella's. All the
blood on my hands, the broken promises, the women I had
used—they were all decisions I had made, wrong decisions that
hurt people, killed people. Finishing off the bottle I sank into
an abyss of shame and self-loathing. The walls around me spun
out of control, just like my life, the ceiling over my head seemed
to be falling on top of me. What the fuck had I done? I had
ruined everything. With that failing thought, I descended into
the sweet silence of unconsciousness.

***

*As I walked down the narrow hallway of the crumbling
building, my heart pounded with fear. Not fear of my own
death, but those around me. My fellow soldiers at arms, Dillon
who covered my back. The heat was unbearable, thick, like a
living entity that coated your skin and sucked the life right out
of you. At the end of the familiar hallway I nudged the door
open and the acrid scent of mortar and death gripped my lungs,
the vision of blood seared my eyes. I fell to my knees, my eyes
squeezed shut with the effort it took not to be sick, but it was
useless. The bile rose in my throat and when I opened my eyes
again, the room had changed. It was Mercy's bathroom, again a
familiar nightmare. The dream has so far replayed with echoing
precision, an exact duplicate of the same dream, over and over,
except for here, now in the bathroom at Mercy's Shelter. It
looked the same, but it felt different, warmer and the air not as
thick, the smell of blood sweeter rather than rotten. I looked
toward the shower stall where I knew her body would lay. I
didn't want to see her again, but I was drawn to her. Looking*

over her lifeless bloodied body was the price I paid for my failure of her. I saw her tiny foot first, followed by the long pale leg, her body crumpled against the wall, blood pooled around her broken form. The whimper from my throat was weak in comparison to the rage I felt at finding her like this. This was when I usually woke, when the nightmare became too much and I screamed myself awake. But not tonight, tonight the lifeless body of Sarah moved and, with a horrified fascination, I continued to watch her. Her eyes blinked and her head rose to take me in. She smiled, like she was happy to see me, no doubt pleased I was still here so she could scream and yell how I failed her. Her head tilted to one side and a surprising look of compassion and comfort consumed her features. I tried to whisper I was sorry but the words would not come. A tear escaped my eye and fell uselessly down my cheek.

Tears wouldn't bring her back. Sarah shook her head slowly, her bright green eyes never strayed from mine. "There's nothing to forgive." My heart lurched at her words. "I'm the one who is sorry, I let you down and I'm sorry, but you have to let me go now, Jax. It's time to let the past rest." With that her head lolled back lifelessly.

I woke with a start, sweat dripping from my still clothed body on the couch in my living room. The sun shone through the drapes without mercy, scorching my skin with its touch. I glanced to the empty bottle of whiskey and my stomach pitched, my head pounding with the effort not to be sick. My mouth was as dry as the desert and tasted like ass, or so I assumed, having never tasted ass before. The lingering impressions of my dream held me rooted to my seat. Perhaps forgiveness wasn't what I needed. Maybe what I needed was to finally accept Sarah's fate and move forward, just like Ella had said. Fuck, this was too profound for a Friday morning. I glanced at my watch—shit, it was after nine and I was late. Mercy would be pissed and, just like clock-work, my phone belted out the familiar AC/DC riff. I held it to my ear but didn't get a chance to speak.

"You're late. David is covering but he did the two a.m. shift, so he's exhausted. You'd better be on your way and if not, a note from your mother won't cut it Jaxon James Carter." I chuckled and rubbed my head, stalking through the house to quickly change.

"Yeah, I'm on my way and I need to speak to David so tell him not to go anywhere. I had a fucked up dream that needs his psychoanalyzing. Tell him I'll be there soon and, Mom, I hate it when you call me that." She was quiet for a moment.

"Jax, is everything okay?" In the blink of an eye, her voice had gone from pissed off momma bear to the angelic guardian I adored.

"Not really, Mom. I fucked up but I'm gonna make it right. I need to talk to David about Sarah and once I get that cleared I can make everything right again."

"Oh, baby. Should I check on Ella?" She didn't even have to ask me who or how I had fucked up, she just knew.

"I'd appreciate that. She stayed with Rebecca last night and she'll be working today."

"Okay, honey, I'll stop by Bouquets before I head home and, Jax, you're only human. We all make mistakes. It's important we learn from them and try not to make them again though." I slipped the phone from my hand while I pulled a fresh shirt on.

"Shit, I know. I'll talk to you later." I hung up and raced around the house looking for my keys. The urgency to my start helped me push the sharp hangover from the forefront of my mind. I had to get to work, I needed to talk to David, but, more than anything, I needed to see Ella.

CHAPTER 25

Ella

The morning after the incident between Jax and Selena, I awoke in Rebecca's bed, still dressed in my clothes from the night before with a pounding head protesting the deflowering of my vodka virginity. I officially hated vodka. Rebecca and I had worked our way through her entire closet and it was indeed full of clothes that had not been touched in years. I found myself with a suitcase full of perfectly decent clothes which made me incredibly happy, but the sting from Jax's actions and words the night before still broke my heart. The next morning I rode to work with Rebecca, we were late but since Rebecca was the boss and she didn't seemed fazed, I didn't worry about it too much. We were met at the store by a worried looking Mercy. She didn't ask any questions, just bought a simple bouquet of tulips and made sure I had her number to call her if I needed to.

The following days crept by slowly. Jax never attempted to contact me and that stung. Annie had told me that he had stopped by the diner to ask how I was doing. The fact he couldn't pick up the phone and ask me himself was absurd and hurtful. Rebecca said he was working with Dave through some issues. He apparently needed to sort his shit out before he even considered seeing me again and helping me to tackle my shit. I considered leaving so many times. I'd even started taking my backpack everywhere I went again, just in case I decided to run. Something held me to Claymont though. Whether it was Jax, Mercy, Annie and Eli, Rebecca or a combination of all I didn't know, but I just couldn't bring myself to walk away. Rita had tried to call me several times, but I wasn't ready to speak to her yet. Rebecca deflected her calls which were apparently growing in angst.

Finally, on the day before Thanksgiving, the day before Jax and Selena's date and the anniversary of my dad's death, she called Bouquets and I answered.

"Damn Ella, I've been trying to ring you for the last week!" Rita shrieked and I pulled the receiver away from my ear.

"Chill out Rita, I'm here, I'm fine. I've been busy, sorry." I grumbled my excuse as pathetic as I felt.

"Do you think I would keep calling, over and over and over if it wasn't important?" My stomach sank. How could I have let some childish boy drama foreshadow the real problems in my life? My hands trembled and a cold sweat broke out on my brow.

"Don't freak Ella," I heard Rita say with calm but firm words. "A man approached me after work last week. He said his name is Dillon Montgomery and he's investigating a man by the name of Marcus Fairmont." Hearing Marcus's name made bile rise in my throat.

"Ella, are you alright?" Rebecca asked from across the room. I wiped my brow and fought to stay focused as I listened to Rita.

"He said that Marcus Fairmont was your step-father, Ella, is that right?"

"Yes," I whispered.

"He asked questions, about you, Ella."

"What sort of questions?"

"He wanted to know how I knew you; had I seen bruises on you; if I knew Marcus." My brain couldn't work out why this Dillon would be asking such questions. If he was working for Marcus, why would he ask about my bruises? Why would he be asking about Marcus?

"What did you tell him?" I murmured.

"Sweetie, I told him nothing, but he said he is working for a friend in Claymont to make sure you are safe and he gave me his card." Suddenly everything fell into place. This must have been Jax's ex-military friend, the man who Jax had looking into Marcus. Why he was there in Dunston had me a little confused, but he definitely wasn't being discreet like Jax had assured me. My panic disappeared, followed quickly with anger.

"Thanks for not saying anything, Rita, I appreciate it."

"Is everything okay, hun, you sound tired?" I was tired, I had been plagued with nightmares and restlessness all week.

"I'm fine, I'll call you in a couple of days. Please don't say anything else to this Dillon, I'll take care of it." As I hung up the phone I grabbed my mobile.

"I just need to make a quick call," I mumbled to Rebecca

who was watching me a little bewildered. I headed for the back of the store, to step out into the small alley behind the shop.

"Ella, are you okay?" Rebecca called out behind me. I turned and nodded, attempting a smile which I knew was a complete waste of time. It was as fake as Selena.

I looked at Jax's number on my screen for at least five minutes before I called. Leaving would be so much easier. My backpack was inside; I could so easily run and leave this mess behind. But running seemed so weak and a part of me wanted to stay. I had made friends, I had a wonderful job and I liked Claymont, even with all the drama that had so far come with it. Jax answered on the first ring.

"Who the fuck is Dillon Montgomery?" I snapped, skipping the pleasantries that I was in no mood for.

"He's a friend, a good friend. He's checking out Marcus for us to make sure he is no longer a threat." Jax didn't hesitate and he didn't try to soothe me with flowery words. He knew I was pissed and direct answers were needed right now.

"He's asking questions. I didn't want that, Jax."

"Yes, he's asking questions. Marcus still has a private investigator looking for you. Dillon is trying to find out where the case is at, what sort of information they have on you." I took a deep breath. I knew Marcus would never give up searching for me. I was going to be running for the rest of my life. Claymont was just another pit stop on the race track my life had become.

"Angel, I need to talk to you. How about I come by tonight?"

"No, I'm busy tonight." I was having dinner at Rebecca's, but even if I hadn't been, I wasn't ready to face Jax Carter just yet.

"Then tomorrow, I really need to see you, Angel," he growled. "Dillon has found out some things that I don't want to talk about over the phone." His words caused a sharp twinge of disappointment while also managing to terrify me. I couldn't imagine what Dillon had uncovered and I wasn't sure I wanted to know. But that was why Jax wanted to see me, not because of us, not because he cared for me and wanted to make things right.

"Tomorrow's not good either, I'm working and you have a date," I spat.

"Angel," Jax implored. "Please, I really need to see you, I've missed you and I know I fucked up. I wanted to call you last week. Fuck, I wanted to call you the minute you turned and left me standing there by that giant fucking Christmas tree, but I knew I had to finally deal with my own shit before I could give you everything you deserved. I talked to David about Sarah. We have a lot to talk about." He had said the words I had wanted to hear but they were like a conciliation prize. He didn't bag me with the first line, so try another.

"I'm glad you're talking to someone about Sarah, that's a good thing, Jax," I sighed. "Don't worry about me, I've stayed out of Marcus's hands for years, I know how to stay safe. Thank you for trying, Jax, I appreciate it." I hung up before he could say another word. My phone vibrated instantly, his name flashing across the screen. I had to leave, it was the only way. I walked awkwardly back into Bouquets and groaned when I saw Selena chatting animatedly with Rebecca, when her eyes found mine they glistened with evil malice.

"Soooo," she said in a sing song voice. "I picked up my dress for the ball, it's divine of course." Her eyes were glued to Rebecca, but I knew her words were for me. "And we've got three nights booked at the lodge up in the mountains after. It's kind of a ritual for us; we've done it every year he's taken me to the ball." Rebecca shook her head and cast me a glare that confirmed just how pissed off she was with Selena.

"Cut the bullshit, Selena. The only reason Jax is taking you to the ball is because there are no more tickets available and it's good PR for Mercy's. Everyone in Claymont knows that whatever you two once had going is over." The look on Selena's face was priceless and I adored Rebecca even more in that moment. Selena spluttered in outrage for a moment before finally composing herself.

"Have the arrangement delivered this afternoon," she snapped.

"Not a problem. Say hi to your folks for me," Rebecca sung as Selena turned and stalked from the store like a diva that was denied her botox.

"Bitch," grumbled Rebecca turning to face me. "So, what's going on tiger?" she asked, her attention now solely on me. I shrugged and scratched my arm nervously.

"I have to go, it's kind of an emergency and I'm not sure when I'll be back. I'm sorry." Her brow furrowed as she approached me and pulled me into an easy embrace.

"What do you need?" she asked. I stepped away from her comfort and support. I had to break this luxury I was quickly growing accustomed to. There was no room for attachments in my life.

"Just deflect Jax for me, just for a couple of days. I just need some space." Rebecca nodded thoughtfully as the phone rang.

"Go, take as much time as you need. You can come back whenever you like. But promise me you will call. Promise me you will let me know you're okay. I need that Ella." I nodded. I would let Rita know and she, in turn, would tell Rebecca. No harm no foul. I grabbed my backpack but hesitated at the door when I heard Rebecca mention Jax's name.

"No Jax, she left early, can I give her a message?" She nodded my way and I mouthed a quick 'thank you' before leaving the warmth and joy that I'd found in Bouquets. I knew Annie was relying on me to watch Eli for Thanksgiving. She had been offered the shift and the money was awesome working the holiday. I had promised I would watch Eli, even though I knew it would be difficult. Thanksgiving was always difficult. I would leave on Saturday and tell Annie then. That would hopefully give her some time to sort out what do to with Eli before her next night shift. Tonight though, I would find a motel to stay in. I was intent on evading Jax anyway I could and he knew to find me at Annie's. Tomorrow night he would be busy and if there was any truth to Selena's words, he wouldn't be in town for a few days after that. My break from Claymont would be messy if I had to confront Jax. I just needed to get through the next forty-eight hours and tomorrow would be the hardest. The anniversary of my dad's death always hit me hard. With my shoulders back and head held high I went in search of a motel.

☐

CHAPTER 26

Jax

Fuck, fuck, fuck and double fucking cluster-fuck. Ella's phone was switched off, she had left Bouquets and Rebecca assured me she had no idea where she had gone. Ella had apparently said she needed to take care of something, but Rebecca eventually confessed her words were more of a goodbye. She hadn't returned to her apartment but Annie assured me she had spoken to Ella and she was fine. Annie had offered to work Thanksgiving and Ella was watching Eli for the night. I was stuck at Mercy's now filling in for a night shift and tomorrow I had that fucking ball. The punches that landed on the bag in the basement were unforgiving. Somewhere over the last week I had found a measure of peace at the thought of broken little Sarah, but now Ella had me tied up in knots all over again. I needed to tell her everything Dillon had discovered, she needed to know about her mother and I needed to make things right between us. The last part I had no idea how to do. Taking Selena to this damn Thanksgiving Ball was a betrayal and downright disrespectful to Ella. Doing it for Mercy's was one thing, doing it for Selena was another thing altogether.

"You think hitting that bag is going to answer all your problems?" Dave stood on the stairs behind me. I cast him a quick glance between punches.

"Nope, but it sure as hell makes me feel better." David grunted and sat down. "What are you doing here tonight? Mercy kick you out?" I joked. It was David's night off and night shift workers really did appreciate going home to a warm house and comfy bed after working a couple of shifts in the shelter.

"She needed sweets and I promised her I would also stop in and check on you. Have you spoken to Ella?"
With one final punishing blow to the bag I stopped and turned to face David.

"Yep, she's running," I growled. David nodded.

"It's how she stays safe. Staying is scary as hell, especially with the shit going on. She doesn't really need or want all this high maintenance drama on top of her own crap." I wiped the hair from my eyes in frustration.

"I don't know how to fix it, Dave. I don't know how to take back what I did, what I said." David thought for a moment.

"You can't take back what you said. You can only make it right, look forward rather than back. I know the ball is a big deal as far as sponsorship and donations go, but is it worth losing Ella over?"

"That's the thing, if I answer truthfully and say no, doesn't that make me a heartless prick? I'd be letting down all the women who need the shelter. I'd be letting down Mercy." David was careful at choosing his words again.

"So, you're sacrificing one for the good of many? You see going to the ball as sacrificing Ella and choosing the shelter?" I leaned against the wall contemplating David's words.
"I want both. I need Mercy's Shelter, I need to keep it running for Mercy, for me, fuck, for you, but mostly for the women who need the shelter and safety. And I need Ella. My need for her is fucking all consuming."
"The need to protect her, love her, fuck it borders on painful, Dave. I don't know how to have both." David shrugged.

"I'm kind of insulted that you would think you're the only man around here who scrubs up okay in a tux." I'm sure the dumbfounded look on my face was priceless and David's low chuckle confirmed it.

"You would do that? You would take Selena Liander to this stupid Ball? It's Thanksgiving David you're supposed to be with Mercy." David rubbed a hand down his face.

"Damn Jax, I have three grown daughters that keep me on my toes. I'm sure I can put up with a spoiled brat like Selena for one night. As for Thanksgiving, as long as you spend it with Mercy, here at the shelter, I'm okay with that and I have no doubt she will okay with it too." I nodded and for the first time in a week, I smiled and it didn't feel forced.

"It will piss Selena off. I need a photo of her reaction when you knock on her door. Promise me you will take a photo." David laughed.

"I'm sure I can do that. Now, get upstairs and clean up that kitchen, it's a bloody disgrace." I pulled off the boxing gloves and threw them onto a nearby table, following David up the stairs.

"I helped Mary cook so that might have something to do with the mess."

David looked back over his shoulder and asked, "Mary let you cook?" He chuckled.

"Yep, I told her I wanted cooking lessons, she accepted and now I know she is regretting it." I grinned at the memory of Mary all flustered and yelling obscenities at me as I apparently ruined the sauce for the spaghetti and meatballs.

Twenty minutes later, as I wiped down the last bench in the kitchen, my phone rang from my back pocket. Glancing at the screen I noted Dillon's name and quickly answered it.

"What's up?" I asked and Dillon's usual grunt confirmed that whatever it was, it wasn't good.

"This cluster fuck makes Afghanistan look like a ball park," he grumbled. "Rita is a good friend, silent, didn't even blink when I asked her if she knew Ella Munroe. I get the feeling she genuinely didn't know Marcus Fairmont, perhaps she doesn't know the whole Ella story."

"Fairmont still there?"

"Yep. He's an easy tail. From home to work, with a quick stop in between to sample his latest flavor, a twenty-four year old waitress named Chloe. Good Doctor Theo is interesting though. I discovered the doc has two files for Ella and her mother. The office file and the home file and since the bastard doesn't have a clue about home security, I was able to have a thorough peek. Seems Doctor Theo has been a longtime friend of Marcus Fairmont, even saw him as a patient fifteen years ago. Our Marcus has some deep fucked up issues, Sarge. Goes all the way back to his own father who beat the shit out of him on a regular basis and a mother who apparently had a never ending supply of men who frequented the home while hubby was working. You'll never believe this, Mrs. Fairmont senior committed suicide, cut her wrists." I groaned, caught somewhere between disbelief and horror.

"I get the feeling Doctor Theo doesn't completely trust Fairmont and is keeping this second set of files, the real files, as his back up. All Ella's claims of abuse are documented in there as well as the apparent suicide. Theo goes as far as to state he believed Ella's claims, even states that he believes Fairmont was entirely capable of cutting her wrists. He's got video footage of all of their sessions and in many you can clearly see the bruises." I suddenly needed to pound something again.

"Son of a bitch believed her and left her with that fucker?" I roared.

"Doctor Theo is well paid, Jax, better than your average psychiatrist. He's fucking loaded and I have no doubt if I dug through his finances, I'd find a trail leading right back to Fairmont or something illegal."

"Then dig. This is good stuff, Dillon. This is the sort of stuff that will put the fucker away for a very long time."

"The devil himself couldn't stop me now, Jax. We're onto something big here and I'm gonna see it through."

"Call me when you have something else." With the conversation ended I was far too wound up to sleep. Beth had the first shift and I collapsed restlessly onto the couch in Mercy's office. I found myself staring at Ella's phone number. My fingers moved across the keys as if controlled by a force outside of my own influence.

JAX: Please don't run, Angel. Trust me. I made you a promise and I won't break it.

There was no reply, but I wasn't really expecting one. I threw the phone to one side and tried in vain to get some sleep. Come morning I needed to find Ella and I would turn the town upside down to do so. ☐

CHAPTER 27

Ella

I woke before the sun had risen, my mind pulled from a deep slumber by the horror that this day brought with it. I don't think even death itself could contain my grief. I wanted to cry, I needed to cry. I needed to scream at the heavens over the injustice of it all. Him up there, He took my dad, He stole him and left me alone, defenseless and today I hated Him for it. Tomorrow I would find forgiveness again, but today I would allow the hate to consume me, but the damned tears would still not come. I dragged the sketch book and charcoal Jax had bought me onto my lap and began to draw. It was the same picture, the same pose, over and over every year on the same day. I was so scared of forgetting what my dad looked like that on the anniversary of his death, every year, I forced myself to confront my heartache and sketch my dad just as I remembered him. His eyes were identical to mine, dark brown and slightly slanted with the Asian ancestry that laced our family tree. His hair was black, like the night sky, and dead straight and he wore it long to his shoulders, sometimes tied at the nape of his neck. In my picture it was out, like a warrior of old—I loved it. His cheek bones were high like mine, his lips not quite as full. His nose was straight and the lines around his eyes and mouth revealed the truth, this man laughed a lot. Not with my mother of course. He tried, he did everything he could to make that woman happy, but only with me did true happiness seem to find him. I remembered everything about my dad. I remembered the stories he told me before bed, I remember the pancakes he greeted me with every day. He worked so hard, but somehow he never missed a thing. Every swim meet, dance recital, parent teacher night, everything, he was there for it all until that day—Thanksgiving ten years ago. I remember waking him with the huge box of decorations and we began decorating the tree and house.

He didn't look well, he looked tired but he didn't stop for even a moment. He lifted me to put the angel on the top of the tree, we hung the wreath on the door, then he moved to the kitchen to make us lunch. That's where it stopped, where my life as I knew it ended. It was likely one of the reasons I hated cooking. The kitchen was the place where I had lost my dad. With the sketch finished I sat and stared at it for a long time and eventually found the strength to carefully fold the picture and stuff it to the bottom of my backpack, where the other pictures of him were folded and crammed away like the painful memory they were.

I sat and stared at the wall for a long time. I couldn't bring myself to eat or drink. A part of me screamed for Jax, for the strength and warmth he was filled with, for the strength and warmth he filled me with. Another part of me hated the pain he was going to put me through tonight. I knew it was selfish of me, Mercy's was above anything Jax and I might have represented. I had no idea if Selena had been telling the truth about the post ball celebrations she claimed her and Jax had planned. A small part of me saw the lie for what it was, but another part of me, the insecure woman inside of me, wondered if there were any truth to her words. Perhaps Jax had realized after spending some time with me that the road to be travelled was just going to be too hard, filled with too many bumps. I wasn't attractive like Selena, I wasn't perfect like her. Perhaps in the week we had been apart it reminded him how easy it was to be with Selena, no strings, just plenty of back scratching. The thought of Jax with Selena intimately made my stomach roll. I glanced at the red digital numbers on the clock beside the bed. It was already after four p.m. I had spent the entire day alone, in bed, staring at a wall feeling sorry for myself. It was time to clear the grief and funk from my head, starting with a scorching shower.

Before I left for Annie and Eli's, I turned on my phone to check for messages. There was one text from Jax; I deleted it before I crumbled and read it. There were several missed calls from him too, along with one from Rebecca. I tucked the phone into my back pocket and left the motel. The sky was dark gray, snow fell in a light flurry around me. Pulling my scarf tightly around my neck I made my way to Annie's.

"Are you okay?" Were the first words out of her mouth and I put on my best forced smile. I didn't want her to worry about leaving Eli with me.

"I'm fine Annie, I stayed at a motel. Where's Eli?" She shut the door behind me.

"He's taking a bath. Have you seen Jax?" I shook my head and threw my bag down on the couch.

"No, I haven't."

"He's desperate to get a hold of you. I promised I would call him as soon as I spoke to you." I shook my head at that.

"Please Annie, not tonight. I'll call him tomorrow, okay?" She grabbed her coat and shouldered her way into it.

"Let's talk about this later. I need to get to work. Thanks for watching him tonight, I know it's Thanksgiving and all but the pay for working tonight was just too good to refuse."

"It's not a problem, Annie. I love hanging out with Eli and I didn't have any plans anyway." Annie pulled me into a hug.

"There's some leftover turkey in the fridge. Eli and I had a small party for lunch. You would have been here for it if I could have gotten a hold of you. What did you do, throw out your phone?" I pulled it out and waved it before her.

"Sorry, it's been turned off. It's on now, so if you need anything just holler." Satisfied, Annie left for work and I dragged Eli's thoroughly wrinkled body from the warmth of his bath.

As we sat reading in the lounge room, Christmas carols played from the small stereo in the background. It was quiet and cozy, reminding me of the many peaceful nights I got to spend with my dad, reading tales of princes and princesses and long lost kingdoms. A loud thumping at the door made both Eli and I jump, interrupting the reverent moment.

"Annie, let me the fuck in, I know you're in there!" an unfamiliar voice roared. I was frozen in place as Eli's little hands gripped my arm.

"Daddy?" he whimpered, his eyes wide with fear, his quiet cry little more than a breath off his lips. Bang. Bang. Bang. The door shook with the force of his pounding.

"Open this fucking door or I swear to God I will break it down!"

"Shit," I breathed heavily, panic threatening to consume me. More banging broke my immobile state and I turned to look at Eli. He was terrified, his eyes wide and in shock. I had to hold myself together for Eli. With a long, deep calming breath I stood and dragged Eli by his hand down the hallway and into his room. I hesitated a moment and turned back to face the bathroom. If Phillip got into the apartment and went looking for Eli, his bedroom would be the first place he checked. The banging on the door grew more forceful and Eli cried quietly behind me as I pulled him into the bathroom. I swung open the cabinet under the sink and pulled out the clean towels, throwing them into the tub beside me.

"Get in," I whispered. Eli hesitated. It was a small space and once I closed the door it would be dark.

"Here," I pulled out my phone and handed it to him. "You can use it as a light. Get in." Eli pulled his knees up to his chest and tucked down his head as he sat in the small space. "Look at me little man." His frightened eyes found mine. "I need you to be a big brave boy and call the police. You know the numbers right?" He nodded. "Good, boy. Tell them the address, tell them to come quickly. You stay right here and don't make a sound til I come get you, got it?" His nod was hesitant. "Promise me, Eli, not a sound. You stay put and you stay still and quiet, no matter what." He nodded and I quickly kissed his brow before closing the door and racing back into the living room. The door splintered apart as an enormous brute of a man stood panting, his eyes dilated and simmering in complete rage.

"Who the hell are you?" I demanded of him, the strength in my words a lie.

"Where's Annie? Where's Eli? Where the fuck is my boy?" he roared moving towards me. I stood my ground. I learned with Marcus that cowering only seemed to excite him, standing tall and proud pissed him off, but also turned him off.

"Annie is at work, Eli is with a friend. I'm Annie's roommate, Ella." I couldn't lie about the apartment not being Annie's place, the photos of Eli on the fridge gave it away instantly.

"Call him. I want him here with me in the next five minutes or I swear to God I will fucking knock you into next week." I slowly nodded.

"I don't have a phone. If you have a phone, I will call him

right now." He slid the phone from his pocket and handed it to me.

"Let me see the number you're dialing, I want to make sure you're not calling the police." I held the phone out with trembling fingers and dialed the only number I could think of, Jax. The phone rang once, twice, three times. Please answer Jax, I quietly prayed. I knew he would be at the ball and this would likely ruin his night, but right now, in this moment, I really didn't give a shit.

"Hello?" I almost whimpered at the sound of his deep strong voice.

"Hey, it's me, Ella. Can you bring Eli home? There is someone here to see him." Jax was quiet for a moment.

"Angel, what's going on? Whose number is this?"

"I know it's late and he's probably supposed to be in bed, but it's kind of important."

"Put it on speaker," growled Phillip in front of me.

"Fuck, Angel, who is that?" I pulled the phone away and put it on speaker.

"Hey, yeah, so could you get Mary to wake him up and bring him home? Annie's not home yet, but she won't be far away." There was a short pause.

"Sure, Ella, I'll have Mary bring him round now. Everything okay?"

"Yeah, all good." Phillip's eyes drilled into mine with unforgiving anger.

"I have to go. Thanks for that, just be sure to bring him straight here."

"Mary's on her way now." Phillip grabbed his phone and disconnected the call. His eyes suddenly appraised me, looking me up and down, then searching my eyes as if looking for something more.

"He's on his way, but I can assure you, when he sees that door and you all freaked out, he's gonna be scared shitless." Without warning Phillip backhanded me and I hit the wall, my cheek screaming with pain. I touched the spot where his hand had connected with me and turned to face him, no tears, no terror, just pure hatred and rage.

"And that's not going to fucking help you either," I spat.

When he moved to hit me again I ducked and his fist connected with the plaster wall. I moved behind the couch, putting both distance and an object between us. He stalked me across the room and I kept moving, keeping distance between us, but always keeping my body between him and Eli. "You need to settle down," I suggested.

"She took my fucking son away from me," he growled. Then he lunged. His movements were faster than I had expected as he jumped over a chair and backed me into the wall. His hand reached for me and wrapped around my neck. His eyes regarded mine as he began to squeeze. For a moment, my brain scrambled, then something clicked and I remembered Jax showing me how easily I could take down an attacker. I raised my knee and found Phillips groin. He grunted and his grip loosened but he continued to push his body hard against mine, not giving me room to kick. As dark spots began to swim in my vision I reached up and pressed my fingers into his eye sockets. With a scream he finally let me go. The roar from the doorway behind us registered as I slid down the wall into a wilted heap.

CHAPTER 28

Jax

I had never driven my Dodge so fast over ice, I literally slid around the corners. As I approached Annie's apartment, I could hear the distant sirens. I had been searching for Ella all day. She had seemingly vanished without a trace. I didn't know whose number she had called from, but I didn't miss the ice in her voice. She masked her terror behind that frightening indifference she was a pro at. I knew that coldness meant she was one of two things; she was either upset or frightened. The confusing call confirmed the later and I quickly put two and two together. Annie's husband, Phillip, had come looking for her and Eli and Ella was caught in the crossfire. I jumped from my truck not even bothering to shut the door. I simply ran taking the stairs two, three at a time. I slowed as I approached the obviously shattered door to Annie's apartment and listened. I had to control myself, Ella and Eli's lives depended on it. I could hear a man's voice, his words low and threatening. I peered around the corner and saw a large man holding Ella by her throat, his body forcing her against the wall. Ella reached up and sunk her fingers into his face and in a fury he let her go and I just snapped.

Moving into the room I grabbed Phillip by the shoulder. He turned and swung blindly, his fist connecting with my jaw. The next punch I easily ducked around and my own fist connected with a sickening crack in Phillips face, blood spurting from his nose like a faucet. He stumbled backwards and Ella scrambled to get out of the line of fire. I didn't stop, I raised my fist and I hit him again and again. Somewhere he found the energy to slip in another quick jab and it connected with my eye, but I barely felt it. I punched him once more, twice and he fell to the floor as the police yelled from the doorway for me to put my hands up.

"It's me, Frank," I called over my shoulder, knowing very well that Frank Brisard was back there with his gun trained on my back. I looked down at Phillip for a moment making sure he didn't move, if the fucker did I would put him to sleep permanently. He was out cold, the slow ragged rising of his chest the only indication I hadn't already killed him.

"Fuck, Jax, what the hell is going on?" Frank demanded.

"This is Phillip Longergan. He has schizophrenia and is currently off his meds. His wife, Annie, and son, Eli, have been in the shelter up until two weeks ago when they moved in here. I only just got here but I assume he came looking for them."

"Is that Annie?" Frank asked as he approached the scene slowly. My eyes fell to Ella who looked up at me, fear bleached into her features. The way she looked at me would haunt me til my dying days. She was terrified and after the violence she just witnessed it was most likely of me.

"Angel," I whispered as I sunk to my knees in front of her. Her eyes wide with shock took me in, then as if in slow motion she moved forward and crawled into my lap, her arms wrapping tightly around my neck as I squeezed her body to mine.

"Don't let me go," she moaned. "Don't let me go, don't let me go," her quiet mantra echoed in my ears.

"Never, Angel," I murmured back, running my fingers through her hair.

"This is Ella. Annie is at work," I said to Frank, my voice stiff as emotion choked my throat.

"Where's the boy?" Frank finally asked. Ella suddenly scrambled from my lap and ran across the room. I followed her into the bathroom as she collapsed onto the floor in front of the vanity. She pulled the doors open and Eli, as white as a sheet, stared up at her. She grabbed him out of the small space and hugged him close. I knelt beside them both and wrapped them in my arms.

"The call for help came through from the boy," Frank spoke gently from behind me. "How do I get a hold of his mother?" Somehow I managed to disentangle myself from Ella and Eli long enough to reach for my phone. By the time I moved them into Eli's bedroom, Annie burst into the apartment, her face laced with tears.

"Eli!" she screamed. She raced through the bedroom door and saw Ella holding him protectively. Her face bruised, her neck red and sore, but not a single tear had spilled. She moved forward to hand Eli to Annie.

"I'm so sorry," Annie sobbed.

"No, Annie, this isn't on you, it's on him. I'm fine, Eli's fine." Annie nodded as she clutched Eli to her chest. She pulled Ella forward and kissed her forehead.

"Thank you," she murmured. "Thank you for protecting him." Annie's tears broke my heart, Ella's lack of tears hurt more. Ella turned back to me and I took her into my arms, holding her close.

"Where's your tux?" she said with a muffled voice into my chest. I bowed my head forward slightly closing the distance between us and kissed her forehead. She was so small, so fragile and I had almost lost her.

"If you had of answered your phone just once I could have explained." She tried to pull away but I refused to let her go. "David took Selena to the ball." I wanted to tell her everything—how much she meant to me, how not seeing her for the last week had almost killed me, how I had found my peace with Sarah. Seeing her only a short time ago in the hands of Phillip had fired a rage in me and holding Ella now was the only thing that would douse the fury. "Fuck, seeing his hands on you, I wanted to kill him, Angel." She nodded, her arms holding me tight.

"Jax, we've taken Phillip to the hospital. He has guards on him. Would your girl there be able to answer a few questions tonight?" I glanced up.

"Tomorrow?" I suggested. Ella shook her head though.

"No, tonight is fine. I'd prefer to get it over with." Annie sat rocking Eli whose sobs had softened. Ella leaned forward and ran her fingers through his soft brown curls.

"You did good, little man, I'm very proud of you," she said with a smile. Eli's big blue eyes blinked up at her.

"He hurt you," Eli gently cried.

"Not really, Eli, it didn't hurt much and now he's going to be taken away and get the help he needs. He won't be able to hurt you or your mom ever again." Eli looked worried.

"What about you? Will he hurt you again?" Ella smiled and shook her head.

"She's got me to protect her, buddy." I glanced over Ella's shoulder. Eli smiled, apparently satisfied. "Might have to find that cape after all," I joked and he managed another smile before I led Ella from the bedroom and down the short hallway.

In the living room, Frank hovered awkwardly. He was fifty-five and ready to retire, but for some reason Frank couldn't seem to part with active duty on the police force. He stayed fit, gray hairs dotted his dark brown hair, the only sign that this man actually had two grandchildren. He turned to face us with a kind smile taking in Ella who clung to my hand, her grip a tight vice that spoke volumes. She wasn't about to let me go and I was more than happy with that.

"Do you mind telling me what happened here, Ella?" Frank asked. I pulled Ella down beside me on the couch. She nervously tucked her hair behind her ears, she wasn't hiding right now and she wanted Frank to know that, to know she was telling the truth and that she stood up to this bastard. As she recounted the evening, Frank listened intently, taking notes. My hand gripped hers in what was no doubt a punishing grip as she explained how she hid Eli in the bathroom cupboard, how she confronted Phillip, how he hit her and held her against the wall, his large hands wrapped around her tiny throat. The marks of his fingers were evidence on her neck and Frank took some pictures. He also noted the bruise beginning to form on her cheek. When Ella was finished she glanced at the destruction around her, the door was splintered off its hinges and the room was a mess. From the doorway another uniform called to someone outside the room.

"Hey, Tom, come help me with this door, see if we can't do something with it until morning." Frank stood and I joined him, shaking his hand gratefully.

"I'll call you tomorrow, Jax. I'll leave my boys here to secure the scene. Maybe you can do something about the door?" I nodded as Frank made his way out of the room, passing a tall, gangly looking cop with a scowl on his bird like face. Ella stood beside me and I glanced down at her.

"I'll call Charlie, have him come over and fix that now. Annie and Eli will be safe here, but I want you to come home with me, Angel. I need it. Beth was organizing a volunteer to cover my shift as I left, so I'm not needed at the shelter. Tonight scared the crap out of me and I need you close by." She simply nodded, her attention moving back to the officers who struggled with the smashed door. As I reached for the phone in my back pocket I felt Ella go tense beside me. Her nails dug into the skin on the back of my hand. I glanced at her and followed her gaze to the tall thin officer at the doorway. He stared back at her, his mouth agape.

"Ella?" he murmured. Ella was pale, her breathing quickly becoming labored as she descended into a full blown panic attack.

CHAPTER 29

Ella

Having Jax right by my side had helped me keep calm, even with the police presence, which always made me nervous. I knew not all police were bad, but the fact Marcus had one on his payroll scared the crap out of me. In a moment of sheer terror and blinding rage, something completely right had happened. Jax had saved me, he had dragged Phillip off me and beaten him senseless. I had crawled into his lap and begged him never to let me go and he said he wouldn't, not ever. When Jax told me he had sent David to the ball in his place, my heart had leapt for joy. Man, what I would have given to have seen Selena's face when he dropped that bombshell on her. Then when he confessed he needed me to come home with him, I wanted to wrap my arms and legs around him and never let him go. Seeing Tom Brennan standing in the doorway, in uniform, was a slap in the face. I was truly cursed. Could not a single good thing happen to me without something shitty following it? My life seemed to be falling into a pattern. Something amazing would happen, followed quickly by something completely fucked up. It was unfair and I wanted to whine like a petulant kid, but as I saw Tom standing there I was drowned in a sea of memories. Tom was always there. He helped make the drug charges go away for Marcus. He dragged me from the back seats of cars kicking and screaming, he saw the bruises and smirked like the vulgar animal he was. It was Tom who found me and returned me to Marcus the first time I ran away, now he was here, no doubt, prepared to return me to him one more time. My mind was seized by panic and my lungs gasped for air.

"Fuck, Angel, deep breaths. Come on baby come back to me." I was on the ground, my head in Jax's lap as he whispered words to bring me out of the attack.

"I knew her in Duntson; she has an active missing persons file." I could hear Tom somewhere in the room and his voice sent me spiraling into another panic attack.

"For fucks sake, will you get him the fuck out of here?" Jax roared. My hand gripped his helping to anchor me to the present. I took long deep breaths, my eyes finding Jax's hovering above me. Those steel gray eyes demanded my compliance.

"Good girl, concentrate on your breathing, let the past go," he whispered. It didn't take long before the panic attack had fully subsided and I glanced around the room. Tom had gone and I wondered if he had even been here at all. Highway to Hell played from the floor somewhere close by and Jax grabbed the phone.

"Charlie, I need you at Annie's, the door is busted. You'll find something in the shop, it needs to be fixed tonight. It needs to be secure." He listened to something Charlie said.

"No, no, everything's fine now. Just get over here and fix it up for me please. I have to take care of Ella, she's been hurt." My fingers rose to the ache in my cheek but Jax stopped them, cupping my bruised cheek with his hand.

"She'll be fine, I just want to get her home. Annie will explain everything. There is a uniform on the door until it's fixed. Maybe check with Annie, she might like you to stay for the night, you can bunk on the couch."

Jax ended the call and helped me to sit. His eyes searched the room til they found my backpack and he slung it over his shoulder.

"Annie," he called. She appeared at the end of the hallway, her eyes tired and still full of tears. "Charlie is coming, he's going to fix the door and he'll stay with you tonight."
Annie went to protest, but Jax stopped her. "Annie, he wants to, he wants to help and Charlie can keep you safe. It will be comforting for you to know someone is here and you know Charlie, I know you trust him. Just make sure you feed him breakfast and you will have him wrapped around your little finger." A small smile played at her solemn lips.

"I don't know how to thank you, Jax," she murmured and he pulled her into a reassuring embrace.

"You don't have to thank me, Annie, it's what friends do, look out for each other. I'm taking Ella to my place tonight, we'll check in on you and Eli tomorrow." I stood on my unsteady legs until Jax swept me up into his arms.

"Jax, my legs aren't broken, I can walk," I murmured.

"I don't care either way, this makes me happy and after the week I've had, after the night I've had, I need happy." I didn't argue, truth be told I loved it when he carried me. I felt like I was being held in a fortress of impenetrable steel. Nothing could hurt me here and it was the closest to home I had felt in a long time.

***

Somehow I managed to doze during the journey from Annie's to Jax's. He lived out of town, surrounded by tall, impressive firs, the houses scattered few and far between. I had never lived outside of a city and for some reason the thought occurred that I should feel isolated and scared, but of course I didn't. The further we got from town, the safer I actually felt. The short drive through thick forest brought us to Jax's house. It was dark and difficult to make out, but I could see it was a log cabin and the porch light was on. Jax used a remote from inside his car to open a garage door and when the car finally came to a stop, he jumped out and strode around to my door before I could even reach for the handle. With my backpack over his shoulder, he scooped me up again and made his way into his home.

I wanted to look around, take in my surroundings, but the warmth of Jax's arms drew me in and I nestled my head in the crook of his neck. He carried me effortlessly up a staircase and I felt myself being lowered to a bed. Once he had seated me I finally looked around. We were on the second floor of the cabin and Jax's bedroom occupied the entire area. His bed was a massive feature against the far wall and in front was a sturdy wooden handrail that contained the space and looked out over the floor below. The slanted roof with exposed beams reached high above us. To my left was a doorway and Jax switched on the light for the room beyond, a bathroom in which Jax disappeared into. To the right was another doorway to what looked like an enormous walk in closet.

Jax appeared back before me. "I'd offer you the grand tour but I think you've had enough excitement for one night." He smiled. "I've laid out a fresh towel for you. Help yourself to anything, what's mine is yours." He dropped my backpack on the floor beside the bed. "Did you eat tonight?" I shook my head. I had barely eaten for the last week, my body had been demanding something other than food and now he stood before me, my protector, my guardian. "You've lost weight, you were already small enough. If you lose anymore, you'll disappear." I shrugged.

"I guess I've had a tough week. I haven't really been all that hungry." Jax sighed and shook his head.

"I did that to you." His words were full of regret and pain.

"No, Jax." I stood to protest but he stopped me.

"Please, take a shower Ella, get warm. I'll get you something to eat; I've got some frozen meals Mary had made up for me so you don't have to worry about me poisoning you." He smiled and my knees became weak at the sight. "Let me take care of you, please." How could I refuse? The answer was I couldn't. I wanted him to take care of me just as much as he wanted to. I nodded and Jax took the few short steps to meet me. With one hand firmly behind my neck he pulled me close and pressed his lips to my forehead, holding me there, secure and safe. Then he abruptly pulled away and moved to the lower floor of the loft.

The bathroom was spectacular, with an enormous double shower which made me question why and who else had shared the space with him. That line of thought just pissed me off. With my always imperative collection of toiletries, I washed my body and hair, grabbed a disposable razor and did some quick landscaping and finally allowed the hot water to soak my tired and aching limbs. I was petrified of what had happened tonight, not with Phillip, but Tom. He was here, he knew I was here and no doubt had already told Marcus. I needed to leave Claymont, but the thought of leaving filled me with the worse kind of dread. Never seeing Jax again hurt. I didn't even think I could bring myself to leave. Jax had protected me tonight, he had saved me and that feeling of protection had me wondering if perhaps he could indeed save me from Marcus if he had to. Glancing at my naked reflection in the mirror I took in the nasty bruise on my cheek. I had had worse. The imprint of fingers around my neck was a new one. Marcus had never tried to choke me. It looked ugly and my throat felt raw. The dark rings under my eyes had resettled into position, my face pale.

The scars on my arms somehow seemed more obvious under the bright lights of Jax's bathroom. I sighed. I simply couldn't imagine Jax wanting this beaten body, but I also knew I couldn't do this to myself anymore. All this negativity and dislike for myself was started by Marcus. It was time to cleanse him from my system. Jax was here with me now. Tonight I saw the entire truth in his eyes, the panic, the fear, the pain, the desire and the love. He didn't care if I was too thin, or not thin enough. He didn't see my scars as ugly, he didn't want my face hidden behind layers of makeup. Jax wanted me as I was—broken, flawed and honest. And never before had I been so utterly consumed and owned as I was by Jax.

CHAPTER 30

Jax

As soon as I heard the shower start up, I made for my office and called Dillon. I needed to know who the hell Tom Brennan was. From Ella's response to him, I was convinced the bastard had some sort of involvement with her step-father. Tom admitted he knew Ella from Dunston, that she was a troubled teen whom he had arrested on more than one occasion. During my conversation with Dillon, he told me he had hired someone on to help him watch Fairmont, and ordinarily, I would have cursed up a blue storm, but I knew watching Fairmont and digging at the same time was impossible. The fact he had entrusted the task of the surveillance to his cousin, Braiden, to help gave me some resemblance of reassurance. Braiden worked for Dillon and was damned good at his job. I had no doubt he would stay glued to Fairmont. Being a former PI, he was used to unrewarding stake outs, long nights and veins running brown with caffeine. Once I'd finished talking with Dillon, I made my way to the kitchen only to be confronted with the mess that was once my guitar displaying my inglorious break down on the living room floor. I tossed the guitar in the fire place for now and swept up the remains into a dustpan. The empty bottle of whiskey got promptly thrown into the garbage and I grabbed the first frozen dinner my hand landed on, some sort of chicken and rice dish. I made Ella a cup of hot chocolate and poured the freshly microwaved dinner onto a plate, grabbed some painkillers, then headed back upstairs. The shower had been off a while but the door was still closed. I placed the food and steaming mug of cocoa on the side table and sat on the side of the bed waiting, my foot beating an anxious cadence on the carpeted floor. Now that I had stopped moving, my body quickly came down from the adrenaline that had fired every cylinder since Ella's phone call some hours ago now. I pulled off my sweater and threw it on the floor. Tugging at the laces of my boots I dragged them off and tucked them under the side of the bed so that Ella wouldn't trip over them. Once I had her fed and safely tucked away in my bed I would sleep on the sofa. Hell, I'd slept there last night quite comfortably. It would be no hardship and knowing Ella was safe and sound in my house where I could keep an eye on her, protect her, I might finally get some decent sleep.

The bathroom door opened and Ella stepped out. My heart hammered in my chest, my mouth was suddenly drier than the Sahara. She wore a pair of flannel bottoms hanging loosely around her small hips and a tight little camisole, with quite obviously, no bra underneath. Her hair was brushed smooth and hung still slightly damp over her shoulders, her bare feet whispered across the carpet as she sat down beside me. I breathed in the gentle mixture of the ocean and coconut that was distinctly my Ella.

"Here," I somehow managed to say. I handed her two headache tablets and she took them without question. She still appeared to be in shock, her body operating in a monotone mechanical manner. I slipped her phone out of my back pocket and placed it on the bedside table. "I've turned it down, not off," I explained bringing the plate of food back. She took it and began to eat without question, finally sighing, her body sagging with exhaustion.

"This is really good. We should ask Mary if she wouldn't mind giving us some cooking lessons." I smiled thinking of my failed lesson the night before.
"I ruined the spaghetti sauce last night at the shelter. I don't know if Mary will let me back in her kitchen."
A small smile tugged at the corner of Ella's lips, threatening to break the solemn expression that had settled on her angelic features.

"Did you eat tonight?" she asked as I watched her eat like a deranged voyeur with a food fetish. I loved watching her eat though. She wasn't like most women who ate small portions of salad and dry nuts like some sort of woodland creature. Ella ate real food with passion, not afraid of where the calories might settle, simply enjoying the taste. I hadn't eaten, I didn't know if I could. Ella stabbed a piece of chicken along with some carrot, held it to her lips and blew gently. My dick began to harden which made me question the weird food fetish thought. She then held it out for me and I gladly accepted. It was either the best chicken I had tasted in my life or I was a starved man. We ate the meal like that, one mouthful for her, one for me until the plate was clean. As Ella rested against the headboard of my bed, the hot chocolate wrapped around her small hands I turned to face her.

"We need to talk, Ella." She took a sip and watched me from over the top of the mug.

"When you call me Ella I know it's serious," she sighed, "I agree, we need to talk but I'm kind of emotionally drained tonight. Let's keep it light and we can do the heavy stuff tomorrow." I grinned and rubbed my aching neck.

"Do you really think there is any conversation between us that won't be heavy?" Ella shook her head.

"No, but I can't deal with it right now, so perhaps we should talk about something else, like, how 'bout those Yankees last weekend?" I laughed at her attempt at what some might call a normal conversation.
"Are you even into sports?"

"Actually, I am. My dad loved sports—baseball, basketball, football, hockey, you name it. He took me to all kinds of sporting events and I actually loved it. Even if I didn't know what was happening, the crazy atmosphere and the noise was a thrill." She sighed. "I guess that would freak me out now." Her smile was lost, replaced with despair that was so heavy I couldn't understand how she didn't drown in it.

"I'm sorry you lost your dad, Angel. Neither he nor you deserved that. I know today is the anniversary of his death, I wish you hadn't had to go through that alone." She looked at me with questioning eyes.
"Dillon told me," I admitted.

"It never used to matter whether I was alone or not, it hurt just as bad. Thanksgiving has always been a private day for me but for some reason this year, I thought if you had of been there, it might not have hurt quite as much." I again wanted to punch myself for fucking everything up a week ago. "Can I show you something?" she asked as I silently cursed myself for being such a dick. I nodded and she climbed off the bed and rummaged around that big backpack of hers. Finally she stood and crawled onto the bed beside me, her hands filled with what looked like sketches. She opened them, one by one, four in all,

all exactly the same.

"This is what I do every year on Thanksgiving. Every year it's the same. I wake up and my chest hurts so bad it feels like I'm having a heart attack, like someone is crushing me from the inside out. I try to cry, I think if I could just get the tears out I will feel better, like purging the grief from my system, but they won't come. My stupid fucking tears only come when people are kind to me. Sorrow, anger, pain, I cope with it differently, my body just kind of shuts down." She picks up one of the sketches and runs her hand over the eyes. They are exactly like hers.

"I draw him because I don't have any pictures. I had one picture that Mother allowed me and Marcus took it from me. I'm scared I will forget what he looks like, so I draw him. I had to leave Marcus's house in a hurry, I didn't take anything so all the other sketches were left there. Before you, before the sketch pad and charcoal you bought me, these were the only sketches I had done since leaving Dunston." I thumbed through the pictures admiring her perfect work.

"They're beautiful, Angel. You look just like him." She smiled at that. I knew right then I should tell her about her mother's death but the words wouldn't come. She had said she couldn't do heavy and emotional tonight, so maybe it was best the words remained stuck in my cowardice. I carefully folded the sketches and gave them back to her. She looked nervous as she stuffed them carefully back in her bag and sat back down beside me, rubbing the scars on her arms in what I was now coming to recognize as a soothing action.

"You should try and get some sleep, I want you to have the bed, I've got an office downstairs with a fold out sofa bed and the couch is enormous. Custom built for me to pass out on, so I'll sleep down there." I stood but she made no move to get under the covers. "Come on, I'll tuck you in." I held my hand out and she took it, but still didn't move. Slowly she raised my hand to her face and rubbed the cheek that wasn't bruised across the back of my fingers.

"Please don't go. I don't want to be alone," Ella whispered. When she looked up at me her eyes were filled with so much need that there was no way I could say no.

198

"You only had to ask, Angel," I murmured, cupping her cheek. She leaned into my touch like a cat starved of affection. I slowly sunk to my knees and raised my other hand to her bruised cheek, cupping it gently as I placed my lips over hers. I tried to put every thought, feeling and emotion into that kiss, I tried to absorb her very essence into me. Our tongues gently explored each other as my hands held her head steady, her hands gripping my wrists with such exquisite demand. When we finally parted, both of us were breathing with sweet, unrestrained abandon.

"I want you so bad, Jax. Take me away from all of this, make me feel beautiful."

I searched those sad eyes and it broke my heart that she needed someone to make her feel beautiful. She was the most perfect creature I had ever encountered, but Marcus had obviously beaten all self-worth from this angel. I was given no chance to respond as she pulled me forward by my shirt. Wiggling back onto the bed she drew me with her and I gladly lowered myself onto her precious body.

CHAPTER 31

Ella

    Part of me was terrified that Jax would push me away. He had been so slow and gentle with me prior to the night of the tree lighting, when all I had wanted was his raw male heat and passion. I had been watching his eyes carefully since coming out of the bathroom and I had observed every look of longing and need. He wanted this as much as I did and as his mouth pushed hard against mine, as his tongue explored my mouth, I knew I was done for as far as Jax was concerned. I could never leave him and he would never allow it anyway. I was his and he was mine, it was that simple.

    Jax nipped my lower lip and led a trail of kisses to my battered cheek, across my closed eye lids and to the other side of my face where my scar echoed the memories of my previous battles. His kisses continued down my jaw and to the sensitive line of my neck where fresh marks stained my skin. He kissed them tenderly before finding a path that led to my arm. I tensed when he reached the first of my scars there, the spot where hate had found its way into my soul, where I had weakened and attempted to cut the revolt from my body. He began kissing the marks on my skin, kissing the parts of me that weren't beautiful, that not only maimed my skin but branded my spirit and with every single touch it felt as though he was fixing me, replacing the ugly with something beautiful, making me whole again. Once he was finished on one arm, he crossed my body and began on the other. After what seemed like an eternity, he pressed his lips to my chest. My fingers gripped at his long blonde hair as his hands crept up under my camisole, his scorching fingers slipping across my ribs and ever so slowly to where I needed them most, but he didn't touch me there yet. Instead he pushed up my top and I raised my arms, letting him draw the thin fabric from my body. Then finally, blissfully, one of his hands cupped my breast as his lips found the other. Slow licks and demanding tugs on my nipples created an unrelenting hunger which began in my stomach and ended up at the throbbing center between my legs. The central loving station, as Rebecca had fondly renamed it. I would have laughed at that thought had Jax not lowered his hand under my pajama bottoms right at that moment. He pushed with determination past the barrier of my panties and slipped his fingers straight into my sopping wet core. There was no preamble with his movements, he was like a man on a mission and, fuck, I loved it. It had been so long since I had been touched intimately and even then it was wrong. There had been no passion, or fire, just disorderly and awkward touches with a quick and unsatisfying ending. With Jax's mouth capturing my nipple and his fingers relentlessly exploring my core I knew this encounter would end with me being deeply and thoroughly satisfied. I grabbed his shirt trying to pull it from his body, I needed his skin on mine I wanted no barriers between us. Much to my horror he left my body to give in to my demands, pulling his shirt off, then proceeding to shuck his jeans over his hips. He stood before me, his smile seductive, his eyes hungry as they took me in. His shoulders were heavenly and wide, chest carved like a marble statue and a rippling stomach that ended with the magic V that led to every woman's wildest dreams. I almost blanched at the sight of his impressive cock. It was huge, like the man himself. A small sensation similar to fear crept into my mind wondering if Jax inside me might actually hurt. It had been a long time for me and I even wondered if it were possible that I had somehow become a virgin again during the many years of my abstinence. I scoffed at that ridiculous idea and lifted my hips as Jax hooked his fingers into my pajama bottoms and began to slowly undress me.

Any fear quickly disappeared under his adoring gaze. He took his time, kissing my hip bone, my thigh, my knee and eventually the inside of my ankle. He came back for my panties, his fingers tracing lazy circles over my skin that drove me utterly insane.

"If you don't hurry I might nod off up here," I quietly teased. Jax's sinful grin and sparkling eyes told me he knew perfectly well there would be no nodding off while his hands were on my body. He did comply though, swiftly removing my panties. His rough hands slid up the outside of my legs until his face drew level with my hips, then without taking his eyes off me, he lowered his lips to mine, and not the ones on my face. No one had ever touched me like this before and part of me was mortified, but the feeling of Jax's tongue tenderly caressing my core consumed me with a lust that had no room for inhibitions. My hips now had a mind of their own as they thrust against his face. Jax devoured me like a man possessed and when he pulled away, far too soon, I actually moaned in outrage. Jax chuckled and snaked a path up my body, stopping briefly to kiss my breasts.

"I'm greedy, Angel, I want to be in you when you come for me the first time. Next time it will be around my tongue," he growled wickedly in my ear. He reached for the bedside table and produced a condom, covering himself so quick I barely realized he had stopped touching me to do so. He positioned himself at my core and gently nudged my wet lips, pushing forward to find my entrance. He kissed me again and I could taste myself on his lips, I blushed remembering the wickedness in the way he had just devoured me. I grabbed his firm ass and encouraged him to move forward. With long demanding strokes, he gradually entered me. He groaned in my ear and shook with the effort it took to control himself.

Once finally seated deep inside he stilled giving my body time to adjust to the somewhat foreign intrusion. He rose above me on his forearms and took in every inch of my face.

"So beautiful," he breathed, his words laced with awe. Jax placed a lingering chaste kiss on my forehead before he began to move. My eyes rolled back and my lids floated closed as I hovered in what felt like another dimension, a place where nothing existed except me, Jax and this bed. I quickly grew bold and wrapped my legs around his hips urging him deeper and faster.

"Fuck, Angel, you're going to undo me," he groaned in my ear. His hand lifted my knee, opening me, exposing me and he lifted so he could sink deeper with a new angle that seemed to touch every nerve ending. I arched my back trying to find more, of what I didn't really know, rational thought eluded me right now. Jax slammed a little harder into my body as if he knew exactly what I needed and with the relentless and demanding pace he had set, I began to climb, my body throbbing with need. Jax bent down to capture my nipple in his mouth, sucking and tugging hard at the small pink bud. I groaned loudly.

"Jax," I pleaded as an unfamiliar feeling of rapture built from within my body. His mouth left my nipple only to find the other, sampling it with equal ferocity and passion. "Jax," I moaned a little louder and he leaned forward, covering my body with his, his pelvis rubbing with unyielding insistence over my clit and just like that my body climbed, hovered and fell over an invisible wall of pleasure. My back arched, my head bowed and I screamed his name, my breath coming in ragged pants as I found the release my body had been aching for. I felt Jax's body slam hard one last time as he groaned not my name, but 'angel', followed with short shallow thrusts as he emptied his seed. Finally, he slowed and allowed his head to collapse, his forehead resting against mine. When I eventually opened my eyes he was staring at me like he had just discovered a new treasure.

"What do you see?" I whispered.

"The woman I love," he whispered back without hesitation. He grinned and captured my lips in a passionate kiss. "I probably shouldn't say that to a girl who's spent far too many years running and has her packed bag beside my bed. I'll scare you away," Jax confessed. I ran a finger around the smooth skin of his eye and jaw, noting the slight discoloration from being hit by Phillip. Jax took my fingers away from the bruise and kissed them softly.

"You don't scare me, Jax Carter. I've been waiting a long time to find a man who could love me again. My heart is yours, so please be careful with it." He sighed, his eyes closed as he absorbed my words, his fingers laced with mine beside our heads.

"I will cherish it like the treasure it is," he murmured. Reluctantly he left my body to get rid of the condom and tidy himself up. When he returned he climbed in under the sheets and draped his big strong and very naked body around me. We were completely entwined, our bodies wrapped up in each other, our hearts beating steady beside one another, our souls permanently merged. In that moment, no demons or nightmares could disrupt the peace we had found in each other.

CHAPTER 32

Jax

I owned her heart, I had once more gained her trust. I would never let her down and I would never leave this angel's side. If she tried to run, I would follow. As my eyes flickered open, I realized Ella wasn't by my side and, after a fleeting moment of terror, I noted her backpack propped against the wall where I had left it last night. I knew she wouldn't leave without that damn bag. Climbing out of bed, I pulled on my jeans from the previous night and moved to the bathroom to wash my face. My eye was black but not swollen, my jaw a little tender but otherwise fine. Fucker, I thought, my mind racing over the details of my encounter with Phillip. I glanced to the shower stall and saw Ella's body wash and shampoo sitting on the shelf and I smiled. The night may have started in terror, but it ended in sheer bliss. Losing myself in Ella's body was like stepping into paradise. Sex had never been so fucking perfect, most likely because what I had enjoyed with Ella had not been sex. It was pure unadulterated love. I had told her I loved her. I imagined the first time I whispered those words to a woman it would be a little different. Perhaps over a candle lit dinner or while watching the sun's colors bleed into the night sky during a magnificent sunset. But when all is said and done, the magical thing about telling someone you love them is saying the words when the moment demands it, when you can no longer breathe without that person knowing and last night was that moment for me. Ella's reply that my heart was in her hands was as good as an 'I love you' back.

I climbed down the stairs and found Ella staring at the picture she had drawn of Mercy. I'd had it framed and it currently hung by the fireplace in my living room.
I leaned against the wall at the bottom of the steps and Ella glanced over her shoulder in my direction. I watched her take me in, her eyes beginning at my bare feet, travelling over my legs, the unlatched button on my jeans, my stomach, chest and finally settling on my eyes. I liked the proprietary in her gaze and the desire in her eyes and I grinned like a man who had just won lottery. She was wearing my sweater and nothing else;

she looked utterly adorable. Her face was bruised, which sent fire through my veins, her neck marked by Phillip's hands. I knew these marks would fade, but it was more brutality on Ella's soul and fuck knows she didn't need that. As if sensing my eyes on her fresh bruises, her fingers delicately rubbed her neck and she shrugged.

"It doesn't really hurt," she murmured, glancing away and stepping cautiously around the fireplace.

"I haven't seen a piece quite like this. It's interesting, kind of retro destructive?" She was mocking the smashed guitar shoved carelessly into the fireplace and I laughed.

"It's a new piece called 'Jax loses his shit'." She moved on, looking over the pictures of me with Mercy, another of Charlie and his mom and one of me dressed in my fatigues in Afghanistan.

"What did the guitar do to you?" she murmured.

"The guitar was innocent, simply caught in the crossfire when I realized what an asshole I am."

Ella shook her head. "You're not an asshole, but you might have moments of irrational and foolish thought but that's part of every man's DNA. You play?" She turned to observed me as she wandered aimlessly around the large room. I nodded.

"I used to. I haven't for a while and it's unlikely I will for a while more considering the state it's in now."

"Bummer, I would like to have heard you play," she confessed.

"Next trip to town I'll buy a new one." If she wanted to hear me play, I'd damn well play until my fingers bled.

"You have creaky steps and floorboards." she commented and I found the observation a little unusual. "And the faucet in the kitchen rattles when you turn it on." I couldn't help but laugh.

"I guess a builder's house will always be in need of repair. Other jobs generally take priority." She shook her head and smiled.

"No, don't fix it. It's the way a home is supposed to sound. Houses are supposed to make noise, it's like they talk to you, protect you." I considered that for a moment.

"I take it Marcus's house was quiet?" She nodded that

painful solemn look that often settles over her eyes. As she drew even closer to me I restrained the need to reach out and take her into my arms.

"My real home, with my real dad, it was noisy. The doors creaked, the pipes rattled, there was always music and we laughed all the time. Marcus's home was silent for the most part, other than the occasional raging outburst and the sound of his fist meeting my flesh." My own fists clenched in rage and I couldn't stand it any longer, she was close enough to touch and I reached out and pulled her to me. She came willingly, her arms snaked around my waist holding me close.

"I want to learn you," she murmured. I brushed her hair aside and leant forward to kiss her neck.

"I thought we learned each other last night." I grinned while kissing the fresh bruises. I felt her shiver under my gentle touch and kisses.

"That was a learning of our bodies and I think you learned more about mine than I did about yours." She pulled back to look up at me, her cheeks flushed with either embarrassment or desire I wasn't sure. The memory of her taste, her body beneath mine, my body inside hers sent blood immediately to the only organ in my body that was outside my mind's control. "You like music?" she asked. I nodded and she pulled away moving to my large CD collection. "It's a very orderly collection. Everything is in alphabetical order. Are you sure you don't suffer from OCD? This house is very clean for a bachelor." I grinned and moved behind her, wrapping my arms around her waist. She tensed under my touch and I expected her to. This position was a trigger for her memories.

"Tidy and orderly is a must for soldiers, I guess that it's something I can't quite let go of. If you would prefer it messy, be my guest. Mess it up." She gradually relaxed as she concentrated on my words, my hands on her stomach holding her close. She slowly turned around and wrapped her arms around my neck and I lifted her feet from the ground so we could be face to face. "If you feel more comfortable in a mess, make a mess," I encouraged. She shook her head.

"If I were any more comfortable I would be comatose. Here, in your arms, it feels like nothing can touch me. This here feels like home." I kissed her, how could I not. My lips worked hers until she opened for me and my tongue swept in ruthlessly. When I finally managed to pull myself away she looked thoroughly kissed and thoroughly speechless.

"You're wearing my sweater," I noted, rubbing the end of her nose with mine.

"Uh-huh," was all she managed.

"I think we could fit three of you in there." My lips found hers again and the faint sound of her tummy rumbling brought us apart. "I need to feed you," I said lowering her to the ground. I led Ella to the kitchen where she promptly perched herself on the bench her feet swinging in lazy delight. I grabbed the skillet and some bacon and eggs from the fridge.

"You're going to cook?" She gasped. I laughed as I grabbed the remote for my stereo system and powered it up. Nickleback's Savin' Me filled the house, the speakers set out and positioned to fill every room with noise just as Ella had moments ago wished for.

"I promise it will be edible. Bacon and eggs is kind of my specialty. I hope you like your eggs sunny side up or over easy, that's as adventurous as I get." Ella smiled.

"Either will be fine with me, go ahead. Impress me with your breakfast prowess." We still had to have our talk; she needed to know that her mother had died. I couldn't even begin to imagine how she would take the news and a small insecure part of me was scared shitless that she would run again. Her mother had been a cruel bitch. She had knowingly left Ella in Marcus's punishing hands; she had not offered the protection every child is owed. I hated her for that, but at the end of the day she was still Ella's mother, her only mother and possibly the only family she had. Outside the sun was up, the fresh snow on the ground gave the outside world an air of fantasy. I followed Ella's gaze to the work shed further out in the yard.

"That's where I work. I can show you later if you like."

"When do you have to go back to the shelter?" Her eyes didn't stray from the shed.

"I've got the next two days off. I was supposed to go into Carter's today but I can do what I need to do from my home office." Ella nodded reflexively, her thoughts obviously a thousand miles away. I allowed her to keep them to herself. If she wanted to share she would, but something told me her mind was racing with memories that belonged to her and her only. From the whimsical look on her face, they were good memories, the kind I wanted her to have.

CHAPTER 33

Ella

I had a dream once, a long time ago, when I was no more than nine, ten at most. I remember it distinctly because I woke up crying, my daddy crouched at my bedside brushing back my hair and whispering calming words.

***

"Tell me your bad dream, baby girl. Let it out so that it can no longer hurt you." Tears rolled down my cheeks as I gazed into his dark concerned eyes. I always told Daddy my bad dreams. He said holding them in was bad for us, that we needed to let them go so our minds were free to be filled up with all the good stuff. But this dream wasn't really a bad dream, not like the ones I usually had anyway.

"I was in a house and it was warm like this house, but it looked different. I liked the house, Daddy, but you weren't there, you were gone and I couldn't find you." I broke down into uncontrollable sobs and once I had control, I continued. "I looked everywhere and then a big man told me you were gone, he said you had died and I needed to be brave, I needed to be strong." I cried some more as my daddy shushed me and rubbed the palm of my hand in a soothing way. After I finally began to grow quiet, the tears no longer blinding me I looked to my daddy who sat so patient and calm by my side.

"Daddy, do you think he was my angel?"

"Maybe, he did tell you not to be scared, to be strong. That seems like something an angel might say."

"If you can't be with me, you will send my guardian angel to look after me, right?" He smiled, his smile always made everything okay, it made the bad dreams less scary, the dark less empty and the fear that one day I might lose him less real.

"You will never be alone, baby girl. I promise you that." My tears stopped falling and the fear I had felt in my dream drained from my body.

"My guardian angel is big, bigger than you," I whispered.

"Wow, perhaps your angel is a warrior," Daddy marveled.

I considered this and nodded.

"And he has a work shed, just like yours that sits in a field of snow." Daddy laughed.

"True angels have hands that build and protect. I hope you get to meet your angel one day sweet heart. But until then, I'm afraid you are stuck with me." I shuffled over. It was my silent plea for my daddy to not yet leave me alone. He climbed onto the bed and I settled my tiny head onto his chest, where I soon found sleep again.

I stared at the work shed sitting in a field of white glistening snow as Jax plated up our food somewhere behind me. Mercy had said perhaps my finding the shelter was fate. Perhaps I didn't find Mercy's at all, but maybe my guardian angel had finally found me. Suddenly, I was flooded with the fear of losing Jax—he could be taken away from me so easily, just like my dad. I turned just as Jax approached me and, in a rush of emotion, I wrapped my arms tightly around his neck, my breathing ragged as I was swamped with feelings I could barely comprehend.

"Angel?" Jax asked worried.

"You can't leave," my voice wavered with panic,"Daddy promised me you would come and you would keep me safe. Promise me you will, promise me you won't leave me?" I was terrified something would happen to Jax. His arms held me tight.

"I promise, Angel."

My hands found his face as I forced his gaze to mine. His brow creased with confusion as he saw the irrational, yet real fear in my eyes.

"Don't leave me like my dad did," I whispered. Jax's hands captured my face and we held each other like that, searching for the truth in each other's eyes.

"Never, baby, I'm not going anywhere. What happened just now, where'd you go?" I shook my head. I wasn't ready to tell him, I didn't know if I ever could. It was a moment between a little girl and her father, perhaps a profound moment— personal and significant. I glanced back at the shed, the clarity of my dream from so long ago fresh in my mind.

"Just a memory," I murmured, my thoughts trying again to drag me away from here and now.

The mood at breakfast picked up after my moment of anxiety. Jax teased me about the enthusiasm with which I ate; it was always curiously entertaining for him. I assured him he had some sort of bizarre food fetish and, with the kitchen cleaned up, Jax carried me back to his bed where we made love again. He told me he feared he wouldn't be able to let me leave his bed and I told him that things might get messy if he didn't allow a bathroom break.

***

Jax was in his office as I curled into a ball in front of the fireplace, a fire freshly lit minus the splintered guitar. I wore a long sleeved shirt that was pushed to my elbows. I glanced at my arms and the crisscross pattern of scars on them, ending with the deep ugly gash across both my wrists. Apart from Jax's loving attention to them last night, he seemed to barely notice them. I ran a finger over one of the scars, mesmerized by just how insignificant they really were. The cuts I had given myself were not deep; therefore, the scars were pale and at a quick glance barely noticeable.

The scars at my wrists were more obvious, but looking at them didn't seem to hurt like it used to. Marcus had put those marks on me as a reminder of how he owned me, but he didn't own me. All the scars really represented were how I had survived battles that no human being should ever have to endure. A gentle hand around my wrist broke the moment of my epiphany. Jax rubbed his thumb across my scar as he sat down beside me, lifting my feet into his lap.

"You know, these might remind you of where you've been, Angel, but they don't have to dictate where you're going," he said softly, his fingers brushed lightly across my scars. I couldn't help but climb up into his lap and wrap my arms around his neck. The intense need to be close to him, completely wrapped up in him was powerful. Jax held me firmly to his chest.

"I know that now. They are just scars, old wounds. It's time to put them behind me and move forward." With a sigh Jax whispered in my ear.

"We need to have that talk now." Reluctantly I nodded and sat back, giving him my undivided attention. Jax still held on to me, his fingers rubbing a soothing pattern into my hands.

"Tom Brennan was the arresting officer on nearly all your arrests in Dunston, he is known to be a personal friend of Marcus." He wasn't asking me, he was telling me and of course I knew this for fact.

"Tom was Marcus's doormat, his yes-man. Marcus had eyes and ears all over Duntson. He always seemed to know where I was, who I was with and he would send Tom out to fetch me and drag me home. Tom saw my bruises more than once, he knew what Marcus was doing and he did nothing to stop it." Jax nodded.

"I need to call Frank, he needs to know what kind of a man he has working in his precinct." I shook my head fiercely.

"Jax, it will be Tom's word against mine. He has evidence to support all the shit I did. I was a troubled teen, into drugs, alcohol, making trouble for my family, running away. Tom just looks like a cop doing his job." Jax rubbed his jaw seeming to consider that and then eventually gave in with a short nod.

"I'll keep my eye on Tom. If he so much as breathes in your direction, I won't hesitate to rip the man's heart out." It was a blood thirsty declaration but it made me feel safe and cherished. "Your therapist, his name was Dr. Theo Stojanovic?" I hadn't heard his name mentioned in four years now and my fists clenched with irritation as memories of the doctor filled my mind. He was a thoughtless drone who treated me as Marcus asked him to. He never listened to a God damn thing I said. My silence was confirmation enough for Jax. "Dillon has discovered that Dr. Theo kept two sets of files for you, one at his office and another at his place of residence." I tilted my head, contemplating the information Jax had just given me. "Dillon's business is security, so as you can appreciate, he has a certain set of skills that come in advantageous when one needs to gain entry to a house for instance." Jax wiggled his eyebrows and I laughed.

"I never got the hang of breaking and entering. Maybe Dillon can give me some pointers," I joked. Jax shook his head and laughed before soon becoming somber again.

"The files that Dr. Theo keeps at home are startlingly different from the files he keeps at the office. They appear to be a little more honest and for Marcus Fairmont, a whole lot more damning." My mouth dropped open.

"Dillon can't just take the files and present them to the police. If the police asked how he came to be in possession of them, he can't exactly say he broke into the doctor's home, not quite legal enough for our good law enforcement officers. We can try though to convince Theo that Marcus is going down. I can only assume that's why he kept the files, as backup, insurance if you like." The contents of those files could perhaps mean jail for Marcus. Never before had my future felt so, possible.

"Dillon wants to spend another week or two in Dunston putting together a case and then he will visit us here. He needs to speak to you, Angel, we need to verify dates, injuries. You missed a hell of a lot of school which will work in our favor."

"Marcus used my behavior as an excuse for any school I missed. I might have been at home covered in bruises, but he had me visit Dr. Theo, made it look like I was having an episode or something." Jax nodded.

"But Theo has the second set of files to confirm his beliefs about the injuries. The doctor also recorded all your sessions. He has hours of recorded data at his home. Dillon hasn't viewed it all but what he did see clearly shows your injuries." A part of me was dancing with delight, but a much larger part of me was horrified over the thought of the video evidence. Pretty much everything that came out of my mouth during those sessions was a lie. I basically said what I knew Marcus wanted me to say. I was a mindless patient; nodding when it was appropriate, saying what was expected. Under duress, I admitted that I was acting out because of my father's death— that I used drugs and alcohol to escape the memory of the day he died, that I slept around in an attempt to fill a void that my father had left. God, those words made me want to throw up. Sure I missed my dad. I hated the memories of the day he died, but the drugs, the alcohol, the boys were all an attempt to escape Marcus. I was mortified of what Dillon would think of the videos, even more worried about what Jax would think if he ever saw them.

"I know what you're thinking, Angel, but the videos are a good thing, baby. It doesn't matter what you said, with Dr. Theo's written files, the real ones, the evidence of the abuse in the videos, the dates you missed school, we will be able to tie it all together. It will be the truth and it will make a solid case against Marcus." I nodded, my head now throbbing with the all the information I was trying to absorb and understand. Jax ran his hand nervously through his messy hair, pushing it out of his eyes.

"Fuck angel that was the easy part, the next bit is going to be bad and I wish I didn't have to tell you." He set his shoulders back and looked me square on. "You're mom." he rubbed a hand down his face and groaned. "Shit, Angel, you're mom passed away, about twelve months ago. Twelve months ago yesterday to be precise." Jax had said the words but they took a long time to sink in. My mom was dead. My brow furrowed in confusion. "The autopsy report says she committed suicide—large traces of the sleeping pill, Ambien was found in her system and her wrists were cut." Images of my mother flickered through my mind like an old video projector. All of them were the same—my mother's expressionless face, her heartless smile, her cold eyes. She didn't care about me. She didn't protect me or try to save me. If she was dead now, then good riddance. That's how I should have felt. Instead, like all the other times I tried to hate her, I couldn't. All I could feel was sorrow and I began to buckle under a wall of guilt. If I hadn't of run she might not have died.

"Marcus?" I whispered.

"There is no way to be sure, but I'd put money on it. It's not hard to see that Marcus is a mental case, he was once a patient of Dr. Theo's and he has major mommy and daddy issues. His father beat him and his mother was unloving—detached, spoiled, brought different men home regularly when her husband worked late or went away.
She died the same way—full of drugs with her wrists slit. It's not hard to see a pattern developing here." Bile quickly began to rise in my throat.

"I think I'm going to be sick." My hand clamped over my mouth and Jax grabbed me, pulling me to a small downstairs bathroom where he held my hair back as I emptied my breakfast into the toilet. When there was nothing left to offer the porcelain throne, I sat quietly still, my mind trying to comprehend exactly how I felt. Dejected, guilty, glad and indifferent, how could I possibly feel so many different confusing emotions at once? Surely I was either one or the other? Jax wet a wash cloth and wiped my face.

"I'm so sorry, Angel," he said as he wiped my forehead. The sensation of the cool cloth on my hot skin was a balm to my senses. I leaned into the coolness wanting more before I remembered I had just thrown up and now sat on the floor of the bathroom with Jax mere inches away.

"I need to brush my teeth, I need a shower." Jax scooped me up into his arms with ease and climbed the stairs to the large upstairs bathroom. He placed me on the counter while he started the shower, then turned to help me undress. Once I was under the steaming hot water I closed my eyes, shutting out the world as I let my body deal with the stress. I felt Jax behind me as he carefully washed my hair, massaging my scalp for the longest time before washing the soap free. Then he proceeded to methodically clean my body. It was intimate even though it wasn't sexual. After he was done, he wrapped me in a clean towel and dried off my hair, then tucked me into his bed, wrapping his body around me like a protective cocoon. No words were spoken. Jax patiently let me absorb the news, process it and deal with it the only way I knew how—without tears, numb from the inside out. After what felt like hours, I finally found my voice, though it was low and strained.

"She died because of me, because I left, that's why he hurt her." Jax tensed beside me and although we were skin to skin, every inch of our bodies touching, he somehow managed to pull me closer.

"No, baby, you can't think that way. That's how Marcus would want you to think. Your mom knew what he was like, she made that bed she needed to damn well lie in it. Anyway, if you had stayed, who's to say he wouldn't have killed you then moved on to your mother anyway?" I didn't want to think anymore, I didn't want to feel and somehow I forced my body to shut down as I sank into a blissful abyss of darkness.

CHAPTER 34

Jax

I wanted Ella to cry, to scream, to rage. She was more than entitled. Marcus Fairmont had yet again marked her world with violence and hate and he did it on a day that was sacred to her. But not a single tear fell. My tears are for kindness, not pain, not hate, not fear, her words echoed through my mind. As I held her in my arms, her body still radiating warmth from the hot shower, her hair still damp, she was utterly still and excruciatingly silent. Eventually, her breathing evened out and I knew she had fallen asleep. The fact that she had felt guilty for what happened to her mother crushed me. I refused to allow her to feel the guilt that rightly lay at the feet of Marcus and somewhat her mother too. She had to have known the abuse that Ella endured and yet she did nothing. As long as she was happy in her own little bubble, that was all that mattered. I hated her for that, but I certainly didn't wish her violence and death because of it, much like I'm sure Ella would be feeling. Ella's heart beat was a steady rhythm against my chest and I watched the gentle rise and fall of her chest, listening to the soft whisper of air that escaped her slightly parted lips and eventually I fell asleep too. I woke much later to the feel of a gentle hand tracing a small scar on my shoulder.

"Shrapnel," I murmured my voice husky from sleep. Ella pushed up onto one arm and began a careful inspection of my body, finding my scars, not that there were that many. "Nail gun," I said as she traced the small round scar on the back of my hand. "Motor bike," I groaned as my body began to respond to her delicate touch, her fingers lingered over a large scar on my knee. Ella nudged my side and I rolled over as she began to inspect my back.

"Bullet ricochet," I murmured as she took in the large round scar that marked my right shoulder blade. It was hard to make out as it was partially covered by my tattoo. Her sharp intake of breath was the only acknowledgement as her fingers continued to caress my body. She would find no more. That was the history of Jax Carter's physical pain. Other than a couple of broken bones, my body had not been through the same violence that hers had, which seemed completely unfair since my body was so much larger, so much stronger. If I could have endured her beatings and taken that agony for her, I would have.

"What is your favorite color?" Her sudden and unexpected question caught me by surprise, my mind was hazy with lust and it took me a moment to answer.

"White, like the snow," I murmured, enjoying her fingers as they traced my tattoo.

"Your favorite movie?"

"Clerks. Charlie and I can still quote just about the entire movie, it's scary."

"If you could be a superhero, which one would you be?" I couldn't stop the laughter that racked my body. This line of questioning was pretty damn cute. I rolled over and grabbed her waist to hold her above me, straddling me completely naked. Damn she was a sight to behold.

"Batman, he's just your everyday Joe with a cool suit and wicked toys," I said a little breathlessly and Ella smiled. "I would like to see you dressed in a Batman costume." She blushed.

"Be careful what you wish for, that could be arranged." I folded my hands behind my head, allowing her to continue touching me, exploring my body which was responding appropriately.

"Favorite song?" she continued with the questions.

"Dust in the Wind, by Kansas."

She was biting her bottom lip, no doubt trying to think of her next question. She looked so darn sexy I could no longer keep my hands to myself. I grabbed her thighs and rubbed my hands slowly up them.

"Since we are playing twenty questions, it must be my turn. You're favorite color?"

"Blue, like the ocean." Her voice had a breath of longing and I knew my touch was affecting her in the same way her touch had affected me.

"If you could go anywhere else in the world, where would it be?"

"Hawaii, to see the ocean." She smiled.

"Hmmmm, I'm beginning to see a pattern here." My hands had reached her waist and I wrapped them around her, marveling that I could just about encompass her body with my hands.

"And what does Ella Munroe see for her future?" I bravely asked, knowing her future was not usually something she thought about. Her eyes that had been watching my hands, snapped up to meet mine. It was a long time before she answered.

"A gallery, filled with art—some mine, some others. Perhaps a coffee shop attached to it, because I love coffee." Her face was filled with longing. "And I see my blonde haired, much too tall warrior wooing me with flowers, picnics under the stars, serenading me with music because he plays the guitar when he isn't smashing it to pieces." I knew my grin was one of those shit eating, smug, arrogant ones, but I couldn't help the satisfaction that flooded my heart at her words. My hands slipped up the smooth skin of her stomach and cupped her breasts. They fit perfectly right into my hands, they were flawless, she was flawless. Ella moaned before slowly moving out of my reach.

"Where are you going, Angel?" I groaned. The seductive play in her eyes excited me as she moved down my body and kneeled over my dick.
Then, with an excruciating long slow lick, she followed the vein from base to tip. It took every ounce of self-preservation not to blow at that second. The sight of the angel before me, worshipping me in such a way was enough to make my brain cells fry. As she took me in her mouth I thought of anything except the sight and feel of Ella consuming me, otherwise, I would not last more than five seconds. Ice hockey, basketball, the miserable hot fucking desert, oh shit, I groaned as she took me deep. Her eyes watched me with pure female contentment. When I knew I could not go a second more without coming, I hooked my hands under her arms and dragged her up my body. I pulled her to my lips and kissed her like a starved man. I needed to be in her this instant. I grabbed a condom from the drawer, pissed off that I had to stop for even a second. Once I was covered I lifted her hips to my cock and allowed her to

slowly, torturously sink onto me. She rode me leisurely, her back arched, her beautiful long hair cascading down her back, brushing against my thighs. I needed to be closer so I sat forward, wrapping my arms around her, kissing her lips, her cheek, her neck while she road me into fucking oblivion.

Later that night as I defrosted another of Mary's miracle frozen dinners, Ella phoned Annie and Eli, then Rebecca, which led to our first argument.

"You're not going to work on Tuesday," I said matter-of-factly. I knew I sounded like an ass, but there was no way I was letting her out of my sight.

"You will know if Marcus leaves Duntson. If he does, it's a sixteen hour drive, at least. I'm sure you can get from Mercy's to Bouquets in that time," she argued.

"What if he gets on a flight? He can be here in less than two hours!" I tried hard not to raise my voice, knowing she would flinch at any sign of hostility.

"You can get to Bouquets in like five minutes, Jax. You know it won't be a problem." Her calm attitude was beginning to piss me off and freak me out.

"What about Brennan?" I asked incredulously and she shrugged.

"He's a police officer, he's not going to haul me out of work in the middle of the day for no reason, it's too public. Anyway, Rebecca would eat him for breakfast if he tried." I didn't want to admit that she had a point.

"You're having one of those moments of irrational and foolish thoughts that men are prone to, you're being a domineering asshat, Jax." I looked at her as she flicked through a magazine on my kitchen table, absorbing every page as if it held the answers to every question she had ever had. I knew she wasn't really reading it. It was a trade guide for fuck's sake.

"Did you just call me a domineering asshat?"

"I did. I also mentioned irrational and foolish." She glanced up at me from under her thick lashes. I could see the insecurity in her gaze. She wasn't used to speaking to men in this way and even though she trusted me, an instinctive part of her was expecting rage, perhaps violence. I grinned and shook my head. She had a smart mouth when she wanted to and I loved it.

"Well, this domineering asshat was watching a man wrap his fingers around your throat only a night ago. I'm not ready to let you out of my sight yet." She sighed, her gaze moving back to the magazine.

"I think I have a building and construction magazine around here somewhere once you're done with the trade guide." I laughed. She smiled as she finally noted what she was reading and threw the magazine across the table. She got up and strode right to me, her arms wrapping around my neck. I lifted her easily so our eyes were at the same height.

"I don't want to hide away anymore, Jax. You can even drop me off and pick me up. You've shown me how I should be living my life without fear. I refuse to let Marcus control me any longer." I looked into her beautiful brown eyes that I could no more refuse then stop the sun from shining.

"So you're saying this new found lease on life is my fault?" I grumbled. She nodded.

"Most definitely, but it's a good thing. Otherwise I'd be five hundred miles from here by now and you'd be lonely and horny." Laughter rumbled from deep in my chest and I kissed her nose before placing her feet back on the ground.

"Okay, but there are rules. You won't go out for breaks; if I'm so much as five minutes late, you will wait inside the store; you will carry your phone, fully charged, on you at all times." I shook my finger at her like my mother used to. I remember being intimidated by that finger, but Ella just laughed and nodded. Fuck, I'd created a monster.

CHAPTER 35

Ella

Over the next week, I followed Jax's rules to the letter. It had seemed as though Rebecca had joined Team Carter and wouldn't allow me to step out of line even once. She had the shortened version of what was going on in my life. Jax thought it was important she knew, for my safety and hers. If she decided she didn't want a part of it, then I would help Jax at Mercy's. But of course Rebecca puffed out her chest and showed me her little fist. "Any man so much as lays a finger on you and I will break the bastard in half," she growled like a protective momma bear.

I had to beg her to take me to her doctor during one of our lunch breaks. I was eager to get myself on the pill. Since my body had discovered the joy of real, heartfelt, passionate sex I wanted it every spare second and condoms were somewhat of an inconvenience when it came to spontaneity. She had taken me straight there, watching over her back nervously then directly back to the safety of Bouquets when we were done. I hated that she felt she had to watch her back, that she was so anxious suddenly. I had brought this unease into her life, but Rebecca wouldn't allow me to feel guilty for even a moment. She even went as far as to throw a bunch of gerberas at me when I approached the subject of guilt, telling me to suck it up and stop being such a little girl.

During the day, Mercy and Charlie would drop in to Bouquets unannounced, most likely to make sure I hadn't broken Jax's rules and left the store alone. Each morning Jax dropped me to the door and he was there to greet me at five. Somehow I seemed to have moved in with Jax. We had taken the suitcase of clothes that Rebecca had given to me and Jax had made room in his closet for them.

It was weird putting my clothes away. They usually only left my backpack to be put on my body or washed. I noted two sealed garment bags in the back of Jax's closet and curiosity got the better of me. I zipped open the first and found a formal military uniform, pressed crisp and clean. I ran my fingers reverently over the collar and imagined Jax dressed tall and proud in it. I closed the zipper and moved to the second bag. In this one, I found a sharp expensive looking black suit. I guess this is what he wore to functions like the Thanksgiving Ball and that he was, most likely, going to wear it last week when he was supposed to take Selena. I found myself wondering how many times she had seen him in it, held onto his arm as he guided her into an elegant restaurant or ball. They would look perfect together, beautiful. Had she stripped it from his body in moments of passion? Jealousy was not an emotion that sat well with me. I was completely unfamiliar with it, ill-equipped for dealing with it.

"What are you thinking?" asked Jax, standing at the doorway and I sighed.

"This looks like something Bruce Wayne would wear. Are you sure you don't have a Batman suit back here somewhere?" I teased. He came up behind me and wrapped his arms around me, kissing my neck. The first time he had attempted to approach me from behind like this, in the basement at Mercy's Shelter I had lost it, panic had consumed me. Now I didn't even flinch. How had I come so far so quickly? The answer was easy, Jax had made it so.

"You won't find it in here, I keep it in the bat cave." He chuckled. "Do you like it?" he wondered. I did, but I hated that it represented a life I was not a part of. "It's new. I bought it months ago when I thought I might be going to the Thanksgiving Ball and we all know how that ended. Perhaps you will allow me to buy you a dress and take you somewhere special one day, it's a shame to be wasted in a bag for all eternity." My eyes fluttered closed as he continued to kiss my neck but unease still crept into my thoughts.

"I'm not really a dress kind of girl," I whispered, wondering if that's what he wanted in a woman.

"You can wear jeans and t-shirt for all I care. Hell, you can go naked and we'll just laze around the house. I'll be all dressed up like Bruce Wayne and you in your birthday suit. Actually, I like that thought more than any pretentious restaurant or ball." His hands began to flick open the button on my jeans and, at that moment, a loud knock at the front door broke the growing desire and I jumped.

"Easy, Angel, Dillon texted me an hour ago. He drove through the night, it's most likely just him." I tried to relax, but truth be told I was a little nervous about meeting Jax's ex-military friend, Dillon Montgomery, the man who had, over the past few weeks, come to know all my secrets in all their gory detail. I followed Jax down the stairs from his loft, but stood glued to the bottom step, consciously noting I had three exits from the room—front door, back door and stairs. I shook my head, annoyed that I would be thinking like this. Dillon was Jax's friend, Jax trusted him more than any one. He had been working tirelessly to bring down Marcus, to free me and we had never even met. Jax quickly checked out the corner of the blinds and smiled as he opened the door.

"Been too long, soldier." Jax laughed, embracing Dillon like a long lost brother.

"Sarge," Dillon chuckled, "since when did you start cuddling?" Jax pushed him away and stepped aside so Dillon could enter. He was tall, almost as tall as Jax, but not as muscular. He was lean and toned, his hair cropped army style short. He wore a black jacket over black cargo pants, with shiny black army boots. He looked dangerous and deadly and I couldn't help but take a small step away. Jax of course noticed and moved to my side, wrapping his big protective arm around me.

"Dillon, this is Ella Munroe, Angel, this is Dillon." Dillon smiled and nodded. His eyes were full of understanding and compassion, no anger, no violence.

"It's a pleasure to finally meet you, sweetheart," he said easily. And here, now, under the kind thoughtful gaze of this stranger, my eyes grew watery and a lone tear dropped from my lashes and down my cheek.

"Thank you," I said when no other words would come. My senseless, inane tears that were spared only for kindness felt like a weighted weakness in my chest.

"You're welcome, honey," he acknowledged as Jax pulled me into his arms.

"We need never be ashamed of our tears," Jax murmured the quote I knew well.

"You're quoting Great Expectations now?" I sniffled.

"Shhhhhh, Dillon will hear," he joked.

"Too late, I heard and you will never live it down." Dillon laughed, which made me laugh.

"Excellent, now that we're all laughing at my expense shall we have something to eat?"

"Not if you're cooking," Dillon scoffed.

Dillon was exhausted, but he still insisted on dragging out his laptop and going over everything he had—and he had a lot. Dr. Theo Stojanovic was ready and waiting to cut a deal. Under some 'mild' pressure, as Dillon put it, Dr. Theo admitted he was originally blackmailed into treating me. Apparently Marcus had proof that Theo had helped one of his patients win an unlawful insurance claim that netted a whopping five million dollars, which Dr. Theo was humbly paid off for, an easy one point five million.

So, while Theo stood to go down, his time would be reduced if he cut a deal and helped put Marcus away. As a gesture of goodwill, Theo willingly handed over all his legitimate files on me and my mom, who had apparently been a patient for nearly two years prior to her 'suicide'. All too soon, Dillon came to the video evidence from Theo. He cast me a nervous glance before playing one of the tapes. I looked to Jax wondering what he would think and he took my hand squeezing it. "It doesn't matter what you said in these tapes, we want to use them for the physical evidence they show. We know you were forced to say things you didn't mean." I nodded, unable to speak, my heart racing as I took a long calming breath, concentrating on relaxing my body just as Jax had taught me to help prevent a panic attack.

"Go ahead, Dillon," Jax mumbled. The video began before I had entered the room. Dr. Theo sat behind his desk. He was a short, balding, sniveling excuse for a man, in appearance and person so it seemed. The video was of a high quality, clear with sound. The door to the small office opened and I held my breath as a tiny, fragile little girl stepped through. She looked as beaten and defeated as she felt, after all, I should know, I remember this day like it was yesterday. It was ingrained into my memory like an open wound that would never heal. It was a week after my fifteenth birthday, after an officer, someone other than Tom, had found me in a drug induced slumber in the back of Henry's car. I was charged with possession and this was the first time I had faced court over my actions. I was sentenced to drug rehabilitation, with Dr. Theo of course, and Marcus had to pay a hefty fine. As punishment for embarrassing him, he had beaten me to within an inch of my life. My eyes were blackened, one still partially swollen shut. My lip was cut and swollen, one side of my face darkened with nasty purple and black bruising.

I moved weakly in the video and sat carefully, as if any sudden movement might break me. Jax's hand gripped mine almost painfully as we watched the video. Dr. Theo seemed to dismiss the injuries and started asking questions about drugs, the charges against me, wanting to know how I felt about them. Dillon stopped the video.

"The hidden files from the doctor's home document as many of the injuries as possible and claim that he believes Marcus inflicted the injuries. He documents your reaction to Marcus's name as fearful, exactly what one might expect of someone who had been abused." Dillon explained. He shut down the footage and moved the curser to another file and opened it. The date at the bottom made me shudder. This was the day after I was released from hospital after the 'incident', where I apparently tried to kill myself, accused of taking a knife to my wrists and slicing like I had done so many times before, only this time with the intent to end it all. Subconsciously, the hand that Jax wasn't holding went to the scar of my other wrist and started rubbing, as if I needed the proof that it was really there. Old Ella, defeated Ella, whose eyes were distant and crushed, walked silently into the room.

"Have a seat, Ella," Dr. Theo said his voice low and gruff. The little girl sat stiffly in the chair beside the desk as Dr. Theo began to scrawl notes in a file before him. "And how are you doing today, did you take the painkillers?" The little girl nodded once, but otherwise remained perfectly still. "Can we talk about Tuesday night?"

"What do you want me to say?" the little broken girl asked.

"Can you tell me what led you to harm yourself this way?" Dr. Theo asked, still yet to look up from the damn file.

"Obviously I miss my daddy so much I want to join him."
My voice laced with sarcasm. I was beaten, but not down.

"Have you had thoughts of suicide before?"

"No." And I hadn't, never, not once.

"The scars on your arm tell another story, Ella."

"Self-harm, not suicide, Dr. Theo." The resolve in my
words betrayed the defeat in my body.

"Of course, you mutilated your body as punishment. You
used drugs, alcohol and sex as an escape from the memories of
your father and when that didn't work anymore, you tried the
only thing you had left, death." You could clearly see that my
fists were clenched in the video footage and, as if still feeling
the same pain, loathing and anger, my fists instinctively began
to tighten now. Jax held my hand tighter.

"Looks like you have me all figured out Doctor." Dr. Theo
finally looked up from his notes and seemed to contemplate the
scared little girl before him.

"Perhaps I do, Ella, perhaps I do," he murmured.
Dillon stopped the footage again. "The file in front of Theo
clearly states that Ella is a classic self-harmer caused by the
stress of her father's death. He recommends intensive therapy
and a prescription to help with sleep. The other files; however,
are a different story altogether. Dr. Theo is clear when he says
he believes Ella would never try to kill herself—her resolve is
too strong, her will to live and to defeat Marcus too powerful.
His entry admits that Marcus Fairmont is fully capable of
carrying out this sort of injury to Ella. This, sweetheart," Dillon
tapped the files before him, "this will send Marcus Fairmont
away for a very long time."

CHAPTER 36

Jax

Two things happened over the next week that made me slip from a domineering asshat to a completely irrational dictating bastard. In my defense, all I wanted was to keep Ella safe, but when Tom Brennan up and vanished my senses kicked into overdrive and when Braiden reported from Dunston that Marcus Fairmont had taken a short leave of absence from the advertising firm he owns, I kind of began having a meltdown. Thankfully, Dillon was hanging around to help me compile all the evidence we had on Fairmont into something we could present to the police. If he hadn't been here to help me keep my sanity, I'm fairly sure I would have locked Ella up in my home, chained her to the bed if necessary, and probably screw up any chance at a real future with her. Between Dillon and I, we were able to make sure Ella was safely escorted to work and home again, but after a week she was starting to get irritable and restless with all the fussing. When she pleaded to have a night with the girls I would have easily said no, but Dillon was, once again, the voice of reason, suggesting that it would be safe enough to drop her off with the girls and pick her up again later that night. They weren't allowed to go out though and it was agreed that Rebecca's was close enough to Andy's Office and secure enough for the girls to let loose for a few hours while the boys had a couple of quiet beers down the road. So on Saturday night instead of chaining her to my bed, I was delivering her to Rebecca's where Annie and Mercy were already waiting with drinks in hand. I couldn't remember the last time my mother had a carefree night out with the girls, so it was good to see her there. It was also good to see her so easily embrace Ella—no awkwardness about our relationship that had quite literally snuck up on all of us.

"You can't come in," growled Rebecca from the doorway as I stood in front of her holding Ella's hand tightly.

Rebecca was dressed in her usual crazy old school clothes and her white blonde hair pinned back to one side with a flower. I didn't know anyone else that dressed or looked quite like her. Although it was a little overstated for me, the look really did seem to work for her. She had the confidence to pull it off.

"Really, why, what's going on in there? You all stripping down to your underwear for a pillow fight?" I asked and Rebecca's eyes sparkled with mischief.

"You like to think of your momma in her underwear?" Well, there went my sexy all female pajama party fantasy I had often entertained. Mercy laughed from beside Rebecca.

"I think it's safe to say that my son believes I sleep in full flannel pajamas every night rather than the silk negligee I actually wear and I'm sure he has also convinced himself that I never have sex, which I do, regularly. Dave is a wizard in the sack." My mouth dropped open and I have no doubt I went several shades of red. Rebecca grinned at my stunned and uncomfortable response to my mother's declaration.

"Fuck, Mercy. That imagery was really not necessary. You've most likely scarred me for life," I grumbled and complied with Ella's silent demand for me to lean closer as she kissed my cheek. Rebecca winked.

"Don't worry, Jax, by the end of this evening my little tiger here will have spilled her guts about you too." I was officially worried as Rebecca dragged a giggling Ella through her door.

"Don't worry, it will all be good," my angel winked. I reluctantly left to join Charlie and Dillon at Andy's Office for a quiet drink while we waited for the girls to thoroughly emasculate us.

Ella

"How you holding up, honey?" Mercy asked. I shrugged. Marcus apparently hadn't left Dunston and I honestly didn't think Tom Brennan was up to anything other than perhaps running off in an attempt to save his own hide. I was truthfully beginning to feel a little trapped in the guise of security that Jax and Dillon had created. I popped the top off a fruity cocktail mix Jax had picked up for me on the way over and took a long drink.

"There really isn't much I can do right now. I'm getting tired of jumping at every little noise and my nerves feel a bit frayed. It will be nice to finally relax tonight." Rebecca swung her arm around my neck.

"Of course it will. Come sit down, I have a gift for you." I let Rebecca lead me into her cozy living room and sat down obediently, Mercy to my left and Annie to my right. Rebecca disappeared and soon came back with a large potted cacti with a big red bow wrapped around it. She placed it on the coffee table and smiled at me expectantly.

"A cactus. Thank you." I smiled back at her in confusion.

"Ahhhh, not just any cactus though. This is the variegated form of the Echinopsis lageniformis, otherwise known as the penis cacti." I took a closer look at the cactus and started laughing when I realized that the upper parts of the stems were spine free and smooth and did in fact resemble a penis. Mercy carefully ran a finger over one of the penis shaped bulbous stems and Annie laughed so hard she snorted.

"This fascination you have with plants that resemble genitals is a little worrying," I teased Rebecca. She shrugged and threw herself back into a big cozy recliner.

"Well, I'm not getting any so maybe I'm taking out my frustration on plants." Annie choked back a laugh.

"You do realize there are other ways to take out your frustrations that are far more pleasant than buying unusual plants?"

"Yes, but I refuse to lower myself to inanimate or plastic objects for self-gratification," Rebecca said stubbornly.

"There not all plastic, some are silicon," admitted Mercy. Rebecca threw a cushion at Mercy and she caught it easily laughing.

"You're supposed to be the responsible one here, Mercy." Rebecca chuckled.

"What about Charlie?" I innocently asked. Rebecca shook her head and looked away, blushing which made me wonder if her feelings for Charlie were more than she had previously let on.

"Charlie is Charlie," she groaned.

"Yes, he is," admitted Annie confused. "He's handsome and seems like a nice guy. He's great with kids, he's even babysitting Eli tonight. And apparently, you have seen each other naked, so what's the problem?"

"You've seen Charlie naked?" Mercy yelled and Rebecca blushed again.

"Louder, Mercy, my neighbors might not have heard you," said Rebecca sarcastically.

"Charlie and I had one glorious night and I'm telling you, it was A-mazing! That man's body has been cut straight from granite, I'm sure of it. And what he can do with his tongue, one word—wicked! But two nights later, in fact the night before you came knocking on Bouquets door, Ella, I saw him having a cozy dinner with Caitlyn Brown at Luigi's, so apparently the night was what it was, a night, nothing more. We didn't talk about what the night meant and Charlie made me no promises. Anyway, that was forever ago, I'm over it now."

I had seen the way Charlie looked at Rebecca and there was definitely interest in his eyes. Rebecca grabbed us fresh drinks and deftly changed the topic of conversation.

"I have a great idea, Ella, how about you draw me a sketch of Dillon. Now that is one fine piece of soldier, I think I could be persuaded to self-indulge if I had that fine face to look at. In fact, you could sketch me a picture of Dillon, Jax and Charlie. All three are very swoon worthy!" I laughed at Rebecca's swooning impression.

"Eye's off number two, weird genital flower lady. He is bagged and tagged," I complained with a mocking pout.

"Alright, alright settle down tiger. You can just draw me his chest, or ass cause that man has one fine ass. Seriously, Mercy, thank you for the addition to the sexy male gene pool!" It was

Mercy's turn to laugh.

"Why thank you, Rebecca, but I'm pretty sure my son's behind is for one lady's eyes only." Mercy winked my way. Annie sighed beside me, sipping on a glass of champagne.

"I wouldn't mind a sketch of Dillon's rear end, but, to be honest, it's been so long since I was intimate. I'm pretty sure Barney the dinosaur would do it for me these days." We all laughed loudly at Annie's solemn declaration. "Seriously, he's all cuddly, has a great smile, good teeth and he's purple, I do love the color purple," Annie continued dreamily.

"Well, Dillon has a great smile and great teeth," I said helpfully, enjoying this little game that seemed to be developing into match maker. Annie shook her head.

"I don't think I'm ready for another man just now, especially after having Phillip beating down my door a week ago." Just like that the mood grew somber.

"What if he has a purple cock?" Rebecca murmured. Our horrified looks of surprise quickly turned into unstoppable laughter.

It seemed we could always trust in Rebecca to turn a serious moment into something that we could laugh at and God knows we all needed that.

CHAPTER 37

Jax

I was on Rebecca's doorstep at exactly eleven p.m. as promised and seeing Ella safe and sound brought me no end of comfort. Though seeing her intoxicated sway as she approached me at the doorway made me cast Rebecca an annoyed glance.

"What?" she asked innocently. "She had four drinks and, as promised, none of it was vodka!" Rebecca held her fingers up clearly showing me the number five. "She's a light weight." She grinned. Annie followed Ella and she wasn't in much better form. Dave had picked up Mercy an hour ago and he had given me a quick text telling me the girls were well on their way to being inebriated.

"Oh, don't forget you're penis cacti, Ella!" shouted Rebecca, disappearing into the house and reappearing a moment later with a cactus with stems that were shamelessly formed into the shape of a penis.

"I'm not carrying that," I balked. Ella took it from Rebecca.

"What, this plant unmans you?" Rebecca giggled.

"The cactus has nothing on, Jax," Ella hiccupped from beside me and I grinned at my girl's sharp defense at my honor.

"No bragging about the fact you're getting laid and I'm not," Rebecca pouted.

"Right, I've once again heard more than I needed to. Goodnight, Rebecca." I got the girls into my truck and dropped Annie home where Eli was tucked into his warm bed and Charlie was uncomfortably sprawled on the couch snoring like a trooper. Ella didn't stop talking the entire way home. Apparently she was far too fascinated with her girl's night to even contemplate sleeping.

Seems she fancied herself quite the matchmaker and was planning on manipulating Dillon and Annie into some sort of relationship as well as Rebecca and Charlie.

"I got the impression Charlie and Rebecca already had something going?" I asked as I waited for the garage door to draw open. The lights were on inside, which meant Dillon was still up.

"He's your best friend, how can you not know these things?" she asked indignantly.

"It's all part of the guy code, Angel. We don't talk about our feelings or relationships, unless it's to brag and apparently, Charlie doesn't want to brag about Rebecca. I guess that means she was un-brag worthy, or he actually like likes her." Ella looked a little horrified.

"Did you brag about me?"
I grinned and winked at her as I pulled her into my arms from the front seat of my pickup.

"Not in the way you think. I like like you remember? So bragging is all above board and completely sex free." She bit down on her lip considering that for a moment.

"But am I brag worthy, you know, if you didn't like like me?" she asked. I pulled her close and kissed her senseless.

"Angel, you are so brag worthy it almost drives me crazy that I can't bring myself to share every damn sordid detail." She smiled as I pushed open the door from the garage to the house.

"Well apparently Charlie and Rebecca had one A-mazing night, but then the ass, and by ass I mean Charlie, went and took Caitlyn Brown out for dinner two nights later. I think Rebecca was pretty hurt and jealous, so things didn't go any further. But I've seen the way Charlie looks at her and he is completely into her. So what gives?" The irritation in her expression made me laugh.

"Caitlyn Brown is a client who wants some renovations done. Charlie isn't interested in her at all, in fact, I'm pretty sure Caitlyn has a girlfriend."

"Really?" Ella gasped. I nodded as I strode into the kitchen with Ella in my arms. Dillon looked up from the table.

"It's always a good sign when you have to be carried in from a girl's night out," he laughed.

"Dillon, how do you feel about children?" Ella started. Poor Dillon, he was in for it now. He looked at me confused and I shrugged as I deposited Ella on the kitchen bench by the fridge and quickly poured her a tall glass of water.

"They serve their purpose," he joked. "Are you asking me to help you produce one? Because I am pretty sure Sarge there knows all the basics, but if he's not getting it right I will give him a talking to." Ella blushed and quickly drank down the entire glass of water.

"No, Sarge has it covered. But Annie has a little boy, Eli, he's six." Dillon stretched back in his chair and laced his fingers behind his head with an amused look on his face.

"Sure, I remember him, cute kid totally into Transformers. And?" he urged Ella on to whatever she was hopefully getting to sometime soon.

"Just wondering what you thought of them, Annie and Eli." Dillon nodded and looked at me with a knowing smile.

"Annie's pretty and she's a good mother, Eli is a breath of fresh air." Ella beamed, seemingly satisfied with herself. Then her mood suddenly changed. Not sad, or angry, but pensive.

"Was my mother cremated or buried?" Dillon's smile became sincere.

"She was buried, in the same cemetery as your father though not together." Ella nodded.

"It's been a long time since I was there. Maybe one day I will go back and visit." Her words were not filled with sorrow but quiet deliberation. She smiled at me. "I don't mean to be a buzz kill, let's go upstairs and practice making babies."

"Right, bed!" I scooped her off the bench with enthusiasm and made for the stairs as Dillon coughed from behind us, hiding his laughter.

"What the fuck is this?" Dillon had finally noticed the cactus.

"Oh, that's my penis cacti. It needs warmth so maybe it should go by the fireplace. Oh and not much water! It usually lives in the desert," Ella called out over my shoulder as I made my way up to the loft. I caught Dillon's astonished look as he took in the unusually shaped cactus before he shook his head and turned away.

I lowered Ella to the floor of the bathroom and started up the shower. I helped her undress then held her hand as she stepped into the stall.

"You should join me," she said seductively and I hesitated. I knew if I did, one thing for sure would happen, but she had been drinking and it would feel as though I would be taking advantage of her if I allowed it.

"Jax," she sang my name. "If you don't get in here with me, I will have to take care of things myself. After all the sex talk tonight I'm feeling a little…hot." She looked so cute leaning against the wall of the shower her hands rubbing lazy circles over her stomach and slowly moving higher. I couldn't refuse her. I stripped like my life depended on it and joined her in the large double shower. "Why do you have a double shower stall?" she asked as I began soaping up a wash cloth.

"Have you seen the size of me?"

"You don't need two shower heads though." I could tell she was irritated, her mood tonight swinging so quickly from one extreme to another, obviously brought on by the alcohol. I washed her back then leaned over and whispered in her ear.

"Baby, you are the only woman who has ever stepped foot in this shower. I had two shower heads installed because I was waiting to find you and bring you home with me, so we could do this." My hands lathered the soap against her stomach and eventually found her perfect breasts.

"Really?" She breathed, enjoying the soft massage as much as I was.

"I promise you." She turned in my arms and began washing my chest and arms, finally her hands slid down my abdomen and brushed my quickly growing dick.

"I love your body," she sighed. I leaned forward and kissed her neck, licking the water that ran in rivulets down her front.

"Are you just using me for my body?" I laughed at her as she gripped my dick harder and began to stroke. I groaned.

"No, I really do love this shower too, especially knowing I'm the only woman that's been in it," she teased. My hands lowered and slipped into her core, which was wet and hot. Her body responded to my touch and I absorbed her moan with a kiss. I had quickly passed the point of no return as I carefully lifted her, resting her back against the wall and gently lowered her onto me. We both groaned at the sensation, of me filling her and her walls squeezing me, it was perfect. With demanding strokes I began to pump into her body before abruptly realizing my mistake—I forgot the condom. I slowed, trying desperately to get control.

"Fuck, Angel, I need to grab a condom." Her eyes, glazed with desire locked onto mine.

"I had Rebecca take me to her doctor last week on our lunch break. I'm on the pill and I've had health checks over the years, I'm safe." Her grin was breathtaking. "It was meant to be a surprise, so I guess this is it…surprise." As I absorbed her words her smile fell. "Unless you don't want to, we can stop." I thrust forwards into her leisurely and grinned.

"Not a chance. I have yearly checkups along with all the staff at Mercy's and I've never gone without a condom, I'm as STD free as a boy scout. And we'll talk later about you leaving Bouquets to go to the doctor." She smiled again as my pace quickened. I kissed her passionately, fiercely, appreciating the feel of a woman without the barrier of a condom for the first time ever. I was glad it was with Ella. It was a perfect representation of the trust and love we felt for each other. When I felt Ella tense and shudder with her orgasm, whispering my name into my ear, my body could do nothing but willingly join her.

"I love you Jaxon James Carter," she breathed. I chuckled.

"You've been talking to my mother," I growled playfully, kissing and nipping the sensitive spot under her ear.

"Uh-huh, I know all your secrets now." She shivered and that was the truth. Over the last few weeks we had talked about war, Sarah, the little I knew about my father. Ella knew everything about me, more than any other person could ever claim and I knew everything there was to know about her. It was almost as if our love for each other washed away the bullshit and left nothing but perfection. Ella owned me—my heart, my soul and all my secrets. I lowered her carefully to the floor as the water was quickly growing cold. Once we were tucked under the thick warm blankets of my bed, I pulled her back against my chest.

"I love you Ella Mai Munroe." I kissed her cheek and felt her smile, before sinking into a deep sleep.

CHAPTER 38

Ella

When I woke it felt as though my head might actually split in two and my stomach protested severely at the slightest movement. Once again, Rebecca had cast my body into a nightmare of a hangover. I silently cursed my boss as I hung my head over the side of the bed trying to find some release from my pounding frontal lobe. Jax chuckled as he climbed the stairs to the bedroom.

"Good afternoon," he said.

"Must you be so loud," I groaned. His laughter felt like a hammer on my skull. I looked up and took him in. Damn he was sexy. Faded blue jeans, white shirt, his blonde hair had that messy look that only fingers can create. He crouched down before me with a glass of water and two pills. I graciously took them and allowed my head to hang back over the bed. Jax carefully rubbed my neck.

"Afternoon?" I mumbled

"It is. You slept all day. I had to check your pulse twice just to make sure you were alive. Can I get you anything else?" he whispered and it still made my head pound. I groaned loudly.

"Can you kill Rebecca for me? This is the second time I have woken up feeling like this because of her." Jax tilted his head in thought.

"When was the last time?"

"The night after the tree lighting ceremony," I grumbled. Jax forced me to roll onto my back as he sat down beside me. His eyes carried the weight of regret as he gazed down at me.

"I'm sor…" I quickly placed my hand over his mouth. "That's in the past, Jax. We're here now, that's all that matters." Jax's hand roamed unhurriedly over my naked body.

"Couldn't even get me into pajamas, huh?" I joked. He smiled, his dimples lighting his face with the boyish charm I adored.

"I have a new rule. No clothes allowed in this bed." I eyed his state of dress and he laughed.

"I have to go to the shelter for a bit. Mercy wants me to pick up some supplies and drop them off. Dillon is in the study, he wants me to bring back some groceries; he's craving pancakes."

"Mmmmm, pancakes." It seemed to be the only thing my stomach was willing to tolerate. Jax kissed me but before he could draw away I pulled him closer and kissed him deeper. He groaned loudly when we finally parted.

"Fuck, Angel, I'm going to be walking around Claymont with a hard-on now." He laughed.

"I'm sure the chill outside will help with that." He gave me another chaste kiss before leaving me to my suffering. I somehow slipped back into sleep, like my body was demanding nothing today except complete oblivion.

When I woke some time later, the house was dark. I pulled myself from the bed and in the darkness found my drawstring pajama bottoms and a sweater. I pulled some fluffy socks on my cold feet and lifted my hair into a messy pony tail before tiptoeing downstairs. I wondered what time it was. Had Dillon laid down for a nap? Jax was obviously not back from Mercy's yet. In the kitchen, I flicked the switch for the light and nothing happened. I looked around the room noticing the digital display on the microwave was also out. I made my way over to the fireplace, found the matches and lit a candle which sat on top of the stone hearth. I carefully lifted it and headed for the study to wake Dillon. He would surely know how to replace a fuse if that was the problem. I tapped on the door softly.

"Dillon, are you in there?" When there was no answer I turned the knob and pushed the door open. The loud creak made me smile. The house was letting him know someone was intruding in his space. I loved noisy houses. "Dillon?" I crept into the room and used the candle to light up the space. It was empty. I rubbed at my chest nervously and picked up the phone at the desk. There was no dial tone, but if we were without electricity it might mean the phone didn't work either. I checked the garage which was quiet and empty then made my way back upstairs to my phone which sat beside the bed. I flicked through the phone numbers until I found Jax and pressed the green ring button. I stood at the window looking out over the snowy back yard. Jax's phone went to voice mail.

"Hey, the power is out and I can't find Dillon. I don't know anything about these things, fuses are man's business as far as I'm concerned. How far away are you?" I hung up and threw my phone onto the bed just as I noticed something glowing amongst the white snow outside with a neon brightness that only a phone screen can bring.

I stood for some time watching, contemplating before noticing the dull light from the work shed. Maybe Dillon had made his way out there and lost his phone on the way. I grabbed my thick jacket and snow cap and climbed back downstairs, pulling on a pair of Jax's boots that sat by the back door. They were way too big but they would protect my feet from the freezing snow. The early evening was still and silent, the only sound was the ice that crunched under the big boots as I crossed the big back yard. I stopped at the phone I had noticed from the upstairs window. Picking it up, I confirmed it was definitely Dillon's. He had six missed calls and five text messages ranging from three hours ago to just now, all from the same number.

 I glanced nervously at the work shed door and when curiosity got the better of me I checked the messages.

BRAIDEN: Answer you fucking phone

BRAIDEN: Where the fuck are you?

BRAIDEN: Dillon, I'm not shitting you, we need to talk

BRAIDEN: Fairmont has left!! Fucking call me

BRAIDEB: Fuck it, I'm on my way

I glanced to the door of the shed again. My sixth sense was screaming, demanding I return to the house. What if Dillon was in there just chilling out though? What if Dillon was in there and needed my help? My hand shook as nerves racked my body but I still took purposeful steps to the shed and turned the latch, pushing the heavy wooden door open. I hadn't yet been inside Jax's work shed and the size surprised me; it was large and clean. The scent of wood filled my lungs. A lamp was glowing from a desk on the opposite side of the room, but other than that, the place seemed quiet and empty. I took a few steps inside.

"Dillon, where the fuck are you?" I called out as I neared the center of the room. The gentle click of the door closing behind me sent a splinter of sharp fear through my body. I wanted to run while the need to turn around and face the possible threat was just as consuming. The stand and fight nature of my being won as I turned around and was confronted with my demon, my nightmare—Marcus Fairmont who stood with a gun pointed level at me.

"You always did have a dirty mouth, Ella," he drawled. The sight of him standing before me after so many years was as terrifying as I imagined it would be. I stiffened, paralyzed with fear. He had not changed a bit. His perfect blonde hair styled into a perfect GQ magazine cut. His hazel eyes still filled with hatred and loathing as he looked me over.

He wore a sharply pressed chocolate brown suit for fuck's sake with perfectly polished brown Salvatore Ferragamo's. He was dressed for a boardroom meeting while standing in a dusty wooden work shed in Claymont, sixteen hours away from his home and business during the middle of winter. All for me. Why the fuck couldn't he just leave me alone? Anger thrummed like an electric charge through my body as I faced him.

"Found me, huh?" I said, my voice calm, betraying the anger and fear that swirled like a tidal wave inside me.

"I believe I told you I would. I can find a needle in a hay stack if I so wish. Remember that, Ella?" My fists clenched at the memory of that night. Marcus sighed and took a few steps forward. He was a tall man, but for some reason I didn't find him quite as intimidating as I did all those years ago. Perhaps I had grown, found my strength and was no longer afraid of him like I used to be, or perhaps I had gotten used to Jax who literally towered over Marcus.

"Your lover is out back, gunshot wound to the back, likely dead by now. Unfortunately, he shot Tom first, but it's no big deal. Works in my favor really. Looks like Tom came here with nefarious intentions and cornered your boyfriend; there was a shootout and they both died. Tragic story for a small town like this and right on the eve of Christmas." Jax couldn't be dead, he wasn't even here. It must have been Dillon and I ached with the urgency to go check on him, to get him help, but for now I could do no more than stay away from Marcus and stay alive.

"All this just for me? To get me to come home with you?" Marcus laughed and the sound sent a shiver down my spine.

"I don't want you to come home with me, Ella. I am here to finish this. We didn't get the chance last time." I balked at his statement.

"So you just want to fuck me?" I screamed. He shook his head, slipping the gun into the back of his pants.

"Fuck you and," he paused, "cut you." He took another step forward and I backed away. "None of this went the way it was supposed to, right from the day your daddy died of a heart attack. That wasn't meant to happen, Ella. He was supposed to live, live and see the destruction of his family. All this…" He waved his hands to encompass him and I. "This isn't really as rewarding without him watching. I guess though, if God and heaven does exist, he will be watching. He will watch me fuck you, then cut your scarred little wrists and you will bleed out. Tragic little broken fuck up from Duntson who already tried to take her life once finally does the job right after her lover is killed in a shootout with a corrupt police officer. Poetic, don't you think? Has that Romeo and Juliette heartbreaking ending that all good romances need." My mind raced with confusion trying to process Marcus's words. I didn't know what he meant by his reference to my father and Marcus obviously thought Dillon was my lover. He didn't realize that Jax was alive and well and likely minutes away from getting home. I just had to stall Marcus and keep enough distance between us until he did.

"Why did you want to hurt my dad?" I asked.

"Because, Ella, he took what was mine. He stole one of the biggest clients in the northern hemisphere—worth, literally, billons of dollars—from me. They was supposed to be mine, they belonged to my firm. He lied and sniveled his way into my client's lap and then had the fucking nerve to die! It was too late of course, I was already fucking his wife and thought, what the hell might as well keep on going and destroy his only daughter too," Marcus was yelling, his eyes filled with manic rage and then, without warning, he leapt at me. I tried to back away but Jax's heavy boots got caught and I fell back with Marcus on top of me. He hit me hard and I brought my knee up connecting with his balls.

He yelped, clutching at himself and rolling as I scrambled out of the massive boots and made for the door. His hand pulled at my hair, ripping me backwards. I ducked and turned escaping his large arms and another blow landed on my face. I punched blindly hitting his throat which caused his grip to loosen as I scrambled away once more. I barreled out the door into the freezing snow, my feet aching with the bite of ice surrounding them, as I slipped and struggled my way across the backyard toward the house. From behind, I was tackled, my body forced down into the frigid ice. Winded, my lungs burned for air as Marcus ruthlessly rolled me over. In one hand was the gun pointed straight at my head, in the other hand was the knife. After all these years he still had the same fucking knife. His eyes quickly took in the blade before his gaze switched back to me.

"I killed your mom with this," he admitted. "And my own mother. This knife and I have history and you, Ella, are about to join the prestigious list of pathetic women who have died at its sharp edge." He shoved the gun into the back of his pants and grabbed my wrists, one of his large hands easily holding both of mine above my head as I attempted to buck him off me. "I'm going to cut you, then fuck you to death—quite a beautiful and fitting ending really." He lifted the knife above me and I felt the blade cut into my flesh. Like before, the knife slicing into my wrist burned with pain and became a curious throb immediately. I awkwardly glanced above me and watched the bright red blood seep quickly into the snow, too quickly, too much blood. Marcus's eyes were filled with manic excitement as he watched my face carefully. I fought the darkness and lethargy that was beginning to take over my body. Marcus pressed down against me, his sickly arousal pushed against my thigh.

My mind raced with images of Jax finding me like he had found Sarah, wrists cut in a pool of blood. I sobbed at the thought and tears began to fall down my face. Marcus's eyes glistened with excitement.

"I finally found a way to make you cry," he murmured with disbelief.

"Noooooooooooo!" Jax's roar was frightening enough to raise the dead as I heard him smash through the back door and out into the snow. The look of surprise in Marcus's cold eyes made me smile. He reached back and grabbed for his gun, pointed and fired, just as my world fell into dark oblivion.

CHAPTER 39

Jax

When I had received Ella's voicemail I had literally dropped the box I was unloading and I ran for my pickup. I knew something was up. When I got a hold of Braiden he had told me he'd been trying to get hold of Dillon for the last three hours and Marcus was AWOL, I knew right away that shit had officially hit the fan. I quickly gave Braiden Frank's number and told him to call and explain the situation. I told him to call the national fucking guard if he wanted, but I needed backup, like yesterday. Arriving at my house, which was still in darkness, I grabbed the gun from under the seat of my Dodge. I had started carrying it everywhere I went almost two weeks ago. The house was quiet and seemed empty and an unfamiliar voice from out back caught my attention as I crept silently to the kitchen and peered out the window. Seeing Marcus lying on top of Ella's limp body in the back yard triggered a switch and without even thinking to open it, I smashed my way through the closed kitchen door that led outside. The stunned look on Marcus was pure ecstasy as I raised my gun and he fumbled for his. While still running through the snow I fired, no hesitation and I knew my weapon would find its target, I rarely missed and when it was Ella's life on the line, I wouldn't miss. I felt the bullet hit my shoulder—flesh wound. It stung like a bitch and burned like hell, but didn't stop me as I continued to race towards Ella. When I reached her, I pulled Marcus's heavy, limp body up by the jacket and simply threw him to the side. One shot right through the eyes. The fucker was dead; he was as good as dead the first time he decided to lay his hands on my angel. Ella was still as I sunk to my knees beside her. I ripped my shirt and quickly wrapped it around her wrist tightly and gathered her into my arms trying to instill some heat into her freezing body.

"Come on, Angel, open those pretty eyes," I demanded. After a few moments they flickered open and I sighed loudly with relief. "You scared the shit out of me, baby." She glanced at my face, then took in the blood that had seeped through my shirt from my shoulder. "It's nothing, just a scratch." I pushed the hair back from her face and noted the bruising. The fucker had hit her and I suddenly wanted to kill him all over again. There was movement from behind me and I swung around, clutching Ella to me with one arm while my other hand held my gun poised and ready to take down the new threat. My finger immediately withdrew from the trigger.

"Fuck, Dillon, I nearly shot you," I growled. He looked like shit. He was too pale as he collapsed to his knees beside me.

"Someone beat you to it," he groaned.

"You gonna live, soldier?" I demanded.

"Course, Sarge," he panted, knowing better than to give me any other answer.

"You're hit," he noted and I shook my head ignoring the irritating ache from my shoulder.

"Flesh wound." Dillon checked Ella's pulse.

"It's weak." He pulled off his jacket and I helped him wrap her in it. "Police?"

"On their way, you'll hear sirens any minute," I said gruffly. I heard Ella sigh then and I pulled her closer to my chest, kissing her forehead.

"I waited for sirens once," she whispered, her eyes never leaving mine. "My dad was already dead on the kitchen floor while I waited for the sirens. When I heard them I thought they were the sound of angels, but it meant nothing, they couldn't save him." Her eyes were heavy and dull.

"Fuck that, Angel, you're not going anywhere, I won't allow it, so keep your damn eyes open." Dillon chuckled from beside me, looking worse by the minute.

"You too, soldier. I still have to kick your ass for letting someone shoot you in the back." The worshipful sound of sirens finally found my ears but I didn't relax. Ella fought for consciousness in my arms and Dillon quietly tried to explain what had happened from beside me, his voice faint and weak. He told me how not long after I had left he spotted someone out back. He took his gun to investigate and was surprised as fuck to find Tom Brennan out back, blubbering about how he never wanted to hurt Ella. How he knew it was wrong but Marcus knew he had taken bribes, so he was black mailing Tom to help keep Ella under his control. Dillon was so shocked to see Tom and hear his sniveling excuses that he missed Marcus coming up behind him. He barely got off a shot before taking one in the lower back, but his shot found a mark, like all good soldiers, right in the center of Tom Brennan's cold heart. When Frank finally arrived with backup and an ambulance he tried to call another stating there wasn't enough room for all of us in one. Reluctantly, I agreed to follow behind in Frank's patrol car while Dillon and Ella rode in the ambulance. Ella's eyes pleaded with me to stay close and it broke my heart, smashed it to pieces to see the fear in them and only when Dillon took her hand did she seem to settle a little.

At the hospital, we were separated briefly while I was stitched up. Dillon was taken away to surgery and Ella needed stitches and blood, she had lost too much. After a quick phone call to fill Mercy in, and a lot of grumbling and bitching to a nurse who decided right there and then that being a nurse wasn't worth my shit, I finally found Ella. A doctor and two nurses hovered over her as I entered the room without even asking permission.

"Jax?" one of the nurses asked.

She seemed familiar, but I could barely take my eyes off Ella long enough to put a name to her face.

"Is she okay?" I asked, my voice broken. The doctor nodded.

"It looks like she's tried this before." He nodded towards her wrists and it pissed me off.

"She didn't do it. The fucker who did it is lying in my back yard with a bullet between his eyes." The doctor went a little pale at my confession. "Frank Grier is outside, he can confirm everything."

"She's lost a lot of blood, but we are already replacing it— she'll most likely need a couple of bags. Some bruising, but other than that she'll be fine. She's obviously a fighter, it would take more than this to knock her down." I nodded and approached Ella's side while the doctor quietly left the room with one of the nurses. The one that had called my name checked the drip that fed the precious blood back into Ella's body.

"We went to school together," the nurse said in a low and

sympathetic voice. I finally dragged my eyes from Ella's fragile beaten face to take in the woman standing before me.

"Dee Witherborn," I whispered, finally noticing her. She smiled and nodded.

"Your friend will be fine, she just needs some rest. The loss of blood will make her weak." I nodded woodenly.

"She's my angel. She needs her strength to kick my ass for not keeping her safe." Dee smiled.

"Seems to me, if you shot the man who did this to her, you did your job. She's here, she's alive." I ran a finger carefully down the side of Ella's face that wasn't bruised and Dee slipped out of the room. I laid my head down on the bed beside Ella. Holding her hand, I closed my eyes, trying not to see her pinned under Marcus's body as he cut her wrist again.
I shuddered and lifted my hand, placing it over her heart. Feeling the strong steady beat there helped me to relax. A small weak hand covered mine and I glanced up to see Ella staring at me. She looked so tired.

"Get some rest, Angel, I'm not going anywhere. Everything's okay now." She watched me carefully for a moment and moved her hand to my bandaged shoulder—the blood on my shirt revealing the evidence of my injury. I captured her hand and kissed it. "Another scar, nothing serious." At that her eyes flickered to her heavily bandaged wrist.

"Me too," she said as her eyes rested sadly on the latest addition to her scars. "Dillon?"

"He's in surgery, but he'll be fine." She nodded, her eyes closing.

"Thank you." She had been quiet and still for so long I thought she was asleep.

"For what, Angel?"

"For saving me again." I shook my head.

"I told you I would protect you, I promised you wouldn't be hurt again." My fingers brushed the bruises on her face.

"What happened to him?" She shivered and I somehow managed to fold my large body into the bed beside her, taking care not to jostle her about too much. I pulled her close and she rested her head into the crook of my arm.

"He's dead. He's gone from your life, Ella, your free now, baby." Her hand settled over my heart and she seemed to gain just as much comfort from the steady beat as I did from hers. She took a long deep breath and slipped back into sleep.

EPILOGUE

Ella — 12 Months later

My feet were buried under warm soft sand as I sat with my sketch pad in my lap. The sun was like a blanket, wrapping itself around my body, warming me from the skin right down deep into my soul. My hand feathered the charcoal into soft shading around the hair line and neck of the face before me. The crashing ocean to my right caught my attention again. I found it hard to concentrate out here, my eyes were constantly drawn to the endless blue water.

"Finished yet?" Jax lazily yawned before me, stretched like a big lazy and very sexy god on his beach towel. He wore board shorts sitting low on his hips, his skin kissed with a warm bronze tan, his hair, as usual, too long and messy, but I loved it. His eyes were closed but his arm stretched out and easily found my leg, his large hand wrapping around my calf. I smiled at his touch.

"No, so stay still." I demanded and he grinned that lazy Cheshire cat grin that turned my knees to jelly. I kept drawing, finding both security and reassurance in Jax's innocent touch. I tried to be brave. I talked the talk, but didn't really walk the walk, not yet. It still took Jax's presence to make me feel completely safe, but it had only been twelve months. As Dave always reminded me, time is the best healer and you can't rush it. Jax's physical injuries had healed within a couple of weeks, a small scar his only reminder. Dillon took longer. He needed surgery which kept him in the hospital for two weeks, followed by a few months of physical therapy, but he was doing well now. Neither of the men seemed to show the mental scars that I struggled with. Jax didn't like being away from me for too long though and rarely allowed me out of his sight when we were together, but otherwise he was the same ol' cheeky, arrogant Jax Carter.

Police investigations were carried out, the evidence that Dillon had accumulated was checked out and Marcus Fairmont was proved to be in fact guilty of the crimes he was accused of. Not that it mattered, he was dead and I was finally safe. Tom

Brennan was confirmed to be one very corrupt cop and again, it didn't really matter because he was dead too. Dr. Theo was currently facing charges, too many to recall. He would do time in jail and never practice again. I faced my demons and went back to Duntson, visiting both my father's and mother's graves. I sat at my father's grave for a long time, talking to him, explaining that I was safe now, that I had found my guardian angel and that he was, in fact, a warrior and would forever protect me. I sat at my mother's grave for a long time too, but didn't really know what to say. Finally I told her that I forgave her and I was sorry for what happened to her. I could spend the rest of my life trying to hate her, filled with anger and unresolved disappointment, or I could let it go. Letting go was by far the easier option. Before heading back to Claymont, I took Jax to meet Rita, BJ and Larry. Seeing them this time was different. I guess because, for the first time in a long time, I wasn't filled with fear, I wasn't running, I was living and loving my life. My reward for being so brave and my Christmas present from Jax was a three week trip to Hawaii to finally see the ocean. He wasn't a fan of the heat, or the sand, but he said he would endure it for me and apparently seeing me in a bikini wasn't a hardship either. I thought of Mercy's Shelter back in Claymont as I continued to work on my portrait under the Hawaiian sun. It was freezing back there and, as of yesterday, Mercy's was unfortunately a full house. Rebecca had closed Bouquets. She had grizzled and moaned the entire three days it took to move her shop into the larger premises that would be big enough for my gallery, her flowers and a small café that Annie now managed.

We called it Mercy's Angels and it was doing well. I glanced at the silver cuff style bracelet around one of my wrists, a thick leather strap watch around my other. I wasn't comfortable with the curious glances that these scars drew, so Jax had bought me the jewelry to cover them. As for the other scars on my arms, they didn't bother me like they used to. They were really quite faint and difficult to distinguish. I think I was more scared of how I felt when I saw those scars then what other people thought of them.

"Taking too long, Angel," growled Jax as he suddenly sat

up. I smiled and put the sketch book down, crawling into his lap. His arms immediately encircled me and I melted into his embrace, enjoying the strength and warmth only his body could give me. "What were you drawing?" he wondered out loud, grabbing the sketch book. It wasn't what he thought I was drawing. I had asked him to lie before me perfectly still while I did this portrait and it wasn't because I was sketching him. I didn't want him watching over my shoulder like he usually did when I sketched. While he had been quietly napping before me, I sketched the face of a girl. Long dark hair, parted down the middle and hanging like a fall of water over her shoulders, dark eyes, slightly slanted, full heart shaped lips, high cheek bones and a small scar by her right eye. She was pretty, no she was beautiful.

"Looks like you finally got it right," Jax murmured. As part of my 'healing', David had commissioned me to sketch a picture, a portrait, of myself. I had been attempting to do it for months without success. It was up to Jax to tell me if I had it right and so far I hadn't even been close. The fear, darkness and sadness in all the previous drawings meant I had to keep on trying until Jax finally gave my sketch his approval. The admiring gaze in his eyes told me I had finally gotten it right. For some reason, I finally saw myself this way—happy, peaceful, beautiful.

He threw the book aside and pulled me down, positioning me right on top of him. On the beach, under the sun, in this man's arms, I finally felt reborn. I finally felt like the woman I was meant to be. Marcus Fairmont may have stolen a portion of my life, he may have marked my skin, but he didn't defeat me. He hadn't taken my heart and soul.

"Such a beautiful angel," Jax whispered. I kissed his lips gently and gazed down into his steel gray eyes and, for the first time, I didn't marvel about how this man could possibly love me. I simply accepted that he did. As my forehead rested against his, our lips only but a breath apart, I whispered the words that would forever rest in my heart.

"I love you Jaxon James Carter. Thank you for saving me."

The End

"Never be bullied into silence. Never allow yourself to be made a victim. Accept no one's definition of your life."

☐

Other Reads by Kirsty Dallas

Fighting Back – Mercy's Angels Book 2
Tortured Soul – Mercy's Angels Book 3
Breeze of Life

☐

ACKNOWLEDGMENTS

I have to thank all my family and friends who put up with a few months of the mindless, monotone life I existed in while my head drifted in a constant daze of Jax and Ella. Being a writer can send you into a catatonic state for long periods of time and no one but a writer can comprehend the feeling. Thank you to my awesome sister-in-law/friend/manager and everything in between, Kylie, who kept me focused, motivated and moving through the entire Saving Ella journey. She didn't have to pick up a whip once! Her enthusiasm and love for the story was motivation enough for me. Jax and Ella were her babies. I hope the story is everything you dreamed it would be Kylie; it's yours my friend...

My life and love of writing was cultivated by so many people, but began with my mother who read to me endlessly as a baby. Thanks, Mummy, for starting my dream. Also a big hug for my Aunty Robyn on the Sunny Coast, thank you for providing me one of the most valuable tools a writer could ever possess— Stylewriter editing software...A-mazing!

Thank you to the awesome bloggers and reviewers out there who really are the backbone to a writer's existence. The likes of A Love Affair with Books (& my favorite stalker Desiree), Blushing Reader, The Reading Vixens, Reading Fiction for Life, Can't Read Just One, Bookslapped, Totally Booked, Fab, Fun and Tantalizing Reads—you guys literally keep us indie author's afloat and inspire us to create these awesome characters and as always, the all-important book boyfriend!! I hope you all drool and swoon over Jax and he ruins you for all other mere mortal men!!

Thanks to my team of Beta readers—TEAM W.P. (only the privileged members of that team will understand what that means): Sandy, Kylie, Trish, Kim and Nadine. All your advice and notes helped mold Saving Ella into the perfect tale. And a

MASSIVE thank you to Ami, who offered a professional edit of Saving Ella and did an UNBELIEVABLE job!!
A shout out to my models, Kyle Low and Danielle Suffredini, my Jax and Ella who were used for the book cover and or book trailer and teasers. You guys were utterly amazing!!!
I have so much love and appreciation for my father who is the most beautiful, gentle soul in existence and the best photographer in the world. It was his eye behind the camera lens that gave me my cover photo and my mum's expertise with Photoshop who put on the finishing touches!

Thank you to Ami Johnson who did a beautiful last minute professional edit.. You are my savior!!!

To my fellow writers who fill my Facebook newsfeed and keep me dreaming the dream: Amy Bartol, C. J Roberts, J. Sterling, Shelly Crane, Paullina Simons, Kresely Cole, Jessica Sorenson, Abbi Glines—thank you!! Your books and words fill me with inspiration. You all rock and, man, I hope to meet some, if not all of you one day.

And lastly, thank you to the readers, the fans of romance that live for that moment where they slip into an alternate universe and become immersed in a life outside of their own. A world where anything is possible, where love is never perfect but so all-consuming and passionate that it is worth every hiccup and shit fight that it endures. Thank you fellow book geeks, you are all so awesome!

ABOUT THE AUTHOR

I'm just a little Aussie girl with a big imagination, so much to write and so little time to do it. When I'm not writing (or reading), I am kept smiling and sane (for the most part) by my 5 year old daughter. She is the light in my world. I have a wonderfully supportive family who keep me completely grounded. Trust me, they will never let any success go to my head!! And I love them for it. I enjoy ice cold ciders, barbeques, music and art. My feet rarely grace anything other than flip-flops and even in the middle of a hot Aussie summer, I love my jeans!!! To sum me up in a few words—easy going, laid back, dreamy and passionate.

I hope you all love reading my novels as much as I love writing them.

www.facebook.com/kirstydallasauthor

www.kirstydallasauthor.com

www.twitter.com/kirstydallas

BCPL
Baltimore County
Public Library

Made in the USA
San Bernardino, CA
26 March 2017